KC KEAN

Ruthless Rage
Ruthless Brothers MC #1
Copyright © 2023 KC Kean

www.authorkckean.com
Published by Featherstone Publishing Ltd
This book is licensed for your personal enjoyment only.
All rights reserved.

This is a work of fiction. Names, characters, places, brands, media, and incidents
are either the product of the author's imagination or are used fictitiously. The author
acknowledges the trademark status and trademark owners of various products referred
to in this work of fiction, which have been used without permission. The publication/
use of these trademarks is not authorised, associated with, or sponsored by the
trademark owners.

Cover Design: BellaLuna
Editing: Zainab M. - Heart Full of Edits
Proofreader: Sassi's Editing Services
Interior Formatting & Design: Wild Elegance Formatting

Ruthless Rage/KC Kean– 1st ed.
ISBN-13 - 978-1-915203-36-6

To C,
Congratulations! I wish you all the beauty and love in the world. Here's to words that can't be said verbally, but deserve sweet attention all the same.
Much love.

Let the enemy burn bright as we rise from the ashes of today and reign hell down on their souls. We're filled with rage, we're ready to riot, and we're as ruthless as ever.

RUTHLESS BROTHERS MC

ONE

Ryker

The storm brews above us, dominating the sky like a villain with purpose. It's one of those moments where tingles race up your spine and goosebumps erupt over your skin, but not in a good way.

No.

Nothing feels good about this.

The vote went to Church. The majority of my brothers sitting at the engraved oak table went in favor of the Prez's—Banner's—idea and the knock of the gavel confirmed it. I'm stuck in the middle of the madness that I fucking knew would come someday, but as the only the son of the Vice President my thoughts aren't always considered worthy.

Fuckers.

"Pull your head out of your ass, Ryker. You were right, but that doesn't get us out of this shit until there's at least a mile or two between us and this fucked up mess." Emmett slaps a hand on my shoulder and squeezes the leather of my cut.

I'm soaked to the bone, and to top it all off, I can barely see through the haze of the rain.

This might be the first time I utter *I told you so*, but I save it for later. First, we need to get the fuck out of the Ice Reaper's territory, before there's a bullet in my chest and I don't get the opportunity.

"We can't go anywhere until Prez and VP have finished in there," Gray grunts, pointing over his shoulder at the warehouse. We've been standing watch as instructed, outside this damn warehouse in the Reaper's territory for the past twenty-five minutes. How much more time do they need?

Annoyed, I shake my head as Axel attempts to light a cigarette beside me. No one else in the world would even fucking bother to try in this weather, but this guy is a man of his own making, so I don't attempt to stop him.

Despite not appreciating being here, I'm grateful to be with my three closest friends. My brothers. If Prez had put me on a job with anyone else, I would be pulling my hair out by now.

I believe in the club. I believe in what we stand for. Even if it's all I've ever known, I've never considered if the grass may be greener as a ninety-nine percenter. Cut me open and my blood will run black for my club, just as it will when I die in its honor.

These old timers refuse to adjust to the changing world. The longer they continue like this, the further they'll hold us back. I would never speak those words out loud though. Not to anyone but the three men standing with me. If I uttered a word to anyone else, they would see it as me committing treason against the club, and it's so far from the truth that it's not worth the battle. Not yet anyway.

Pushing soaked strands of hair back off my face, I glance at my watch, noting the additional five minutes that have ticked by. It's on the tip of my tongue to call time, but the buzz of my cell phone interrupts me.

"What's up?" I ask Euro with a grunt. No pleasantries, no small talk. We don't have time for that shit.

"I've got five bikes heading your way, Ryker. They need to call time right fucking now."

I end the call without another word as Emmett, Axel, and Gray all seem to stand taller, waiting for my next orders.

"The Reapers are on their way. Get ready to roll out." With that, I race to the side door of the warehouse.

Stealing weapons isn't my idea of fun, nor is it my way of running this damn club. It isn't my father's either, but VPs can't overrule the Prez, so that's what we're here to do. Euro's positioning, however, was my doing. An extra layer of protection at a safe distance to give us more time to act if necessary. I wasn't wrong.

My hand wraps around the steel handle of the door when the ringing of a gun goes off, making my spine stiffen.

The pounding of the rain becomes more distant as I rush inside and head toward the other side of the room where another door waits. The light shining through from the other side lures me closer, but a moment later, a glimmer of crimson seeps under the door.

Blood.

What the fuck is going on?

From the call I got from Euro, the Reapers were close, but not *this* close. Right?

Drawing my gun from my waist, I press my back against the wall beside the door as I glance through the gap. I frown in confusion when I don't see anyone.

Until I look down.

It's our VP. With a bullet between his eyes and a puddle of blood framing him.

My father.

A sharp pain constricts my chest, numbing my body from head to toe, as my breathing becomes labored.

There are murmurs coming from the other side of the door, but I can't see who they belong to, and no matter how hard I strain, I can't hear a word they're saying over the ringing in my ears.

Who the fuck killed my father?

Determined to avenge him, I almost step inside when Banner yells, "Reapers, the fucking Reapers are here. Roll out. Roll out. Roll out."

With uncertainty coursing through my veins, I stutter over what my next move should be. Emmett calls my name from the door behind me, pulling me from my inner turmoil. Glancing over my shoulder, my eyebrows furrow as I debate whether to stay or go.

My heart pleads for me to stay at my father's side, while my head sees the bigger picture.

The third order in the club's list of rules flashes in my mind.

Every man for himself to protect and serve the greater good of the club.

Glancing down at my father, I burn the image of him lying in his own blood into my mind one last time before I retreat. With Euro's earlier warning and the chatter behind the door being calm even after the shot rang out, this somehow links to Prez. There's no proving that though, not here, and definitely not now, but there will be, in time.

I move toward Emmett; every step purposeful as my mind rumbles like the sky.

I'll find the answers.

I'll charge at it all in the name of my father.

I'll learn the secrets that were hidden here today.

I'm a Ruthless Brother, and ruthless is my game.

TWO

Ryker

TWELVE MONTHS LATER

I force a smile to my lips as *another* club whore perches herself on the bench next to me. Molly twirls her light brown hair around her finger and places her other hand on my thigh. She squeezes for good measure, but I still couldn't give a fuck about what she has to say. Even if they are words of sympathy.

"I can't imagine how it must feel losing your daddy, Ryker. A whole year without him. We've all missed his presence, but it's nothing compared to what you must be dealing with."

I hum, biting back the scoff that tempts my lips as I grab her hand and tear it from my denim-clad thigh.

What she misses most is the fact that my *daddy* fucked

her without beating on her too, unlike half the other men she spreads her legs for, but I refrain from commenting as such. Instead, I repeat the same words I've said since I stepped out into the compound yard thirty minutes ago.

"Thanks, Mol. I appreciate the condolences, but I need some time alone to process everything right now."

Her eyes drop in disappointment, but she still pushes up to her feet as I release my grip on her hand. None of those that have approached me like what I have to say, but they take the hint all the same.

"If you change your mind, Ryker, you know where to find me," she murmurs, planting a kiss against the stubble on my cheek before sauntering off.

I don't wait to see if she glances back, that would only offer her hope, and there's none of that here.

Gray smirks as he nudges Emmett beside him. "Look how happy he is with all the attention." Gray sits taller in his seat, raising his brows at me as Axel grunts in agreement from my right.

"If the attention was specifically on his dick, I'm sure he would be more accepting of it."

I wag my finger at Axel, agreeing with him as I reach for my beer bottle with the other. I guzzle half of it in one go, appreciating the chilled, hoppy taste on my tongue.

"All this talking just doesn't work for me," I grumble as my friends chuckle.

That night, when my father died, I was there. As his lifeless eyes stared at me. But nobody except the three guys sitting at the table with me know that. The rest of the club don't know how hard I've been trying to piece together the events of that fateful night. There were moves made, chess pieces eliminated and strategic plays that didn't need the club votes or approval from the table, and I'm so fucking close to uncovering it all.

I'm done with the pleasantries, done with the fake fucking smile, and done with the Prez who takes no responsibility for my father's death.

If this afternoon wasn't in honor of my father, I wouldn't fucking be here. But this is bigger than me, and it's bigger than the honored death that befell him. It's about his legacy, my legacy, and the club's legacy.

"I'm sure if you offered a wink to one of the whores, they would take you inside. It serves as a distraction as well as an excuse to get the fuck out of here," Emmett whispers. It almost sounds tempting, but I have zero interest in any of the girls in this place, not even enough to get a semi.

There's too much rage coursing through my veins today, outweighing every other feeling or emotion that teases my mind. Fuck, anger is all I've felt for the past twelve months, but nothing has been as intense as today.

It's like I'm right back in that room again, my clothes drenched, soaking me through to the bone as my gun weighs heavy in my hand. Vivid memories assault me – the smell of cigarettes, the bullet in my father's head. The night replays in my mind without my approval. I can hear the gun ringing out, the beating of the rain outside. All of it.

I've made progress since that night, each dot connecting me more and more back to Banner, and somehow the Ice Reapers. Still, something stays amiss. Without real evidence or proof of Banner's actions in his death, I have nothing to bring to the table.

I'm close, I can feel it. I just need a little more time.

"Are we still taking Euro with us to meet with the informant?" Axel asks, the words slightly muffled around the cigarette between his teeth.

I crack my neck before nodding, but any response is interrupted as a fist knocks on the table. "Boys, Prez is going to make a speech and he wants everyone over there."

My shoulders tense at Eric's words, but the glaze in his eyes intrigues me, so I opt to alleviate the stress from my own body to focus on him instead. The last thing I want to listen to is this man's bullshit, but there's nothing I can do about it. Yet.

"Everything okay, Pops?" Emmett frowns at his father as he rises from his seat, and the rest of us follow suit, falling into step with Eric.

"It's all good, son. I'm just… all of this would piss Brian off, yet here we are, celebrating his life like this anyway."

I grip his shoulder firmly with a tight squeeze, shaking my head in disbelief as I indicate toward where Banner stands with the rest of our men and their old ladies. There's even a few whores mixed into the crowd too. "No truer words have ever been spoken, Eric, but we all know this isn't really about him. It never is. It's about the club. In the depths of the night, when we're all alone, we'll remember him the way he wanted."

A small smile creeps up at the corner of his mouth, but it doesn't straighten the frown lines on his face. "That's with a glass of bourbon in one hand and a hand-rolled smoke in the other."

My solemn smile matches his, but Gray cuts in front of the group, distracting everyone as he pouts. "But if I have a glass in one hand and a cigarette in the other, where's my cock going?"

Emmett clips him around the ear without a word of response, but my friend's words did exactly what they were intended for; breaking the moment, cooling my heated emotions, and lightening the mood.

Eric's right hand crosses over his body to pat mine, before he steps away. "One day that boy will learn that his cock wasn't made for his hand; it was made for a cunt or a cunt's mouth. Either way, both hands are fine where they are."

I smirk at the cheeky fucker as he winks, causing

Emmett to groan, before he leaves to go stand with the older members of the club. His wispy gray hair still manages to get in a ponytail at the back of his head, and he wears that fucker with pride.

The image of our club's emblem stitched into the back of his cut reminds me why I'm here and what my purpose is. The skull and pistol combo, edged in lime green, mean everything to me. It represents family and home. It also forces me to turn my attention to the Prez as he moves to stand on the boulder that randomly sits in our yard.

"We're all here today to both celebrate and mourn," Prez starts, raising his beer to the sky in salute as everyone goes quiet, waiting for him to proceed. "We may have lost our VP on this day twelve months ago, but his legacy lives on with his son, Ryker, as our new Vice President."

I manage to tuck my hands into my pockets before they clench with frustration. My grin widens. Pride shines in the eyes of the club members as they all turn to look at me, reminding me that there are more people I love here, more people I consider family, and more people I will forever protect.

His words ring true. A lot has changed since my father died. Everyone thinks I accepted the role offered to me from Prez to honor my legacy, but what they don't know is I'm more set on keeping my friends close, and my enemies even closer. It may be a cliche, but it's far too fitting for this moment. Nothing will ever be the same again. I'll make sure of it.

Prez's words fade into the background as I face him to show how united we are as a club, as leaders.

Am I two-faced? No, I'm just biding my time. I want the whole truth, and nothing but the truth when I bring this man to Church and watch him burn in front of my brothers. I want to serve justice in honor of my father, and my time is coming. I just have to be a little more patient before I put a bullet through his skull. A complete mirror image to my father's.

A nudge from my right has me side-eying Axel as he nods ahead, making me pay attention to the shit tumbling from Prez's mouth.

"As a club, we are stronger together, taking all odds on survival, while we deal with our enemies. We will bring justice to the Ruthless Brothers by bringing the Ice Reapers down in honor of our late VP, and I have devised a plan that I'm going to share in Church this evening." He holds his arms out as excitement zips through the crowd.

That's news to me, but as I spy the older members of the club, I notice Billy smirks knowingly. *Does he know? Was he in on other things too?* It could explain why he wasn't in attendance that night.

Prez tips his beer bottle in my direction. "Ryker, we shall—"

I don't recognize the telltale whoosh that whips through the air until I watch in slow motion as a bullet pierces Prez's skull. Before I can even blink, the metal has penetrated his head from the left and exited to the right as the screams ring in my ears from the women and children present.

He drops, the life leaving his body too quickly for my liking, and his head smashes into the boulder, splattering his brain matter and blood even further.

Dumbfounded, I'm unable to pull my gaze from his lifeless body. A new reality dawns over me.

He's dead, and it wasn't at my hands.

Motherfucker.

THREE

Scarlett

The side stand rests against the ground as I lift my leg over the seat of my bike, my baby, and I take a moment to appreciate her, just like I do every day I get the chance to feel her hum between my thighs.

She's made of hopes and dreams, along with the metal and leather that makes her a classic Harley Davidson. She's my most prized possession. I know the moment I step through those doors up ahead, I won't get to see her until I'm *allowed*, and it pains me.

Fuck.

Ruffling my fingers through my tousled hair, I bite back the nerves brewing in my gut, then reach into the saddle bag to grab my belongings and hang my helmet on the handlebar.

My hair is knottier than I appreciate, but I couldn't

keep it braided back off my face any longer. They had been done too damn tight, so the second I was finished, I pulled the fuckers out. The wind whipped through the ends of my hair as I made my way home, and that definitely served its purpose in making me happy.

Pulling the drawstring tight on the bag, I put my headphones on and press play on the podcast I had paused earlier. The monotone voice of the man describing yet another murder investigation filters into my ears as I make my way up toward the clubhouse.

I nod at the security guy at the main gate, but I don't offer any conversation, opting to listen to the podcast instead. Not that he would expect any words from me, I'm not known for my chitchat that's for sure.

Tucking my cell phone into the pocket of my leather jacket, I reach into the other side to retrieve the burner cell phone I have on me at all times. A text message flashes across the screen, and I smile in delight at the figure written there in black and white.

Perfect.

Another job well done.

Pleased, I tuck the cell away and lift my head high as I near the large double doors of the clubhouse. The green and black snakes spray-painted onto the wood makes me cringe, the symbol for the Ice Reapers glaring at me square in the eye.

It's my life, whether I like it or not. I've never known any different, but until the day I die, I will never accept that the snakes represent me.

My gaze drifts to the left, noting the five men sitting around the bench with cigarettes in their mouths and beers in their hands. Froggo and Denz are among them, but the other three aren't familiar. Which can only mean one thing.

More new prospects.

Like that's what we need right now.

Shaking my head, I keep my stride as I focus on the spray-painted symbol once more. A group of men turn their attention in my direction.

One of the younger guys I'm not familiar with rises from his spot, tucking his hands into his pockets as he nods in my direction. His mouth moves, but with the podcast on, I don't hear a thing.

Irritated with the interruption, I drop my headphones to my neck, staring the guy down as he rakes his gaze over me from head to toe.

"Didn't you hear me, whore? I said—"

His words are cut short by Denz punching him in the gut without muttering a word, and the grunt that falls from the new prospect's mouth echoes around us.

"Sorry, Scar," Froggo hollers, raising a hand in surrender. "He's new and clearly doesn't know what his life is worth," he adds as I remain rooted to the spot with a deadpan look.

"Yeah. Dickhead just earned himself the shittiest road name that has ever been given to an Ice Reaper." Denz offers another swift fist to the guy's stomach as the other new prospects watch with wide eyes.

"I didn't think it was possible to get worse than Denz or Froggo," I comment, biting back the teasing smile on my lips, but the pair of them grunt with laughter.

"Yeah, yeah. I'm sure we can make it nastier… maybe we should just name him whore."

I purse my lips at Froggo's suggestion, shaking my head as I come up with one of my own. "Or maybe whoreless because he sure as shit won't be getting any candy with that mouth." I head inside then, but I don't miss the laughter that clings to the group.

Fucking men. Fucking *Reaper* men. None of them are worth a dime, not even Denz or Froggo. I've seen how they *actually* treat the whores around here, and it's not worth living for. To be beaten and discarded like a used rag is not my vision or dream. It's far from it. Especially after I've watched them trade whores at this clubhouse for as long as I can remember.

I step inside with a gray cloud looming over my head. Despite the spring in my step moments earlier, a reminder of who I am and where I come from quickly brings me back down to earth.

"Get it done, boys. Get. It. Done." Prez's voice booms from the other end of the bar area, giving me hope that I may be able to tiptoe around the room without being noticed, but I barely make it two steps past the doorframe when he spots me instantly. "Finally. Where are my fucking funds?"

His upper lip curls as he looks at me over the rim of his glass, downing the remainder of the whiskey in there, before pouring another. Yes. A drunken fucking fool is exactly what the Ice Reapers need to lead them to greatness.

It's embarrassing. *Really* fucking embarrassing.

"Bubba, can you at least let me shower first? Have you seen me?" I run my hands down my sides, bringing his attention to the dirt marks covering my clothes as I continue toward the door leading to the bedrooms, but he doesn't seem so forgiving.

The glass shatters into pieces when he slams it down and then charges toward me. Club members are seated around the bar, but I keep my gaze on him.

He doesn't slow his approach until we're standing toe to toe and he's practically spitting in my face. "You may have been my brother's fucking offspring, bitch, but you're a whore's bastard at best," he grunts, using his usual verbal attack, but it doesn't even graze the surface. I have far thicker skin than he realizes. "You would do well to remember your place," he adds for good measure, and it takes a lot of effort to stop myself from yawning.

"I didn't realize asking to take a shower went against one of the club rules, Bubba. But I haven't had confirmation come through for the transaction yet," I lie, keeping my body relaxed and calm as he bares his teeth at me.

I'm sure in his mind he thinks he looks like an alpha lion marking his territory out in the wild, but he's struggling to look any better than a stray fucking cat.

"Get out of my fucking face, bitch, before I do something I really *won't* regret."

I force myself to take a step back, not commenting on the fact that it was actually *he* who entered my space. A reaction is likely what he wants, and I'm not giving it to him. I have to choose my battles if I ever want to leave this godforsaken place, and this moment isn't the time for my anger to explode.

I may be able to handle myself, but he still puts a roof over my head and food on the table.

Relieved, I step into my bedroom at the end of the hall with a sigh. I lean back against the wood, making sure to turn the lock on the door as I try to calm my heart rate down.

This isn't my forever, I fucking refuse to let it be this way.

I may have spent every day of my life in this prison, trapped in a compound with a club I want nothing to do with, but the end is near. I can feel it. I can taste it.

I've been skimming off the top of my jobs for a while now, trying to build up enough cash to secure my future. It will be the dream—me, my Harley, and the open road. Shit, if I can skim enough this time, I could be set.

That just leaves the escape plan I've been thinking about for the longest time. I need to make sure I can get my hands on my bike, otherwise it won't be worth it.

But the sooner, the better, and I'll be fucking out of here, free of the chains that pin me down.

RUTHLESS BROTHERS MC

FOUR

Emmett

Horror at the scene that unfolded in front of the women and children causes an uproar among every member here.

"Get everyone inside."

The prospects hovering beside me nod before rushing to the women and children who are frozen in place as they stare at the lifeless body in the middle of the crowd.

Prez is dead.

As everyone moves around us, calling out to draw our weapons and take shelter from any further attacks, Ryker, Axel, Gray, and I remain in place. Our gaze is rooted at Ryker, who hasn't taken his eyes off Prez's body since it dropped.

I know what's going through his mind, and it isn't pain or compassion over a life lost. Far from it. The tightening of his jaw, the clenching of his hands, and the widening of his eyes, is pure frustration that he's dead, and he didn't get the vengeance he's been chasing for the past twelve months.

"We need to move," Gray murmurs, reaching for the gun at his waist. "If there's another shot coming in, we don't want to be the target."

As if hearing his concern, a gurgling sound echoes around us moments later, and I turn, only to find Billy flat on his back. His hands engulf his throat as he struggles to breathe for a moment, before the life seeps from his body. Blood drapes over his fingers, bathing his neck and cut in the same crimson color.

"Everybody move," my father hollers, kicking me into action. His concerned eyes find mine as he points in the direction of the clubhouse, but he must be a fool if he thinks I'm going anywhere without him.

Fuck the clubhouse rules. My sister has lost my mother already; I'm not spending my evening telling her our father is gone, too. No way in hell.

"Where are the shots coming from?" Axel grunts, tossing his cigarette butt on the ground with a huff as he reaches for his weapon.

"I don't know, but I'm not sharing the same death day as that fucker, so let's get moving."

I scoff at Gray's choice of words, but follow the other members as everyone heads for the clubhouse. Nobody rushes to grab Prez or Bill. We can retrieve the bodies later. Right now we need to take care of ourselves and figure out what the hell is going on.

It doesn't bode well that Ryker still hasn't spoken a word, leaving him lost in his head as he watches his revenge slip through his fingers. There's no need for us to meet with the informant tonight now that it's all gone to shit.

Axel grabs the door and holds it open for the last of us to get inside the clubhouse, and when he pulls it closed behind us, I internally groan at the level of noise. Children are crying, women are sobbing, and members of the MC are demanding answers. I'm just as bewildered as they are, but one thing is for certain. We need a meeting. Now.

Heading toward the bar area, I keep in step with my closest brothers, when Ryker clears his throat and pounds his fist on the wooden countertop. Everybody quiets down, apart from the children, but it's not their attention he's garnering.

"Church. Now."

Anger vibrates from him, his voice sharper than usual as he turns and heads for Church. We trudge from the room, following his direction. My fingers run over the skull engraved into the thick wooden door, as they do every time we enter, before I find myself among the men.

Murmurs circulate as Axel and Gray take a spot on

either side of me, and Ryker hovers behind the seat reserved for the VP. I catch a glimpse of my father as he steps into the room, head down and shoulders bunched. He's getting too old for this shit, but there's no telling him that. I'm just thankful Emily is at college and not here to witness this.

Before Ryker begins talking, I pull my cell phone out and quickly shoot off a message to the prospect I have shadowing her on campus. I offer him a clipped version of what's happening here, while wanting to make sure he has eyes on her.

I don't get a chance to even tuck my cell phone away before a response comes through, confirming his visual.

Thank fuck for that.

Raking my fingers through my wavy blond hair, I pull it back off my face and secure a hair tie at my crown, flicking the ends into a bun, as Ryker paces.

The final member steps into the room, closing the door behind him, and the room falls into silence. "I'm trying to figure out what the fuck just happened out there, but I'm falling short because nothing makes sense," he starts, leaning on the back of his seat. "Who the fuck targeted us today? I know we have ongoing issues with the Ice Reapers and the occasional dust up with the Devil's Brutes, but assassination? Surely, that's above their fucking pay grade."

I tug at my short beard as I consider that fact too.

We live a dangerous life, and this is a lethal game, but moves like this have *never* been made before. Someone has gotten bold, it seems.

Ryker's knuckles whiten around the seatback as fury threatens to overcome him. I can practically hear his thoughts, questioning whether or not he actually wants retribution for the man we're sure killed his father. The reality of the situation is bigger than him though, and he knows it.

It's not about avenging Prez or Bill; it's about the club's reputation, the Ruthless Brothers. The question is—Who do we rain hell down on?

"We need to retaliate, Ryker. We need to act fast with total annihilation." Members at the table hum their agreement at Axel's statement, and I can't say I blame them. Ryker will do it for the club, but he should also be doing it for himself.

Whoever took Prez and Bill out today, stole that right away from him.

"The issue with retaliation, Ax, is the fact that we don't have a fucking Prez to make that decision," Ryker retorts as he starts to pace again.

He can't be this crazy or blind to everything we're seeing and how it's unfolding. He must be too caught up in his fucking thoughts to see the reality before him. It's on the tip of my tongue to lay it out for him, when my father speaks first. "All in favor of our VP, Ryker Holden, stepping up to become our permanent Prez, raise your hand."

Ryker's eyes widen as they dart to Gray, Axel, and I, but he doesn't utter a word as every man at the table lifts their right hand in confirmation. The only man that would have likely stood in the way was Becker, but he's no longer here.

After a moment passes, the vote is unanimous. Taking in the raw emotion in the room, Ryker moves in slow, calculated steps around to the head of the table where the Prez's chair sits.

It's an unspoken rule that the Prez must be seated before we go any further with plans, so the tension, excitement, and pride rises around the room as Ryker takes his rightful spot at the head of the table as the leader of our club.

The second his ass is perched in his seat, Gray claps his hands once, rubbing them together as he asks the question, "What's our next move, Prez?"

This whole fucking thing is bizarre as fuck right now, but I don't miss the smile on my father's face as he nods in Ryker's direction.

"We need to figure out where this attack came from," Ryker starts, tapping his fingers on the table mindlessly.

Duffer scoffs from across the room. "It sure points in the direction of the Ice Reapers, Prez. After what happened to your father, on the anniversary of his death… Fuck, I can't see this being anyone but them."

That would make sense, but it still confuses me. We didn't take retribution that night or the following days for the death of Ryker's father, which was another reason that all signs seemed to point to Banner's involvement. So why come here and make a statement like this again today? Did he not follow through on something? Was there more to the picture that we just haven't seen yet?

Shit.

If we don't follow the signs, it will mean we have to share our concerns over the dead Prez, and that would cause uproar right now, which is the exact opposite of what the club needs.

Stability, strength, and family. Three things we have continued to lose over the past few years.

"What's our move, Prez?" I ask, looking Ryker dead in the eyes, and he offers the subtlest of nods. He knows I'm the thoughtful one, the one that considers every option and outcome, and he knows I wouldn't be bringing it to the table like this if it wasn't the right option.

"Retaliation on the Ice Reapers. If not for today's events, then there will be some solace from my father's death as we smear their blood across their home."

Fists pound on the table, thumping in time with one another in a chant of agreement.

Could innocent people die? Yes, but that's the game we play when we choose this life.

"When do we roll out, Prez?" Axel asks, an unlit cigarette hanging from his lips, as Ryker reaches for the gavel.

He twirls the handle in his hand, then makes eye contact with every man in the room.

"There's no time like the present. We leave now."

The gavel hitting the wood confirms it. The first order from our new Prez, and I will stand right at his side.

Today. Tomorrow. Always.

FIVE

Scarlett

A sigh falls from my lips, alleviating the pressure in my chest as the water continues to pound against my skin. My body is a light shade of pink from scrubbing my limbs so harshly, but it's worth it. I need the grime and dirt off me. It's become an almost therapeutic routine for me at this stage. A distraction from the grim and stale, shared shower stalls.

I'm just thankful there's no one else in here.

Humming along to the soft jazz that echoes around the room, my head falls back with another sigh. Nothing helps reduce the tension of a job like blasting soft jazz loud enough so that it's heard over the shower while I wash the day away.

I'm no longer trapped in a motorcycle club with men that make me cringe and a life I wouldn't wish on my worst enemy. Instead, I mentally transport myself to the vibrant atmosphere of New Orleans. I've always wondered what it would be like to see the art, sway to the music in the street, and taste the foods that look like they were served straight from heaven.

As if sensing my joyful moment, the water raining down on me instantly turns cold, and I shiver. Glaring up at the shower head, I turn the damn thing off and step out of the cubicle with a huff.

I wrap my pink towel around my body, disappointed that my moment of serenity is broken. My wet hair clings to my skin, making me feel even colder as I rush to grab my cell phone and head back to my room.

The second I swing the door open though, I'm met by utter carnage.

Two men are rolling on the floor, fists flying and grunts vibrating around them.

Turning my music off, I glare at the assholes blocking my way. It's not the first time there's been a fist fight here, nor will it be the last. That shit doesn't bother me; what bothers me is the fact that I'm only wearing a towel and these fuckers are in my way.

"Can you take your dick measuring contest elsewhere? You're in my way."

Neither of them acknowledge my words as they continue to brawl, making me even more irritated while I tighten my grip on my towel, holding it in place.

I manage to step to the left with one foot, but the second I do, the sound of gunshots ring out from somewhere else, and my back stiffens.

Fuck.

Something tells me this is more than two Reapers fighting over the same club whore.

With another step, I take in the men still throwing punches and realize the guy with the upper hand isn't wearing a Reapers' cut.

No.

That's the complete opposite of a Reapers' cut.

Fuck.

Fuck. Fuck. Fuck. Fuck. Fuck.

Two more gunshots fire off as men shout at the top of their lungs. What they're saying doesn't quite reach my ears, but it's not my problem. This is so far from being my problem, it's the opposite end of the fucking globe.

This is my chance.

A distraction like this would have every man away from their posts, so I can grab my Harley and get the fuck out of dodge.

Quickening my pace, I fling my bedroom door open, my knuckles white from holding my towel in place as I throw a few drawers open and blindly grab an outfit.

Without looking, I know I will find a band tee, a pair of yoga pants, and my plain black bra and panties. It's all

I have; the only variation is the band of choice for the day.

My towel falls to my feet, adrenaline pulsing through my body with every breath I take, and I rush to grab the emergency bag I've had stashed under my bed for the past two and a half years.

It's been collecting dust since the day I turned eighteen, waiting for the right time.

This is it.

I don't need to check the contents, I have it memorized, so I quickly slide it toward the door.

Get dressed, Scar. Get dressed and get the fuck gone already.

As I'm reaching for my bra, I flinch when a fist pounds against my window.

"That's it, baby, show me your tits."

I don't recognize the guy on the other side of the glass. His demeanor is relaxed, there's a cheeky grin on his face, and a flash of want in his eyes. The branding on his cut confirms he's a member of the Ruthless Brothers, but there's no additional tag space for his name. Sneaky.

Not today, buddy.

"The club whores are further down that way. Keep trying," I offer with an exaggerated sweet smile, without rushing to hide any part of my body from him.

That fact doesn't seem to get lost on him as his eyes continue to rake up and down the length of my body. "I think I'm exactly where I'm supposed to be, sweet cheeks." I don't have time for him and his hot-as-fuck blue eyes, so I continue to get dressed. "Don't cover up that pussy, girly, I'm claiming it for myself," he adds, but I flip him off as I race to find my boots.

Just as I put my foot in the right one, someone pushes against my bedroom door, making it bounce off the wall. "Hands up where I can see them, whore."

Not a Reaper. I gulp back the panic that threatens to take over me. There's a hot, blond viking of a man in my room with a gun aimed in my direction. It would be one hell of a way to go, but this sure as shit isn't my time.

I can defend myself perfectly fine, but my fucking weapons are in the small set of drawers which are closer to him than they are to me.

Fuck.

I slowly continue to lace up my boots as I eye him.

"Did you not hear me? I said, hands where I can see them," he repeats slowly, and I scoff.

"You also said whore, so I assumed you weren't talking to me." I proceed to put on my other boot without breaking eye contact.

There's anger in his eyes, a burning vengeance vibrating around him with each breath he takes.

"A club whore is a whore, and since I don't know your name, whore will do," he explains, tilting his head to the side as he squints at me. "So tell me, whore, why are you in here, scampering to get dressed instead of diving for cover to save your life like the rest of them?"

My brain short-circuits for a second. "Does it matter?"

"It could or it could not. Tell me the answer and I'll decide."

Pursing my lips, I glare at him, but before I can attempt to come up with some bullshit response, the blond guy who was outside my window appears beside the viking in my doorway.

"Yes, Emmett, you found the hot one. Good looking out, man," he says triumphantly, patting his friend on the arm as he steps into the room. "Looks like we're good to roll out now that everyone of importance is dead."

Surprised, my heart lurches in my chest as I point a finger in their direction. "Everyone of importance is *dead*?" I repeat, the words foreign on my tongue as I blink with confusion.

It's the viking's turn to smile wickedly as he places his gun in the holster at his waist. "Yup. The Reapers are done. Whatever protection you were getting here, whoever kept your bed warm at night, they're all. Fucking. Gone." He says it almost tauntingly, but he doesn't realize the euphoria that bursts through my body.

I keep my emotions locked down as they both eye me. "That's good to know. I'll make sure to let myself out when

I've gathered my things."

"Nah, sweet cheeks. Pack a bag. We're in need of a new club whore, and your fine ass is coming with us."

With my arms banded around Blondie's waist, I enjoy the wind whipping against us, but it feels strange as hell to have someone upfront.

I ride alone, always, but clinging to a man I don't fucking know, putting trust in him and his ability to handle his bike, I can see a little bit of the enjoyment in being the passenger.

My nerves haven't dwindled, not for a second, and every minute we get closer to his club, the more uncertainty I feel in my decision to play along with being a club whore. I will do whatever it takes to survive, but no two clubs are completely alike. Ever.

As much as I hated the Reapers, I have no idea what I'm walking into, but it's better I step through those doors as a club whore than myself. It's clear they know nothing about me, no one ever does, but now that every Reaper of importance is dead, it's an opportunity to start fresh. It may not be the one I was reaching for, but I can keep myself afloat for now at least.

This gives me time to figure out a proper plan and a

chance at a real future. There will be no looking over my shoulder by the time I'm done, no one giving me orders, and it sends a zing of empowerment through my veins.

If that means being a club whore for a day or two, then I can work with that. I've known enough of them to play the part. I just hope they haven't brought along any of the *actual* club whores, or else, I'm fucked.

The bike slows as someone holds a metal gate open for us. And the Ruthless Brothers' clubhouse comes into view.

Here goes nothing.

I lift my leg over the bike, unclipping the helmet Blondie insisted on giving me. The sun is setting, offering an almost poetic glow to our good-for-nothing town, but like always, I pretend I'm not stuck in fucking Jasperville.

I won't be for much longer.

A convoy of bikes drives into the compound, and I check the back of each one to make sure there are no other girls here but me. When I'm sure I'm alone, my shoulders relax a little.

"You make a good passenger, sweet cheeks. You ride often?" Blondie asks as he strokes a finger down my spine. A reaction bubbles within me. A reaction I don't want to admit to, so I squash it down and turn to face him.

"I have my own, and I ride it whenever I get the chance." I fold my arms over my chest, putting an invisible barrier between us. He doesn't take the hint for personal space as he slings his arm around my shoulders and pulls me toward the doors along with everyone else.

I can't get a read on the vibe in the air. There's anger, a rage rippling through them all, with a heaping of victory too. Clearly, they're just as pleased as I am by the demise of the Reapers, a loss I'm not sulking over in the slightest, but it feels like all of that blood still didn't calm the fury surrounding them.

Blondie reaches the front of the men, making us the first to swing the doors open, and my spine stiffens, unsure of what the reception will be like, but an uproar of cheers are what greets us as women, children, and men clap, stamp their feet, and bang their fists on whatever surface they can get their hands on.

"Three cheers for the Ruthless Brothers," someone calls out as we step further into the room, and everyone does just that, hooting and hollering in delight at the downfall of the Reapers and the triumph of the Brothers. "Three cheers for our new Prez."

My body stiffens at the fact that there's someone new in charge here, an uncertain time in my childhood threatens to rise to the surface, but instead of dwelling on it, I focus my attention on seeking out the new Prez.

Nudged into the middle of the room, a bottle of bourbon in one hand and the other waving around at everyone to calm down, I come face-to-face with Ryker Holden.

We're a small town, where everyone knows the Prez and VP for every club, even if you're not a part of one yourself. I know his story, the passing of his father and how he came to be VP. It's talked about enough among the Reapers, or it was at least. Now there's no more hearsay. Only facts and truth as it plays out before me.

"We're a family, we cheer for our family, we celebrate as a family, and we survive as a family," he states, sending the room into utter silence. His brown hair is messy from his helmet, and his green eyes sparkle with pride, but the way he runs his tongue over his upper lip tells me he's not completely engrossed in this moment.

"Here, here," an older man calls out, making everyone smile, and Blondie's arm around my shoulders tightens.

"With that being said, things are about to get filthy up in here, and I wouldn't want to ruin the pretty eyes of our old ladies and the children. So, get the fuck out."

A few children grumble as a handful of men drape themselves over the women getting ready to leave, following them out of the door as the crowd grows smaller. But the second the door closes behind them, the music is turned up and women in small dresses and barely-there outfits come out of the woodwork.

Whores.

Perfect.

What are the chances I could claim sensitive eyesight

too and get a pass from this shit?

"I'm out."

A huge guy with brown hair curled into a bun pats Blondie on the shoulder before cutting through the crowd and disappearing down a hallway. I expect Blondie to turn to face the party and drag me into it with him, but to my surprise, he tightens his arm around my shoulders and heads for the same hallway his friend took moments earlier.

When we step through the door, the thumping dance music quietens, but is replaced with the sound of heavy metal blasting instead.

"Don't mind the music. Axel likes to drown us all out." I nod, not really sure what I'm supposed to say as he opens a door. Uncertainty flashes through me as I spy a bed pushed against the far wall.

There's an expectation of me now, one I'm not familiar with. He may be hot as fuck, and it's not like I'm a virgin, but shit, I'm nervous.

"What's your name, sweet cheeks?"

I startle at his question as my hands flex at my sides. "Scarlett, but everyone calls me Scar."

His smirk makes him look even sexier as he strokes a finger down my cheek before taking a step back.

"Scar, the name's Gray. Get some rest, this is your room now. Make sure to lock it," he says with a wink, before turning on his heels and heading back to the party.

My brows knit in confusion, completely bewildered by him leaving, and the fact that I'm even here to begin with. But I'm far too familiar with how things go in clubs like this, so I quickly step inside the room and shut the door behind me, not releasing my breath until the sound of the lock clicks.

An overwhelming feeling of being out of my comfort zone and completely swept up in the moment washes over me.

I'm just thankful there's a roof over my head and a fresh set of sheets on the bed. I can handle tomorrow when it comes, but now, I rest.

SIX

Axel

My head pounds with every step I take, but I still move toward the door determined to get on with my day. The pain I'm in is all my own doing and I won't make excuses, but damn does it hurt like a bitch.

I wince as I step out into the hallway, unappreciative of any noise or bright light coming my way. Although it's mostly quiet, I can hear the distinct sound of my favorite podcast presenter coming from the other side of the door to the spare room. My steps slow as I tentatively press my ear to the wood, hearing this week's episode about a man that slaughtered his family.

We live in a fucked up world, and it really shouldn't be entertaining, but it's fascinating to listen.

Not wanting to be caught looking like a creeper, I move down the hallway toward the kitchen as the smell of coffee lures me closer. I hope like hell that there's no one actually in the kitchen because I'm in no mood to fucking socialize right now.

Turning to the right, I come face-to-face with Molly, a club whore who annoys me simply by breathing. She looks rough as hell, likely mirroring my current state, so I know I have no room to talk.

I avoid her gaze as I trudge toward the coffee machine and pour myself a mug with the remnants in the jug. I'm not spending any more time in here than is necessary, so the second I place the jug back on the stand, I'm marching back toward the door.

"Axel," Molly calls out, but I don't pause to see what she wants.

I make my way toward the garage.

The bar area is empty and clean of any mess left from last night's celebrations, not that I was a part of any of it. I was too busy hiding away in my room with a bottle of liquor as I drank alone.

Again.

I need to stop doing it, but more so, I need to stop touching the hard shit that makes me feel even worse, but fuck does it do a good job of making me feel good before I pass out cold. I'm always running from my memories, running from anything that may hurt me in any way, shape, or form, and a couple of lines to take the edge off really does the trick.

Irritated, I tuck my long, wavy brown hair behind my ear as I take a sip of my hot coffee before pushing the door open to head outside. I instantly regret it as the sun burns my retinas, making my brows pinch as I squint in annoyance.

I don't slow my pace as I untuck my shades from the pocket of my cut and place them over my eyes, shielding me from the burning sun and its judgmental glare. Kicking the stones at my feet, I cut across the yard, following the telltale sounds of tools being put to use as I near Ryker.

He's flat on his back with one of our project bikes hanging above him. He doesn't even attempt to rip me a new asshole because I'm later than I told him I would be.

Instead, he lifts his eyes slightly to find me as I come to a stop beside him, my shadow falling over the length of him as he quirks a brow. "You look rough."

I scoff at his assessment as I take a sip of my coffee before placing the mug down on the tool box to my left. "Thanks, I fucking feel it too," I grumble, tying my hair up into a bun at the top of my head so the wind doesn't continue to float it around my face.

Ryker rises to a sitting position as he places the wrench beside him. I don't miss the concerned look that instantly crosses his face.

Fuck.

I know what's coming, it's always the same, but at least

I can shield my eyes from his intense gaze today. Maybe I should start wearing my sunglasses more often.

"We've talked about this, Ax," he starts.

"No, Ryker, you talked about it, and I listened. I just didn't take action like you hoped." My muscles tense, fighting against me and my words, but I don't retract the truth I know I've spoken. "Besides, there's bigger shit going on that we should be discussing first, Prez," I add, hoping to change the subject.

"Fuck off with that bullshit." Ryker stands and wipes his oily hands down his jeans.

"Why? You love it. Don't say that you don't." I'm teasing and he knows it, but I'm probably coming across harsher than I intend to because I really don't want the conversation to turn back to me.

"Of course I do, Axel, but I barely slept a fucking wink last night after everything that happened. Someone called that hit and I have to hope and pray that we retaliated correctly." He sighs, raking his fingers through his hair before reaching for my mug and downing the last of my caffeine.

I bite back a grunt, focusing on the conversation instead. "Maybe dickhead one and dickhead two were supposed to die sooner rather than later, and maybe it was a sign that it wasn't your burden to carry. Their blood wasn't meant for your hands."

Ryker folds his arms over his chest as he looks up at the sky, his eyes falling closed for a brief moment before he sighs again. "That might be true, but it doesn't fill the gaping hole of rage that's been tearing at my insides for the past twelve months."

Cutting the distance between us, I squeeze his shoulder, tightening my grip when he doesn't instinctively turn toward me, and after a moment, he meets my gaze. "I'm sure it doesn't, Ryker, but maybe you're supposed to fill that hole with something else. If anything, it should definitely shift the weight of the world that's been riding on your shoulders this last year."

I don't do deep and heavy, but my friendship with Ryker is different. He's my brother above anything else and if he needs a good fucking pep talk, then I'll happily provide one. Although, I would much rather do the talking with my fists than my lips. That's more my idea of fun.

"You're right, but it's only shifted the *full* weight of the fucking club onto my shoulders now," he grunts.

"Please, like you weren't already carrying us."

A rag comes flying toward my face the next moment before falling to the floor, and I'm more than sure he tells me to fuck off under his breath, but I let it slide as silence descends around us.

I bask in the silence, enjoying the tranquility of the birds chirping in the distance, no engines revving, and the sunshine beating down on us. "You doing okay?"

It's not every day a Prez dies and a new one replaces him. Wiping out another MC with no bullshit declaration of war, just getting the fucking job done, isn't the norm around these parts. But we did it and I wouldn't change a damn thing either. The reality, however, only serves as a reminder that these actions should have been taken in retribution and honor of Ryker's father when he was killed last year. But nothing happened, or, not enough happened.

It's been hard on all of us, but no one more than Ryker.

"I'm good, man. I would be even better *if* you kept away from the white stuff and actually made it out here on time to help me like you said you would."

Fuck, I thought I had gotten away with it.

It feels like razor blades rip at my throat as I swallow back the guilt. The thought of going cold turkey makes the scar on my back burn like a raging inferno. The memories flicker through my head, tempting me further down the dark, tainted path, but I force it to the back of my mind like I do every time.

I'm sure I'm going to have to deal with all of my issues one day, but today isn't that fucking day.

"Less of my bullshit and more of yours," I grumble, patting him on the shoulder before I point toward the clubhouse. "I think you need to wipe off your hands and shake off your cut because a precedence needs to be set today. Which we both know starts and ends with you calling your first meeting."

He eyes me for a moment, like he's trying to find an argument against me, but then he huffs. "Fine, round them up."

With another mug of coffee in hand, I step into the Church with every man behind me. Some look as rough as I feel, others were buried deep in some club whore pussy when I found them but quickly moved to join me when I rapped my knuckles on their doors.

A day in a motorcycle club is like nowhere else. No two days are ever alike, and you really never know how many pairs of tits you're going to see. It's fun.

Ryker nods to me as I move around the table, Gray and Emmett hovering beside him too, and a sense of pride washes over me. Ryker has been a part of this club since the day he was born. I've been right beside him since I was fucking six, becoming prospects at fifteen… and now, here we are. More specifically, here he is, the man of the hour, the one to lead us to victory, and it gets my fucking adrenaline pumping.

He was made for this role, dedicated every inch of himself to this club like no other man has, and now it's time for him to bring us to greatness.

I move to stand beside my three closest friends. Emmett is a Ruthless Brothers' son, just like Ryker is, while Gray lived on the same street as Ryker and I as kids, and we've been inseparable ever since.

Now we stand tall, ready to support our brother and the club with everything we have.

Euro closes the door behind him, confirming everyone is now present, and the four of us take our seats at the table. Ryker naturally taking the head chair makes me grin, and I fall into my usual seat beside Gray and Emmett further down the long table.

"Shall we call the meeting?" Eric asks. It's the job of the treasurer to call the meetings to a start and take notes, but we lost our treasurer yesterday alongside our old Prez.

Ryker clears his throat, spreading his palms wide on the table top, as he looks at every single set of eyes in the room before speaking. "I know yesterday was not how we expected the memorial to draw to an end, but we got our vengeance and created total carnage in our wake, bringing an end to the Ice Reapers."

Cheers echo around the room as delight and appreciation are shown for avenging our club. Cheers that I join in with, pounding my fist on the wood as I do.

"I also had confirmation a few minutes ago, through Duffer, that the police have been over to the compound.

The explosion we rigged erased all the evidence inside the clubhouse. We did a stellar job because they're declaring it a gas leak."

Another round of celebrations vibrate around the room.

"But, with that being said, we can't act so rashly in the future. We need to proceed with caution and take measured steps to create a solid foundation for our legacy, our family, our club."

"Here, here!" I holler, stamping my feet along with my fists pounding the table, and my brothers join in, shaking the fucking Church to its core with our victory and pride.

"I couldn't have said it better myself," Eric announces. As Emmett's father, he's now the oldest member of the club, carrying more wisdom and experience than the rest of us combined. Which only earns him more respect from every single person here. Old ladies and club whores included. "So, now that there's a new Prez at the head of our table, you need to appoint the men for the open positions at your side," he adds, and the entire room starts to chant one word.

"Prez! Prez! Prez!"

Ryker waves his hand around after a moment, lowering the sound in the room as he nods, sitting taller in his seat. "You're right. Especially since we lost two members yesterday, it's important our framework is strong."

I couldn't agree more.

Ryker glances around the room again, it's so quiet you could hear a pin drop, keeping everyone on the edge of their seats.

"I am electing Emmett as our new VP. Any objections?"

A round of 'nays' quickly bounce, and I grin proudly. We've talked about this so many times, but to see it actually unfold is something else entirely.

"Good. Gray will fulfill the role left behind by Brian and become our treasurer. Any objections?" The way he's speaking leaves no room for argument, but a round of 'nays' echo around us once again.

Gray gives everyone a one-finger salute when no one argues the decision and everyone chuckles at his antics that we're all so used to.

Next, Ryker's eyes settle on me, before switching to Eric, who sits across the table from me with a knowing smile on his lips.

"I believe it's time old man Eric stepped down from the role of sergeant at arms and instead became the ambassador for the club. I know we haven't had anyone in that role for some time, but no one represents the true meaning of the Ruthless Brothers quite like you."

Eric's eyes sparkle at the direct acknowledgment from Ryker. Then he leans back and offers everyone a deathly glare. "If any motherfucker declines this shit for me, you're dead. I'm an old man now. I've brought enough blood to this club, and I agree with Ryker's decision. Besides, I have a good idea who the new S.A.A. will be, and no one enjoys getting their hands bloody more than him."

A hum of agreement washes over the room.

"You're right there, Eric. The new sergeant at arms for the Ruthless Brothers will be Axel fucking Braun. Any objections?"

"Not a single fucking one," Euro hollers, before everyone begins to clap and stomp their feet again.

A grin creeps across my face as pride swells my chest, and the essence swims around me, offering me hope of a calmer, brighter, and more structured future. Except, my past takes only prisoners and I have a feeling I will still be my own undoing.

Despite that, I know I'll do this club proud, no matter what. The fact that my accomplishments will be dripping in blood only serves as an incentive to live to see another day.

SEVEN

Scarlett

"*The investigation took a sharp turn when a strand of hair was examined, leading the officers to a different suspect altogether.*"

I scoff at my phone, the signs were there before the strand of hair, but since there was no hard evidence, the cops hadn't considered them as an option. That's the difference between cops and robbers, heroes and villains, good and bad; the ones who abide by the law see things in a very different light than those that don't.

Growing up in a dark world, surrounded by criminals and outlaws, I wear different lenses to view life in comparison to the cops and all that is good. It's not that I believe I'm *not* good, my morals aren't as grim and hellish as others I know, but I wasn't raised like them.

Right and wrong doesn't look the same to me as it does to them, and that's fine by me.

I twirl my cell phone in my hand as the antsy feelings rush through me. I might love listening to these crime podcasts, but there's only so many I can listen to on repeat before I start to go a little insane.

Uncertainty takes a hold of me again.

No one has knocked, no one has forced their way in… No one has done anything.

I'm not sure if they've forgotten I'm here or not. I know the inner workings of a club, and I know there are a lot of people here. Members, old ladies, their families, the whores. They won't all sleep here every night, but the size of the club is far bigger than the Ice Reapers.

If that's the case though, I may be able to go on my merry way and get the fuck out of here. The thought makes my stomach twist, the nerves churning within me. I hate to admit that my detailed plan to get the fuck away from Jasperville, Texas, is met with the worry that I won't be able to survive on my own.

I'm strong, intelligent, and fierce, but I know that only applies to the world I've been raised in. The outside world, the *real* world, feels far scarier to me. Drugs, guns, sex, and abuse aren't for everyone's tastes, but growing up surrounded by it all, I at least know what I'm dealing with.

I need to get out of this room and out of my head for a minute. Turning the podcast off, I rise from the bed and tuck my cell phone into my back pocket as I move to stand in front of the floor-length mirror in the corner of the room.

Running my fingers through my dark locks, I check myself over to make sure I look a little more… whore-ish and a little less… me. I'm struggling since my clothes are limited, but I've squeezed into my low-hanging skinny jeans and opted for my cropped white top that shows off far more flesh than I'm used to. The V falls low, making my cleavage look better than usual, and my hair falls in loose waves around my face and down my back.

It might not be skimpy and perfect, but it will do.

Tying the laces on my combat boots, I make sure to tuck my miniature pocket knife inside too.

Silence greets me outside briefly before my ears pick up on a faint, dull sound coming from the other end of the hall. Following the noise, I make sure to roll my shoulders back and relax into my stride so I don't look as tense as I feel.

A small radio is playing in the corner of a kitchen, but there's no one actually present.

Maybe I could make a grand escape? Am I even a captive? I don't fucking know.

I turn and enter the bar area across the hall, wondering how much of a clear path I may actually have, when I hear the heavy sound of a gavel smashing. My head turns to the double wooden doors across the bar area, and before I can register that the fall of the gavel will be bringing a meeting to an end, men enter the room.

I remain frozen in place by the door, watching as they disperse. Some head straight for the bar while others exit through the front door, and as if sensing my gaze, my eyes lock with Blondie's—Gray.

My breath hitches as he smirks in my direction before my gaze drops to his cut. I notice the slightly tilted title on the left side and my eyes widen at the words I read that I know for certain weren't there yesterday.

Treasurer.

Someone's been promoted.

Just then, a man moves into my direct line of sight, catching me off guard.

"Hey, pretty lady," he purrs, and I scrunch my nose in distaste as he reaches out to twist a strand of my hair.

It takes everything in me not to push him away and put some distance between us, but I remember my place and remain in position.

His hair is styled into a mullet, a look I'm not usually for, but the waves that run through his ends take the edge off. His nose is a little crooked, from what I can only assume is one too many fights, but otherwise, he's easy on the eyes. Which would definitely explain the confidence oozing off him right now.

"Are you the sweet new whore Gray brought home for us?" His eyes sparkle with hope as he manages to inch closer to me until we're chest to chest. "I've got some time on my hands if you're free now," he adds, not even waiting for me to answer as his eyes drift to my chest.

Asshole.

Nipping at my bottom lip, I keep my eyes locked on his. I'm sure I look sweet and innocent, but he definitely likes it with the way the corners of his mouth tip up. But really, I'm just buying myself time to think of a way out of this right now.

I've just gone from planning my escape to being put on the spot to use my body and it's melting my brain.

"What's up, Euro?"

My eyes cut to the man who interrupts us, and I come face-to-face with Mr. Viking himself. His blond hair is loose today, falling around his shoulders and making him look more like a Greek fucking God, but the beard on his face keeps him rugged.

H.O.T.

Now if this guy was asking me for spare time, I wouldn't even be in this room anymore, same with Gray, but mullet-guy... Euro, it's a firm no. Ladies man or not, my vagina is shriveling up at the thought of him.

Euro takes a moment to answer the Viking, who runs his eyes over me from head to toe, and it feels far more assessing and less sexy prowl than I care to admit. Boo me. And in a flash, he turns and addresses Euro once again, like

I'm not right here.

"Euro, you've got shit to be doing. Besides, our new *guest* here has some questions to be answering," he explains, piquing my interest.

I can definitely adjust to being called a guest over a whore, but the questioning has me a little uncertain.

"I do?" I blurt, folding my arms over my chest as Euro moves back and gives me some space.

The Viking quirks his brow at me, like he really doesn't have time for my sass.

"Will that be a problem?"

I shrug and raise my eyebrows. "Depends on the questions."

"Fuck, yeah. She's mouthy for a whore. I like it," Euro interjects, and I manage to bite back my response as Mr. Viking turns to him with a deathly glare.

"Fuck. Off. Euro."

He doesn't last a whole second under the Viking's harsh stare, before quickly scuttling away, and I roll my eyes at the loss of backbone that fucker has.

Clearing his throat, Mr. Viking turns his attention back to me, and my eyes drift down to his cut, intrigue getting the better of me.

Vice President.

No wonder Euro fucked off so quickly; this man is important apparently. Important enough to be Ryker

Holden's right-hand man.

Interesting.

"Now that there's no interruption, you can lead the way," he states, sweeping his arm out in the direction of the room they all stumbled out of.

No one seems to be paying us any attention, except for Ryker, Gray, and the long-haired rocker from last night, who stands just inside the Church doors. I tuck a loose tendril of hair behind my ear as I clear my throat and look back at the Viking.

"You want me to step in there?"

His brows knit as he looks at me in confusion. "Is that an issue?"

"Uh, no. I just haven't been inside one before," I reply, slowly stepping toward the doors as nerves vibrate up my spine. I dig my fingers into my skin as I try to remain neutral and calm.

The Reapers would *never* have let me step inside their Church, not even to clean the fucking thing, so this feels strange as hell.

"I'm not sure how shit went down at the Reapers, but we're a fucking family here. You're not allowed in without an invite, but it's also not so sacred that we wouldn't expect to find you hiding in here if we came under attack." I look up at the Viking beside me, eyebrows nearly touching my hairline as I silently nod in understanding.

Noted.

Things are definitely different here.

The three guys waiting move around the table and take their seats as I enter the room. The Viking closes the door behind me as I move to the opposite end of the large table, running my fingers over the backs of the wooden seats as I go.

I glance from the door to the frosted window behind Ryker's head before I finally give them my attention.

Ryker sits opposite me, his brown hair swept back off his face. Viking takes the spot to his left, relaxing back in his seat as he looks at me out of the corner of his eye, while Gray smirks at me. I get the feeling he's the mischievous one of this group, unlike the guy sitting across from him. He's wearing shades so I can't see his eyes, but tension radiates from him, just like it did last night, and I wonder if that's a constant state he's in.

"Take a seat, Scar," Gray orders, pointing at the seat directly in front of me and I do just that.

"Scar?"

The question comes from the guy with the shades, his head tilting between Gray and me a few times before Gray finally responds. "Short for Scarlett. Ain't that right, sweet cheeks?"

I hum in response. I don't know shit about these guys, so what they want from me can only relate back to one thing.

The Reapers.

As if sensing my thoughts, Ryker leans forward in his seat, pulling my gaze to his as he laces his fingers together on the table. "How long were you with the Reapers?"

"A while."

"That's vague." Ryker raises his eyebrows at me, clearly wanting more, but I'm more than happy to drag this out as long as possible.

"Do you want specifics?"

Mr. Shades huffs, wagging his finger in my direction. "We wouldn't be fucking asking if we didn't," he grunts, but I don't flinch at their harsh tone. Not when I'm used to it.

Sighing, I lean back in my seat, clamping my hands between my thighs as I direct my answer to him. "Longer than I wanted to be. Is that better?"

He shakes his head in annoyance. A trip down memory lane isn't something I'm prepared for today, and I really don't know why that fucking matters.

"Do you know who I am?"

I turn to the guy asking the question and nod. "Ryker Holden."

"Do you know what happened to my father at the hands of the Reapers?" he asks, his expression giving none of his feelings away, and I scoff.

Lifting my hands, I rest my elbows on the table as I

lean forward, mirroring him. All four of them are watching every move I make, and I'm not going to let them see a hint of weakness in me.

"Do you really think that was the Reapers?" The twitch of Ryker's brow gives him away instantly, and that's a key sign for me to continue. "I've heard the stories, but nothing adds up in my opinion. I know what time they left the club, and I know they were speed demons on their bikes, but even by their standards, I don't see them getting there in time. Minutes out, sure, but giving them the credit for killing your father? Nah, that seems far too unrealistic to me."

None of them move, not even a single blink.

"What stories, Scar?" Gray asks.

I attempt to act indifferent, but I know that they fucking agree with me, I can feel it in my soul. "I just heard a few stories about that night from the members."

"Like. What?" The sharp tone comes from Mr. Shades, his nostrils flaring as he slams his fist on the table, making it rattle, but not me. It takes everything I am to keep my shoulders lowered, but I know I need to offer them a slither of truth and stop talking to them in circles.

"I know that a deal was done, but a lot of talk was more around the reality of the other end holding up their part of the deal because the likelihood was weak."

"Weak?" This comes from the Viking.

"Yeah, it was something along the lines of, 'If they were willing to treat their own that way, they didn't see them being treated any better, agreement or not.'"

"Fuck," Gray curses, running his hand through his hair as he tilts his head back, but Mr. Shades scoffs.

"It's all bullshit. We can't trust shit an Ice Reaper says, even if it is one of their whores." The bite in his tone washes straight over me. He doesn't know me and what I've been through, but jibes like that don't even penetrate the surface. Although, it does fucking piss me off, and I can't stop myself from digging deeper.

"Is that what yesterday was about? Retaliation for your father?"

"Yesterday was about retribution for our club. For my father, Banner, and Billy who became one of our fallen men too," Ryker grunts, lips pursed as he finds himself torn between agreeing with the asshole to his right and burying his hands into his hair like Gray.

"So to clarify, you fought fire with fire yesterday. Came in guns blazing without thinking of all the scenarios and consequences that could unfold for you?" My eyes widen, surprised by the fact that they acted so rash.

"We can face anything as a club. Nothing would have stopped what happened yesterday. Nothing." I can tell by the tightness of Ryker's jaw that he believes every word he's saying, and it's not my place to get involved. But one thing is for certain, I need to get the fuck out of here. As soon as possible.

"Okay, are we done here?" I ask, rising to my feet.

"For now," the Viking states with a nod.

"Good."

I think I'm safe from any further questioning, but one of them clears their throat.

"Out of interest, what makes you say that?"

"Say what?" I ask, playing dumb as I glance over my shoulder to lock eyes with Ryker who asked the question.

"About us not considering the consequences that could unfold for us."

I consider whether I should keep my mouth shut, but it's more than the members of this club that could be at risk. It's the old ladies, the children, the innocent, and I can't live with their blood on my hands.

I take a deep breath, turning to face them properly as I open the door behind me. "I haven't had an easy life, but that's really a story for another day that involves a lot of tequila. I've seen brutal men, been raised by them even, but after seeing the state of some of the girls after another club showed up, demanding shit and taking whatever they wanted, I knew I had truly seen evil."

A shiver runs down my spine at the memory as the four Ruthless Brothers frown at me.

"And who was that?"

"The Devil's Brutes, and the Reapers were twisted up in all of their dealings for sure."

EIGHT

Scarlett

I sit perched on the edge of the picnic bench, my feet resting on the seat with my elbows propped on my knees as the sun sets in the distance. The blue skies that blossomed above earlier, are now tinged with oranges and reds, preparing us for the darkness that will follow.

This is always my favorite part of the day. It's like time stands still, the crossing between day and night almost mystical as you watch it happen, unable to stop it from unfolding before your eyes.

I've been out here since I left Church. Mr. Shades and Ryker headed over to the on-site garage earlier, and they've been there ever since, but otherwise, I've been left to my own devices.

At first, I was tempted to hop the fence that secures the perimeter, wave goodbye to yet another biker club, and find the future I've been longing for. But it quickly became apparent that even though Ryker and his main men were leaving me alone, every other man out here in the yard had eyes on me.

No one approached, but the energy and atmosphere it created made one thing certain. I wasn't going anywhere without their say-so.

As the day turns into dusk, the people out in the yard slowly change before my eyes. The kids that were playing on the tire swing earlier are long gone, replaced by bodies of people looking to have a good time.

Sighing, I sit straighter and wince as my stomach grumbles.

I haven't eaten all day. That's nothing new to me. The Reapers would go days without letting me have food, but it still doesn't stop the discomfort and yearning inside of me.

Deciding whether I should venture inside is an easy decision as a group of guys stumble out into the yard and start rolling around in the grass to my right. I'm not in the mood to witness a fist fight, not when I'm hangry.

Jumping off the picnic bench, I make sure my cell is tucked comfortably into my back pocket as I head inside. I keep my head down, slipping through the busy crowd of people in the bar area, hoping to avoid anyone's eye.

I'm very aware I'm here as a whore, and even though I've been left alone while the sun was shining and the kids were around, it doesn't mean the same will apply in the depths of the night.

I've witnessed the change in men in these surroundings before.

If I can slip into the kitchen and find something to eat and make it to my room without being stopped, I'll call that a win. But it's just my luck that I push through the door at the opposite end of the bar area to find the kitchen filled with women.

Some are in skimpy outfits, others in jeans and a tee, but all of them are glaring at me. If I step in there with confidence and my hangry attitude right now, I'll cause a war, which will likely lead to my head being put on a spike and not theirs.

Fuck.

I don't want them to think I'm easily intimidated because I'm not, but I'm just on the right side of sane to know what battles I want to pick, and tonight, this isn't one of them.

Offering a wide toothy smile, I flick my hair over my shoulder and turn right down the hallway to my room. I manage three steps when I notice the room next door is open and the smell of pizza instantly greets me.

Gray is sitting on a brown leather sofa, his feet propped up on the coffee table, with an open pizza box beside him. A video game is paused on the big screen, and I have to force myself to keep moving. But the second I do, I hear my name on his lips.

"Hey, Scar. You eaten yet?" I spin to face him, hands fidgeting nervously at my sides as my stomach grumbles again, giving him the answer he needs as he smirks. "Come on, sweet cheeks."

My tongue runs over my bottom lip as I step into the room, appreciating the fact that the music seems to die down a little more in here from the bar. Rounding the sofa, I take the large slice of pizza from Gray and sink my teeth into the end of it.

Holy fucking shit.

I'm never going to run away and start a new life for myself, not if it means leaving this deliciousness behind.

"Fuck, that's so good," I groan around the food in my mouth.

"Only the best for the Ruthless." He winks as he nods at the empty spot on the other side of the pizza box, and I take it, relaxing back into the leather as I take another bite.

"What kind is this?"

"Meat feast extreme. Pepperoni, meatballs, sausage, spicy beef, mushroom, and a garlic drizzle from Pepe's downtown."

I nod and I continue to devour the greasy goodness sent from God. The second I'm done, Gray offers me another, a smirk on his face that makes me squint at him in confusion.

"What?"

"Do you groan that good for dick too or is it just pizza?"

Shocked, I didn't even realize I was fucking groaning to begin with. The way his head falls back as he laughs though, tells me he's not mad about it. I can take the teasing if it means I get another slice, so I lean in a little closer, making sure my hand touches his as I take the offered slice.

"I groan for anything tasty, Gray. Especially if you whisper 'I'm a good girl'." Taking the pizza, I fall back in my seat, far too fucking pleased with myself as he gapes at me in surprise.

"You are something else, sweet cheeks," he says with a smirk, and I wink.

"You're right, but I'm out of groans for now. You'll have to wait your turn. Right now, it's just me and the pizza."

Before I can even blink, Gray is reaching over the distance between us and grabbing my chin to force my gaze to his. "You're playing with fire, Scar, and I like it." His chest heaves as his pupils dilate and my heart races like crazy in my chest. Holy fuck. "But you need to eat, so I'm going to pause what it is I want to do to you... for now."

This time, I have no response for him, not one, so I quickly stuff my mouth with pizza to stop from responding. He drops his hand from my face and I miss his touch instantly, almost considering something else I could say to bring him back to me, but the moment is broken when a girl walks in.

"Hey, Gray. Have you seen Emmett?"

"I haven't, but I know when he finds you here, he's going to be pissed, Emily." There's no humor in his tone as he assesses the girl. Her blonde hair is swept back off her face, tied high at the top of her head as she pushes her glasses up the bridge of her nose.

She seems sweet. Far too sweet for a place like this.

Her gray eyes flash to mine for a brief moment, before she turns back to Gray and rolls them dramatically at him. "When are you guys going to remember I'm eighteen now," she grumbles, adjusting her backpack on her shoulder as she purses her lips.

"Never," Gray replies with a shrug, pulling his cell phone from his pocket as he smirks at her.

Throwing her arm down at her side to slap against her thigh, she turns her attention back to me. I feel like a deer caught in the headlights with the slice of pizza poised in front of my mouth, but not moving, as I watch the pair of them.

"Are all men like this?" she asks, nodding in Gray's direction, and I shake my head as I clear my throat.

"No. Usually… they're worse."

Her brows pinch as her head rears back a little, and she finally assesses me from head to toe. Once she's satisfied, her eyes meet mine once more.

"You're not a club whore, am I right?"

It's my turn for my eyes to widen as I scramble for a response. "Uhhh…"

"I'm just saying, you're way too pretty to be, and you're not sizing me up like I'm competition, so I can only assume I'm correct."

Still speechless, I panic that I'm not doing a good enough job as a newly assigned club whore. I don't want questions being asked, and I don't want to face the chopping board just yet, so I need to up my game.

Thankfully, my stuttering is forgotten when the blond Viking walks in with an angry look on his face. His jaw is tense, his brows furrowed, and his nostrils flaring as he points a finger at Emily.

"What have I fucking told you about coming here without me? You can't just walk around here like it's a fucking theme park, Em. Get your shit and let's go."

Before I even realize it, my slice of pizza is back in the cardboard box as I rise to my feet and move toward the girl I don't even know.

"Don't fucking speak to her like that."

The Viking, whose actual name is Emmett, goes from glaring to wide-eyed surprise, before glaring even harder once again.

"I didn't ask for your involvement, so back the fuck

up and carry on offering your pussy out to anyone who wants a lick. While you're there, keep your nose out of my family's fucking business." His words are harsh, but they go over my head as I double down, folding my arms over my chest as I move to step in front of Emily.

"You can direct your anger at me. I can stand here all day and take it, but leave her the fuck alone." I have no clue who I'm actually defending, but she's too damn sweet to take his bullshit, and I really do have all day.

I feel a hand at my arm, a gentle and calming touch that makes me tilt my head to look back at Emily. "It's okay. He's my brother," she explains.

Looking between them, my anger and annoyance don't waver as I shake my head. "Honey, he could be God himself, but letting him speak to you like that and get away with it only teaches you to allow *any* man to take the same tone, and I'm sure that's not Mr. Viking's intention. Is it?"

The bite in my tone has me practically grinding my teeth as I settle my glare back on Emmett.

He stares me down, and to my surprise, he wipes his hand down his face before scratching at his beard. The tension from his shoulders relaxes as his gaze softens toward his sister before he glances my way.

"Mr. Viking, huh?"

I squeeze my eyes shut as I cringe at the nickname slip, but the room is filled with chuckles coming from the three of them as I finally peel them open again. At least it broke the fucking tension. Although, Emmett's eyes are still fixed on mine, waiting for some kind of response.

With a shrug, I take a step to the side again, relaxing my stance around Emily as I grin. "You look like a Viking. I'm not the first one to say that and you know it. But don't think changing the subject is going to make me go easy on you if you keep being an asshole to Emily. Understood?"

His gaze intensifies for the longest moment, until he offers me one simple nod. "If that means I have someone else looking out for Emily, then the only thing I can do is understand," he states before waving his arm at her, and she moves to his side instantly.

I can sense the love between them, the care, and even if it is harsher than necessary, it's still there.

As Emily moves to leave, she pauses mid-step, turning back to face me with a curious glint in her eyes. "Hey, I didn't catch your name."

"It's Scar."

"Scar as in short for Scarlett?" she clarifies, and I nod.

"Then I'm going to call you Scarlett because that's a pretty name. Scar sounds like a nickname in a biker club."

"Are you forgetting where we are?" I smirk as I cock a brow at her, and she rolls her eyes at me.

"As if this big *Viking* would ever let me." Her grin is infectious as she turns to leave. Emmett hovers for a split second, looking at me strangely, before he rushes to catch up with her.

Once the room is quiet again, I turn back to the sofa to find Gray assessing me in very much the same way as Emmett had.

"What?" Grabbing my slice of pizza, I stare at him inquisitively, but it seems to take him a moment to figure out what he's trying to say.

"Nothing, you just have a way of leaving an impression on everyone you meet." It's a statement, not an opinion. One I've heard before, but pretend doesn't exist in my memories.

"So it seems," I mutter, taking a bite of the pizza and turning my attention to the television.

Thankfully, Gray takes the hint and reaches for his controller, continuing the shooting game he had paused. We fall into a comfortable silence as I finish my food, but the second I'm done, I'm ready to join in. Nothing occupies my mind like a mind-numbing game.

"Do you have another controller?"

Gray glances at me from the corner of his eyes without stopping the game. "Do you play?"

"If there's another controller, I do," I reply, making him smirk as he points at the television stand.

I run my hands down my jeans before reaching into the unit to find the second controller. Gray gives me a stern look. "I'm not going easy on you."

"I would question your manhood if you did."

"Oh, you're going to be the prettiest fucking loser that ever existed," he retorts with a wink, restarting the game for two players. "Do you want to use my guest account or…"

His words trail off as I shake my head. "No, I'm good."

As I log in to my account, he doesn't utter a word as my skull icon loads in and my profile appears.

x GamerScar9 x
One Friend - Offline

"Only one friend, sweet cheeks? That's bad," Gray says as he takes over, starting the game up.

"I prefer quality over quantity, Blondie," I reply, glancing at him out of the corner of my eye.

"I like it."

"You won't when I beat you." The atmosphere continues to lighten around us, the banter and calmness making my chest buzz with a weird feeling I've never felt before. It has the temptation to make me drop my perfectly placed walls, but I quickly remember myself and take a deep breath.

"Actions speak louder than words, Scar. Let's go."

The game starts without missing a beat, and the online

multiplayer shooting scene appears on the screen moments later. We're on the same team, so we'll technically win or lose together, but the tally of kills and deaths and the ratio it provides will be telling enough.

Neither of us speaks a word, absorbed in the game, until we complete the third game and I finish above him in the team results *again*.

"How the fuck are you so good at that?"

"I have time on my hands," I reply with a grin, and when he doesn't press continue for the next round, I turn to look at him.

"Are we not going again?"

Gray scoffs as his eyebrows almost raise to his hairline. "Sweet cheeks, you're destroying me. It's a good thing I didn't put any money on this because I'd be shit out of pocket right now," he grumbles, waving his hand at the television.

"We can place bets next time," I offer as he rolls his eyes and rises from his seat.

"We're only placing bets when I set you up against someone else so I can reap the rewards too." He stretches his arms above his head, and I catch a glimpse of his happy trail as his shirt rises slightly.

Distraction. Abort. Abort.

He places his controller on the coffee table and offers me his hand. "Let's go."

Frowning at his hand, I place my controller beside me as I remain in position. "Go where?"

If this asshole says to fuck, he has me that hyped up that I would follow him without question, but I want to hear the words first.

"To party. I need to drown my sorrows for losing. You coming?"

That's not what I expected him to say at all, but I can't deny that I like being in his presence. With one final breath, I place my hand in his and let him lead the way.

NINE

Gray

Holy fucking shit. If I'd sat in that fucking room with this mystical being a minute longer, then I'd have been pulling her onto my stiff cock and claiming her as mine. My chest constricts at the thought as my hand instantly flexes around hers.

That's not what I do and it's most certainly not who I am either.

I don't claim anyone. I don't settle down. I don't do any of that righteous shit.

She remains quiet at my side as I lead us down the hallway, and I reluctantly force myself to let go of her hand. I might not be one for claiming people, but I sure as shit still want her in my vicinity. I want her right by my side.

Straightening my cut, I glance at her out of the corner of my eye and the same thoughts continue to race through my mind.

How the hell does a hot-as-fuck chick who has no idea how goddamn alluring she is, who eats pizza like a champ, and beats me at my favorite fucking video game, end up in a motorcycle gang as a whore? An Ice Reaper whore, nonetheless.

Not anymore. I refuse to associate her with those two sickly words that we've brought to an end. She's a Ruthless Bitch now, whether she likes it or not. I may not be willing to claim her for myself, but for the club, definitely.

Fuck.

I need a beer and a distraction from her, but all my mind and body can think about is her porcelain skin and pouty lips.

I'm screwed.

Fucking. Dead.

Cracking my neck, I push open the door into the bar area and the music instantly kicks up a notch. It's surprising how much quieter it can be with the door closed, but at least it seems like everyone is having a good time.

The bar is brimming with members and whores, while some have taken to dancing in the middle of the space. Ryker's in the Prez's booth at the center of the wall to the left, which has a perfect view of the room and exits.

Draping my arm around Scar's shoulder, I steer her toward him as eyes start to glance in our direction. I keep my grin frozen in place as I nod and wave at those who call my name over the music, but I don't offer any more than that.

I need to sit down and hide this boner I've been sporting for the past forty fucking minutes, yet I get the sense it won't be going anywhere any time soon.

"Whatcha drinking, sweet cheeks?" I speak into her ear, and she shivers at my side. My cock pulses against my jeans, begging for attention, but I sink my teeth into my tongue instead, the taste of copper distracting me for a minute.

"I'll take some water."

I frown at her as we come to a stop by the booth. "Water? There isn't any fucking water here."

Her eyes dart around the room for a moment before she sighs. "Fine, I'll have a beer."

Ryker must hear her response because he waves three fingers across the room to the bar staff before shuffling around to make space for us.

"Where have you been, man? You know parties aren't bearable alone," Ryker grumbles as I encourage Scarlett into the booth first.

She's nestled perfectly between us as I sit down and lean back, taking in the room for myself. As the newly appointed treasurer, I was never a part of Banner's inner circle before Ryker, so I've never been privy to sitting here before.

I like it.

"We were hanging out, playing my new video game and eating pizza, weren't we, Scar?" I extend my arm around the booth behind her, my body unable to keep distance between us, and I swear she inches closer to me too. Fuck. I'm either imagining shit or it's getting crazy hot in here. "Besides, I thought you were with Axel," I add, noting the way his brows pull at the mention of his name.

"I was, but when something went wrong on the bike he was fixing up, he got pissed and stormed off." The pain in his eyes is noticeable, no matter how much he tries to keep it at bay.

He may be our Prez, and he may need to keep up a hard front, but that doesn't stop him from worrying about his friend, his fucking brother.

"It's the anniversary, man, it's fucking with his head." I'm acutely aware of Scarlett's presence during a private conversation, but instead of jumping in like most women around here do, wanting to know all of the gossip, she just continues to glance around the room.

"I know. He's just hitting the hard stuff more than ever and I fucking know he's going to go to far. I can feel it in my bones."

Fuck.

If Ryker is worried, we all should be, but none of us are familiar with helping someone like this. Our attempts at an intervention have failed miserably and mentioning a therapist or counselor only sends him into a deeper spiral.

I'm thankful for the interruption as three bottles of beer are placed down on the table before us. I nod my appreciation before taking a big gulp.

My gaze catches Ryker's and I can tell we're both looking for a different topic of conversation. I can sense his desire to grill Scar about the motorcycle gang she mentioned earlier in the Church. The Devil's Brutes. I'm intrigued, but we also agreed that there was some investigating of our own that needed to be done first.

A smirk teases my lips at the memory of what happened with Emmett earlier and I'm just about to catch Ryker up when the smell of cheap perfume and sickly sweet cocktails overwhelms my senses.

The high-pitched giggle that comes moments later has me rolling my eyes at Ryker before I turn to find Molly and Ruthie standing at the end of the booth. They eye me, then Scarlett, then Ryker, followed by the empty spot beside me, but I keep my mouth shut.

They won't take a seat here unless it's offered to them and it sure as shit isn't coming from me.

"Aren't you going to introduce us to the new Ruthless Bitch, Gray?" Molly asks, eyes sharply aimed at Scarlett beside me, while Ruthie nods eagerly.

"Hi, I'm Scarlett." She offers a small wave in acknowledgment before reaching for her beer, and her nonchalance seems to piss Molly off. Everything anyone does that isn't in Molly's favor pisses her off. It's boring. She's desperate to be someone's old lady, but despite her efforts, no one is falling face-first to the ground with love for her.

"I wasn't talking to you," she states, hands planted on the table. "I was talking to *my* Gray."

"Molly, no one here belongs to you. We've had this conversation far too many times and you're just choosing to not listen," Ryker says with a sigh, his irritation clear over the music that fills the room.

"Ryker, baby, I was here first and you haven't invited me into the booth yet. But this new bitch strolls in, offering her cunt out to anyone and everyone and that seems to get her a seat." She folds her arms over her chest while Ruthie sips at her cocktail, clearly quite happy to watch the drama unfold without actually getting involved like usual.

"Actually, I didn't offer it out. Gray just managed to get an eyeful of my pretty pink pussy before I could cover myself," Scarlett declares as she leans forward, bracing her elbows on the table as she locks eyes with Molly.

Fuck. After watching her put Emmett in his place earlier, I knew she was fire, but now, she has my cock screaming in my pants with need. I trail my hand down her spine, knowing Molly is watching my every move as I lean forward a little too.

"Please, Scar, you had ample time to cover your perky tits and needy cunt and you didn't even attempt to hide from me. You can't buy that level of confidence, sweet cheeks. And fuck, let's be honest, with a body like that, I understand why." I offer her a wink as she bites back an almost bashful smile, before I turn to look at the two whores before me.

I know I'm using Scar to piss Molly off, but I can't help it. Not when she seems so willing and has a backbone of steel.

"Fuck, I bet that was hot to see," Ryker adds, smirking from his seat as he runs his eyes over Scarlett, more obvious than ever to irritate Ruthie and Molly, and it works effortlessly.

"You will not believe what she did earlier," I say with a chuckle, meeting Ryker's gaze over Scarlett's head, hoping to change the subject, but Molly isn't giving up that easily.

"Gray, she doesn't know you like I do. I bet she doesn't even know your last name."

When will this girl get the hint and fuck off?

Scar either senses my annoyance and wants to wind Molly up too or she's naive and curious when she places her hand on my thigh and pulls my attention to her. "Gray, I can't believe you haven't told me your last name. I'm going to pass the fuck out with heartbreak if you don't tell me right this second."

Yup. Definitely the first thought. Her eyes sparkle with humor as she runs her tongue over her lips, and I have to force myself to answer before I crash my mouth to hers instead.

"It's White."

Her brows pinch for the briefest moment before her head falls back and she starts laughing. I can hear Ryker joining in with her and the corner of my mouth tilts up too. I was ruined as a kid with my fucking name, but now I think it's fucking brilliant, especially when it makes her laugh like this.

"Of all the options in the world, Gray White is the winner. I love it," Scarlett manages to say around her chuckles, before reaching for her beer. I'm very aware that my hand is still at the base of her spine, but as much as I tell myself to move it. I. Can't.

"It's not *that* funny that his name is two colors." Molly scoffs, like she wasn't the one to bring it up, but Scarlett doesn't get a chance to say anything back when Ryker leans across the table to pat my shoulder.

"You were telling me about something she did earlier."

I nod eagerly, smiling from ear to ear when I explain everything that went down with Scar, Emmett, and Emily. Right down to the fact that I'm ninety-nine percent sure Emily walked out of there in awe of her newfound friend.

"Fuck, now that's something I would have paid to see,"

Ryker finally manages when he calms his laughter down. Scarlett remains quiet, happy to assess the room and ignore the unwanted guests at the table instead of reaping all of the attention that's on offer to her. "I wonder what else we will learn about you, Scarlett."

She clears her throat as she tucks a loose tendril of hair behind her ear, shrugging slightly. "There's not much to know."

"Hey, I've just realized that I don't know *your* last name, sweet cheeks. Don't make me die out on the floor right now. That shit will stain." I fake-gasp as I plant my palm on my chest and pout at her, and she shakes her head in disbelief at my dramatics.

"My name is Scarlett Reeves."

I don't know what I was expecting, something grand almost, like the vibe and aura she gives off, something to match that. But Reeves somehow suits her.

"Hey, I just realized something too," Molly interjects, still remaining at the edge of the booth even though none of us are looking at her. Even when no one instantly turns their attention her way, she continues, "Our new girl needs to do her rite of passage," she announces with a clap, and Ruthie bounces on her heels with excitement.

Fuck.

Fuck. Fuck. Fuck. Fuck. Fuck.

Side-eyeing Scarlett, I don't know what I expect to

see on her face, but it surprises me even more when there's nothing at all. Not a wrinkle to her forehead, no crinkling of her eyebrows, and no sneer on her lips.

Has she heard of the Ruthless Bitches' rite of passage? Was it like this at the Reapers?

"And what if I don't want to be a Ruthless Bitch?" The nickname for our club whores sounds like nails on a chalkboard from her lips, or is it just how I'm hearing it?

Ruthie scoffs this time, stepping closer and finally places herself in the drama. "If you want the Ruthless roof over your head, you're either a Ruthless Brother, a Ruthless Brother's old lady and offspring, or a Ruthless Bitch."

Those are definitely the rules.

Fuck.

My palm flattens against her spine as my other hand balls up into a fist. I'm at war in my own head over shit that has been the club's way for the longest time. Now I'm suddenly questioning it?

What the fuck is going on with me?

It's her. It's Scarlett. Miss fucking Reeves is going to be the death of me.

"The rite of passage at my old club was to fuck a member for all to see. Show you're worthy and willing to give it your all. Is that the same here?" Scarlett looks unfazed as she keeps her gaze fixed on Molly, but I notice the way she rubs her hands on her jeans.

Is she nervous?

If she was a whore there, she would have done it before. Shit.

I need to stop thinking of her with other men because that's pissing me the fuck off.

Sinking my teeth into my tongue once more, my gaze flickers to Ryker who is happily watching this all unfold as Molly confirms that the same rule applies here.

"That's right, *Scar.* Now, do you want to wait right there while I go and find Euro or someone or do you want to leave?" Molly's words ring in my ears along with my pulse as indecision courses through me.

Scar can't leave. Not just because I refuse it, but because there's more information we can get out of her regarding the Reapers and potentially the Devil's Brutes. But staying without doing the rite of passage would only happen if she was... an old lady, and I'm not about that shit.

"Scarlett isn't going anywhere, not tonight at least," Ryker interjects.

She's fucking tonight, and the knowing look glistening in her eyes tells me she knows it too.

I never partake in a rite of passage. *Ever.* Neither has Ryker, Emmett, or Axel. We might fuck the whores on occasion, but not for everyone to see. I know I have no time to decide when Ruthie moves to find Euro, and I reach across the distance between us and stop her on the spot.

"You don't need Euro, Ruthie," I state, and her eyebrows furrow in confusion as I release her arm and drop down into my seat. "If you're on the rite of passage express, Scar, I have everything you need right here, and with the Prez on the other side of you, I don't see that being an issue. Do you?"

Scarlett's chest rises and falls heavier with every breath she takes. She glances to her left to confirm Ryker is indeed nodding in agreement, before coming back to settle those big blue eyes on mine. "I don't see an issue at all," she breathes.

My cock is almost painful from the aching and longing I've felt all night, but he's finally going to be put out of his misery soon.

Then I might finally get this crazy infatuation out of my system.

"But, Gray, you never help a girl out with her rite of passage," Molly shouts, stomping her foot in agitation as she bares her teeth.

"I'm making an exception."

"An exception for me?"

I shrug like it's no big deal. "Sweet cheeks, you destroyed me in there earlier. The least I can do is give you the trophy you deserve," I reply with a wink, thrusting my hips a little, and she rolls her eyes.

A groan almost tumbles from my lips as she places the palm of her hand against the zipper of my jeans. She circles the outline of my cock, and I flex in her hand as she glances at where we're touching before meeting my eyes.

"Is it just for show or does the owner know how to use it?"

Her quick wit is slaying me, her rapid fire banter only making me harder for her.

"Come take the lead, Scar, and you'll find out for yourself," I murmur as she sinks her teeth into her bottom lip. "I'm only doing this if I know you want it, sweet cheeks. So what's it going to be?"

My pulse rings in my ears, begging and pleading with her to want this as badly as I do. The second her smirk teases at the corner of her mouth, I know she's right here with me.

"Fine. You know the rules, Gray. Fuck her in this room, and she becomes a Ruthless Bitch when she's wearing your cum with pride," Molly hollers, pounding the table for good measure, but my eyes are fixed on Scarlett's.

Without missing a beat, she lifts up in the booth and drapes her thighs on either side of mine. I can feel the heat of her pussy through the material separating us and my dick fucking loves it.

"Are you going to wear my cum with pride, Scar?"

"Only if you can keep it off the tip of my tongue by the time we're done."

Fuck.

TEN

Scarlett

My heart beats wildly in my chest, matching the slightest bit of trembling in my fingertips as I look deep into Gray's eyes. I don't know whether I'm stuttering with nerves or raw fucking need for the man beneath me. The sultry look in his eyes has my body moving on its own accord, and I realize I'm straddling his lap. But now that I'm here, there's nowhere else I'd rather be.

When I press down against his length, my core clenches at his hardness. Even with both of our jeans creating a barrier between us, it's undeniable, and I'm needy as hell. This isn't just a show for him, he wants this, wants me, just as much as I want him, and if it's a rite of passage they want, I'm more than willing to follow through *if* it's in the hands of this man.

I can sense eyes on us from all directions, especially from Ryker, who is still in his seat beside us, while the girls continue to drill holes into the back of my head. I'm sure with my back turned, Molly is drawing a crowd and making a spectacle of me, but I refuse to let her get under my skin despite her attempts. I may not have done this whole rite of passage bullshit before, but I've witnessed it unfold too many times to count.

Shit, I distinctly remember what Belinda, one of the club whores back at the Reapers, said to me once, *"Honey, we were put on this earth to have a good time or no time at all, and I ain't living with the latter. They're going to be watching me whether I want them to or not, so what it boils down to is whether I want to put on a show or let the club down. Because what folk don't tell you is, they might call us whores but we're a fucking staple to this club, a foundation the men don't even realize is propping them up just as much as the bar is. Besides, when I'm enjoying myself under this roof, I feel like I'm on top of the goddamn world."*

"What's your first move, Scar?" Gray's voice pulls me from my thoughts. The noise from the club filters into my ears for the briefest of moments before my attention settles back on him.

The fact that he calls me by *my* nickname and not the generic one I'm sure he's used on hundreds of women before has me leaving my inhibitions behind. Relaxing my shoulders back, I don't answer him with words and use actions instead.

I reach for his neck, flexing my fingers along his throat and feeling the bob of his Adam's apple. My tongue peeks out, running along my lips, thirsty for a taste of him. But as I inch his head back, exposing more of his throat to me, I don't go for his skin.

Instead, I move to his cut, where the badge reads *V. President*, and only when his eyes reach mine do I place an exaggerated kiss over the writing. With my eyes fixed on his, I feel his pulse quicken.

Belinda was right; I do feel like I'm on top of the world with this man's reaction when I technically haven't touched him properly yet.

Fuck the rest of them. Fuck whoever is watching. Right now, it's just him and me.

I drag my thumb over the leather where my lips just touched, the cotton of his patch, before I slowly rise up onto my knees. The second I move, his hands grab my waist like he's worried I'm leaving, but that's far from the truth.

The awareness I have of his proximity and the touch of his skin against mine has my core tensing. I can practically feel his fingertips searing into my skin.

Flexing my hand at his throat, I lean in close enough so the tips of our noses brush, when the mouthy bitch that started all of this chimes in.

"I don't think so. Gray doesn't kiss on the mouth." Her words slice through the moment between us, reminding me that we're truly not alone right now.

I don't turn to look at her, keeping my gaze locked on Gray instead as his brows furrow.

"Listen, Blondie, tell this bitch face that you don't get an exception unless you're exceptional, and I'm exceptional as hell," I murmur, brushing my lips against his as I speak.

His throat bobs against my hands as he clears his throat. "Yes, Ma'am."

That's all I need to close the distance between us. Our lips collide in the next breath as his hands instantly move to my hips. His lips are full and plump against mine, making me dive in for more without taking a breath.

He's intoxicating.

Before I realize or anticipate his next move, he's pulling my ass down into his lap as he thrusts up, giving me a feel of his stiff cock.

My nipples pebble with all the sensations running through my body, and my skin prickles with need. I've fucked before, I'm no virgin, but this… this is something else.

Nipping at his bottom lip, I lock eyes with him. "Your cut stays on?" I clarify, more for myself so I don't start tearing at it while I strip him bare.

"It does."

"Your t-shirt?" I run my fingers over the collar of his top as he shrugs.

"Doesn't matter."

Perfect.

Grabbing the material with both hands, I tear it right down the center of his chest. Cheers ring out from behind me as Gray grins, his eyes flashing with appreciation and desire.

In an instant, his hands are at the neckline of my cropped tee, mischief dancing across his lips. But when he grips the material, he hesitates.

As if sensing my worry over the pause, he pulls me in closer before speaking. "Why don't I want anyone here to see your pebbled nipples, Scar?" His voice is darker now, huskier, as he drops one hand to run his thumb over the peaked nub he's talking about.

"They don't have to. I can get up right now and walk away, leave the club and this rite of passage bullshit behind." My chest heaves with every word I speak. It's weird as fuck. Those are the words I should want him to agree to. I need to go, I need to start afresh, and that needs to happen far away from here.

At the same time, I don't want to leave his lap. It's not a case of me being committed to a cause either, refusing to back down or bow out when necessary. It's because I want this, want him.

His eyes darken at the same time he rips at the material, letting the fabric fall to my sides as he reveals my breasts. No bra, no other material between us. Just me and him.

Without wasting a second, he captures my left nipple in his mouth as he cups my right breast with his hand, and a grin teases my lips as my head falls back on a groan.

I suppose that's one way to make sure no one can see them.

The lapping of his tongue quickly turns into nips of his teeth against my needy flesh, and my hands lift to his head. Raking my fingers through his hair, I tug at the ends instinctively as his nips turn to bites, and I gasp.

"Fuck, Gray."

"Fuck, I like my name on your lips," he grunts, bringing his free hand back to my ass as I grind down on him again. "But I fucking hate that you're wearing jeans right now and not some easy access skirt."

I agree with his grumble, wishing I had something that made this fucking easier between us, but I didn't dress with this in mind this morning.

"I hate that I'm wearing anything at all," I mumble, crushing my lips to his once more as our chests are pinned together. His grip tightens on me, but I push back just as much, holding his jaw and moving my mouth to nip at the stubble.

"You are something else, Scarlett Reeves," he mumbles,

thrusting up again before he grabs my waist and hauls me onto the table.

I'm sure I hear one of the bottles of beer smash on the floor, but I don't pull my attention from him. Bracing my hands on the table beside me, there's no doubt people will be able to see my breasts now, but with my back to the majority of the room, I'm not worried.

Gray rises from his seat in the booth, before stepping up onto the leather, and the room cheers once more as a pair of lips suddenly engulf my nipple.

I almost get whiplash from looking to see who it is, and I startle when I find it's Ryker. A shiver runs down my spine as he stares up at me, his lips locked around my taut peak as he swirls his tongue against my heated skin.

Holy. Shit.

I've never been shared before, and as intriguing as this might be, right now isn't the time nor place. As if sensing my uncertainty, Ryker releases my nipple with a pop, before leaning back in his seat.

I take a deep breath as the music cranks up a notch around us. The heavy base vibrates through my veins as I look up to find Gray watching me intently, but my eyes don't remain on his for long when I find his hand wrapped firmly around his cock.

Fuck.

I'm breathless just looking at him.

"Let's put me on display for a minute, sweet cheeks," he says with a wink, and he's barely audible over the music and cheers, but I get the gist of it. As much as I want to roll my eyes at him, I can't say I'm not thankful.

"Lick."

I read his lips well enough to know what he's asking, and it makes my core clench as I lean forward willingly, my mouth opening enough for my tongue to sneak out and skim along the head of his cock.

He's hot against my tongue, smooth and fucking dreamy, so I do it again and again.

"Taste."

He brings his hand away from his length, just using his forefinger and thumb to keep it aimed at my mouth. I press the pad of my tongue against the base of his cock, before slowly tasting him. When I reach his bulging head, I twirl my tongue around him, pleased with myself when his eyes fucking roll back into his skull.

"Suck."

The most important demand of all.

Engulfing his cock with my lips, I tease the end of him before taking more of his hot length into my mouth. I enjoy the realization that crosses his face when I reach the hilt of his dick without gagging. His jaw goes slack and his pupils dilate further as I retreat, only to take him deep to the back of my throat once more.

My thighs clench together as I grab onto the back of his legs, then hold myself still. I'm hoping he'll get the hint as I let my mouth fall looser, and he clearly misses my heat because he nudges past my lips again, making me grin.

A knowing look flashes in his eyes as he flexes his hips, nudging a little deeper into my mouth each time, before he's fully slamming his dick into the back of my throat.

Tears prick my eyes with the force, and I fucking love it, crave it. The thought of his taste on my tongue is enough to make me almost climax alone.

As a tear trails down my face, Gray wraps his hand in my hair and jerks my head back, releasing his cock from my mouth, leaving me to gape at him in disappointment.

"I don't want to come too soon, Scar," he says as he steps down from the booth so we're chest to chest. My cheeks feel warm, likely matching the pink tinge on his face.

Despite my heart throbbing in my chest and ringing in my ears, I still hear the distinct chant that sounds out around us.

"Fuck! Fuck! Fuck! Fuck!"

"Are we giving them what they want?" I ask, and he shakes his head in response, making my body freeze.

"No. I'm giving us what we want, right?"

Relief rushes through me as I nip at my bottom lip and nod.

This man just might be my undoing, or will I be his? I don't care for the semantics, just the actions that are involved.

Leaning up on my tiptoes, I press my lips to his one more time before spinning on my heels and tucking my hands under the waistband of my jeans. With how the booth sits, the table comes up to my waist, leaving little to be revealed to the enthralled crowd.

My eyes meet Molly's instantly, a scowl distorting her face as she stands with her hands folded over her chest. Ruthie isn't matching her stance though; she's down on her knees blowing another member of the club beside her.

It's turning into a fucking orgy, and I definitely prefer that to being the only show.

I almost start to worry that Gray is backing out, then his hands gloss over the globes of my ass cheeks moments later, and I push back into his touch.

"Prez, her tits," Gray hollers as I glance back over my shoulder at him. He places his sheathed dick at my entrance, but doesn't go any further, quirking his brow at me. I'm sure the need in his eyes reflects my own. I'm too far gone on him now to back out.

Before I can edge myself onto his thick cock, hands cup my breasts, and I turn to glance at Ryker once more. His eyes are fixed on where Gray is nestled at my entrance, and he runs his tongue over his bottom lip before flicking his gaze my way.

"He doesn't want others to watch your tits as you bounce on his cock, Scarlett. It's either me holding them, kissing them, or sucking them. Your choice." Ryker's words send a shiver down my spine.

Holy shit.

Is there an option for all of the above?

"Whichever you do, you better hold on tight, *Ryker*," I breathe, before thrusting my hips back and taking Gray all the way in.

His hands tighten at my waist as I try to catch my breath. I feel so fucking full with him right now that I can't move simply because my pussy is clenching around him with desperation.

Ryker's hands pinch at my breasts, a grin tainting his lips as Gray slowly pulls out of me before slamming deep inside of me over and over again. My back arches, my body bowing as my skin prickles.

He keeps up a brutal pace and I'm falling apart at the seams. Shattering into a million pieces at the hands of men that were supposed to be my enemies just days ago.

Gray tugs my head back so my spine arches more and Ryker slips in the small gap between me and the table to claim my mouth with his.

The twist of his thumbs over my nipples, the press of his lips against mine, combined with the pounding from Gray's cock taking me inch by inch, sends me over the edge, and I detonate, coming hard and fast as Ryker swallows every one of my cries.

"That's it, Scar, squeeze my fucking cock. Let your pussy drench me," Gray murmurs in my ear, slowing his thrusts as he prolongs the fluttering at my core.

"We want to see your cum on her, VP," someone hollers from the crowd, and Gray instantly freezes.

"No. Fucking. Way."

Before I even know what's happening, Ryker's mouth and hands are gone and I'm up in the air with my legs wrapped around Gray's waist as I feel someone adjust the waistband of my jeans. "Another time, Reaper," Ryker murmurs into my ear before Gray carries me out of the booth.

Groans and protests sound out around us, but I look at Gray instead. His face is nestled between my tits, yet he somehow manages to get us through the door leading into the private quarters without missing a step.

"What are you doing, Gray?" I ask when it's just the two of us, the music turning to a dull backing track in the far distance as he marches down the hallway.

"I'm not finishing out there," he grunts.

"But the rules…"

"Fuck the rules, Scar. You're not being crowned a Ruthless Bitch tonight."

My heart somehow races even faster as Gray blindly comes to a stop, opening the door at my back, before striding inside and kicking it shut behind us.

"I'm not?"

My question barely slips from my lips before he tosses me down on the bed. His hair is messy from my touch, his t-shirt ruined, and his dick still peeks out of the zipper of his jeans.

"You're not, but that definitely doesn't mean I'm done with you."

The gravel in his voice has me wanting to shatter again. So I rise from the bed and slowly remove every item of clothing that stands between us. He seems more than happy to watch, waiting until there's nothing but flesh.

There's no move on his part to take a single layer of clothing off, and that only turns me on more.

"Turn around."

I preen under his gaze as I follow his order, turning to face away from him as he comes to stand at my back. Now that it's just the two of us, everything feels more heightened, more intense, more intimate.

Stroking his fingers through my hair, he continues to trail his hand down my spine as I tilt my head to face him.

"How do you like it, Scarlett?"

I'm sure he's probably used to women simpering words like 'however you want it, baby', but with the offer on the table, I'm more than eager to get what *I* want.

"I want it hard, fast, and on the brink of pain."

His breath gets heavier in my ear at my words as he strokes his hands down my arms, wrapping his fingers around my wrists before joining them together at the base of my spine. "I knew you would say something like that after the way you took my cock," he murmurs, before kicking my legs out to the sides and forcing my upper half forward onto the bed.

My breath stutters in my chest as anticipation courses through me, but he wastes no time before thrusting into my core. I flex my hands in his hold, desperate to grip the sheets beneath me, but the restraint and inability to do so is even better.

When Gray is deep inside me, my stomach flat against the bed as my face smushes into the sheets, he tries to push deeper, and I cry out in pleasure. He pulls out, only to slam back inside me harder and faster and somehow deeper, fucking me into the mattress as our groans ring out around us.

"I want to feel you come on my cock one more time," he bites, retreating fully as he grips both of my wrists with one hand, before bringing the palm of his free hand down on my ass cheeks in quick succession.

"Yes! Please, yes," I beg, my ass heating under his harsh touch, but the pain quickly melts into pleasure as he slams into me with urgency.

My skin tingles as he squeezes my wrists and brings his other hand to my hair, wrapping in the tendrils as he forces my face into the sheets. Everything disappears around me, and there's nothing but me and the sensations coursing through my veins.

His movements become jagged as he demands to feel me come, while also fighting off his own release. Each thrust of his hips is brutal as he explores me. Uses me. Pleases me.

"Come. For. Me. Scar."

Euphoria explodes inside of me, my body falling apart just as he wants at his command. A cry rips from my lungs, long and breathless, as I feel his cock pulse inside of me.

Collapsing onto the bed in a heap, my muscles weak from being pleasured so perfectly, I know one thing for certain.

I'm well and truly fucked. Both figuratively and literally. And I've never felt more alive.

ELEVEN

Scarlett

Blurry-eyed and completely disorientated, I attempt to prop myself up on my elbow, waking up a little more as I try to understand what's going on outside the room. Noise and rustling greets my ears as I glare at the door, expecting it to reveal what's on the other side without actually opening it.

Do I stay here or investigate?

There's not much time for me to consider anything though, because in the next moment, it's swinging open and the big light is switched on, burning my retinas.

"What the fuck?" I mumble, blinking rapidly as I take in the room.

It takes me a few seconds to figure out where the fuck I am before it all comes flooding back to me. The heat pressed against my back belongs to Gray, the sheets draped over me are his too, but it's Emmett's knitted brows as he stands in the doorway that holds my attention.

"Gray, wake the fuck up. Now." The words are harsh from his mouth, but his eyes are still fixed on me.

Gray shuffles slightly behind me, his cock pressed against my ass cheeks as he starts to harden between us again. I'm shocked he's even got the energy after he continued to take me again and again until I was all out of orgasms and passed out.

"What's going on?" I move to sit up, the sheets dropping and exposing my chest, as I rake my fingers through my hair.

Emmett glances at my chest, his jaw clenching, before he clears his throat and takes another step into the room.

"Gray, now. It's an emergency."

"What?" Gray's response is filled with sleep as he yawns, his fingers gliding over my thigh.

"It's Axel, Gray. Ryker needs us."

Gray's hand stops its pattern over my skin as he sits up beside me. "What about him?"

Emmett looks nervously between the two of us, likely trying to decide whether he wants me to hear this or not. Taking the hint, I rise to my feet, completely aware of the fact that my bottom half is just as naked as my top. "I'll get out of your hair," I grumble at the exact same time Emmett answers Gray.

"Ryker's with him, but he's unresponsive and we don't

know whether he's…"

My gaze flicks between the two of them as Gray's eyebrows furrow.

"Whether he's what?" he asks cautiously, seemingly nervous for any kind of answer as Emmett grips the ends of his hair in frustration.

"Whether he's overdosed or not."

Fuck.

Gray matches my curse, only he mumbles his out loud while I manage to keep my lips closed. Panicking, I start glancing around the room like I can see through walls, but I have no idea where anything is in here so I don't know where to look.

"I need a t-shirt, Gray. "

He drags the top drawer open on the chest of drawers beside the bedroom window, pulling out a plain white tee and tossing it in my direction, before pulling a black one over his own head. His cut quickly follows, along with his jeans and boots as I move toward Emmett.

"Where is he?" I ask, but Emmett quickly shakes his head dismissively at me.

"You're not fucking coming," he grunts, like I'm being completely ridiculous, but it's clear neither of them have ever dealt with anything like this before.

"You're going to want me there. And if you're correct, we don't have much time, so lead the fucking way."

I step out into the hallway without glancing back, and when I notice all of the doors closed in this part of the building, I know they're not here.

Pushing the door open to the bar area, I hear Gray call out my name, but I don't slow my pace as I pad along the sticky wooden floor in bare feet. *I've walked on much worse.* I have no idea what time it is, but there are still a few stragglers in here. The main attraction is two guys fucking two girls between them as they make out.

Hot.

Pity they weren't around earlier to distract the attention away from me. When I don't catch sight of Ryker or Axel, I glance over my shoulder and my eyes instantly meet Emmett's as he nods toward the main door.

I step out into the cold night air, a shiver running through my body. Hearing footsteps right behind me, I know Gray and Emmett are closer now, so I wait for them to fall into step with me before I continue.

There's no point in leading the way if I don't actually have a fucking clue where we're going.

Emmett's strides are longer than my own, forcing me to move my legs faster as I work to keep up with the pair of them.

"So, catch me up to speed," Gray grumbles, rubbing his hands together as he glances up at the night sky for a second, before swiping his hands down his face.

"There's not much else I can say, except that he's out in the garage and it looks like he's in a bad way."

"What does a bad way even fucking look like?" Gray pushes back, clearly not familiar with someone in this state, and I sigh, interrupting their conversation before Emmett has a chance to answer.

"Have you called for an EMT?" I ask, wrapping my arms around my waist as I push past the cold threatening to take a hold of me. The second those three letters leave my lips, they both whip their heads in my direction. They're looking at me like I just grew a second head.

"Are you sure you're familiar with how an MC works, sweet cheeks? Because EMTs are never the first port of call," Gray grunts, raising his brow at me, and I sigh. I am familiar, but I thought that was just a Reaper thing, to be honest. It's stupid as fuck.

"There they are," Emmett states, redirecting everyone's attention as I glance toward the garage and find Ryker hovering over Axel on the ground.

"What the fuck took you so long?" Ryker bites, glancing up at the three of us, the pain evident on his face as his hands continue to grip his friend's cut. "And what the fuck is she doing here? This is private. Fuck off."

I ignore his words as I continue to step closer to them, dropping down to my knees on the other side of Axel. The rough floor bites into my knees, but I swallow down the groan and focus on the man before me.

"How long has he been like this?" I ask, glancing over Axel's form a few times as Ryker scoffs.

"Did you not hear me? I told you to fuck off."

Inhaling deeply, I release a heavy breath before I tilt my gaze to his. "I'm helping in ways you guys clearly fucking can't, but if you've got this, just say the word and I'll leave. Just remember, that puts his life completely in *your* hands."

My eyes are wide despite how fucking tired and disorientated I am, but this is something I've experienced before. The middle of the night is always when I'm needed, it seems.

"Fuck. Just tell me what to do."

Shaking my head, I disregard him as I lean in closer and brush Axel's loose brown hair back off his neck so I can press the tips of my fingers against his pulse. The second I make contact, Ryker's hand grips my wrist, ready to yank me off him, but I quickly lift my other hand, silently pleading with him to give me a second as I close my eyes and count.

I run my tongue over my lips, grateful when he doesn't follow through on his action until I blink open my eyes.

"His pulse isn't too weak. If we could get him seen by someone, they would be able to flush liquids through his system, but I'm assuming you're as dumb in your ways with no medical training like these two buttheads," I murmur, looking directly at Ryker.

Fucking fools.

"We can handle whatever needs to happen, Scar, just no one outside the club if we can help it," Emmett finally says, answering for the three of them as I glance back down at the troubled man beside me.

With him sleeping like this, or passed out, whichever way you want to look at it, he looks peaceful, calm, and pain free, but something tells me his dreams are haunted and his life isn't so serene. It never is when you're a part of a motorcycle club like this. Being a one-percenter, an outlaw, usually smothers the pain we've already been exposed to.

"We need to get him inside."

Ryker nods in response as he starts to rise to his feet, but he pauses when Emmett speaks.

"We can't go through the club, there are still people in the bar, and if they see us walk in with him like this, they'll have questions."

"Fuck."

I'm not sure who the curse comes from. Ryker? Gray? Fuck… me?

"There must be some other access point," I suggest, rising to my feet.

"We can move him around the back. That will allow us to come in through the side entrance closer to our rooms so we don't pass anyone," Ryker states, and I sag a little with relief.

"Perfect, the three of you carry him and I'll make sure to hold the doors open."

The three of them work together, lifting their friend carefully, before Gray nods for me to head toward the right.

Cutting across the grass, I cringe at the feeling of dew dampening my feet, but I'm thankful it's not glass at least. Ryker tosses me a key to open the door. The second they're all in, I shut it behind me and lock it back up.

I turn around to see them opening the door that I saw Axel go through when I first arrived, before he blasted the heavy metal music, and I follow them inside.

Once they have him lying on the bed comfortably, I reach for his right boot, but hands stop me from touching him once more. "I've got this, Scar. He would never forgive us if we allowed you to undress him."

My eyes widen at Gray's words, and I take a step back without pushing for more. There's clearly a sensitive subject here that I'm not privy to, and rightfully so. "Strip him down to his t-shirt and boxers."

"What do we do now?" The solemn question comes

from Ryker.

"All we can do is sit and wait. But it would be ideal if he had some water and pain meds when he finally wakes."

"You can't be in this room when he wakes up, sweet cheeks," Gray explains, and I nod despite my internal need to stay at his side and repeat my childhood like I was so rhythmically used to.

"Okay." The word tastes wrong on my tongue. Being compliant isn't my usual role, so this has me completely out of sorts, but there are boundaries here and I need to respect them.

Turning, I head for the door, but I barely make it two steps before a hand wraps around my arm and I'm forced to stop.

What is it with these men always needing to get my attention physically instead of just saying my name? Anyone else and I would be pissed off right now, but somehow, I'm holding it together.

"How do you know all this?" Ryker asks, the bags under his eyes far more noticeable when I'm up this close.

"All what?"

He rolls his eyes at me as his grip flexes on my arm. "Don't play dumb, Reaper. It doesn't suit you."

I'm not sure how I feel about this new acclaimed nickname he's chosen for me, but I decide to save that argument for later. I glance at his hand on me instead, glaring at it until he releases me. Once he does, I offer him a sliver of my truth.

"My mother was a woman with addictions of every kind. You name it, she wanted it. But her greatest loves were dick, alcohol, and drugs." His features remain neutral, no surprise or disgust playing out across his face. "But he should be fine. The combination of bourbon on his breath and whatever drugs he has in his system have knocked him out. Hopefully, it's nothing more than that, but if his pulse becomes shallower, come find me. He'll wake up feeling like hell tomorrow, and you'll be able to handle that, but you have to know... this isn't okay for him. This isn't the path to survival. If you don't intervene, things are only going to get worse."

Ryker's jaw tightens, his nostrils flaring as he stuffs his hands into his pockets. "I know that."

With a nod, I turn once more, but I don't even get to lift a foot this time before Emmett calls out my name.

"He can't know that you helped him."

I glance between the three of them, and they are all wearing the same understanding in their eyes.

"What?"

"He just... you weren't here. Fuck, I mean you were, but you directed us to do everything you did instead of you actually touching him," Emmett explains as I try to wrap my head around when and how I actually touched him.

"I only placed my fingertips over his pulse to check it," I start, but the rawness in each of their gazes tells me that was still a step too far. "I won't lie to him," I add, my chest tightening in a mixture of pain and concern for him.

"It's for your own good." I frown at Gray's statement as I turn to face them fully again and throw my hands out to the side.

"Why?"

Ryker scoffs, irritation getting the better of him, as he glares at me. "Because the last woman to touch him without his permission is dead, and the reason he's in this fucking state is because of the trauma it caused him."

RUTHLESS BROTHERS MC

TWELVE

Axel

My head throbs with every breath I take, every inch of my body aching in some way as I attempt to run my tongue around my dry mouth. What the fuck have I done? My brows wrinkle even though my eyes remain closed, and it only makes everything feel worse.

Am I dying?

Fuck, I'd rather be dead than deal with this bullshit.

I attempt and immediately fail to blink my eyes open, the world spinning around me as I quickly lock myself away in the darkness again where it's safer.

What was I doing last night? Shit, I don't even remember. I really need to get a hold of myself, but it's fucking hard, now more than ever.

Lifting my hand to my face, it feels like I'm carrying one hundred tons of cement as my muscles burn with the movement. I really did a number on myself last night.

"Oh good, you're awake." The sound of Ryker's voice makes me freeze, my fingers pressing into my temple as I try to process what in the fuck he's doing here. When I don't respond quick enough, he continues, "I can see your fucking lids moving, man. Let's not be a coward now and open them."

A coward? What the fuck is his problem?

"Why are you fucking shouting?" I grunt, confused as hell with his presence, but the scoff I get in response tells me he's pissed. Great, that's all I need on top of everything else I'm feeling already.

I slowly blink my eyes open, fighting against the burn from the dim light coming from the lamp on my nightstand. When I can focus properly, I find Ryker, Emmett, and Gray hovering around my bed with a mixture of emotions playing across their faces, but one remains the same on all of them—exhaustion.

Ryker stands with his arms folded over his chest, his jaw tense, with bags under his eyes as he glares at me. Emmett has his hands stuffed in his jeans pockets as he looks at me with concern, while Gray has his hands on his hips, yawning with tiredness as his gaze flicks between the rest of us.

"What time is it?" I ask, pressing my palms into the sheets as I attempt to sit. I wheeze through the pain until my back is pressed against the headboard, but even then, none of them have changed their stance. Letting my head fall back for a moment, I slowly catch my breath as pain continues to radiate through me.

"Fuck what time it is, Ax, that's irrelevant. There are far more pressing matters to discuss first." That comes from Gray, who offers a tight smile, but it does nothing to ease the tension rising inside of me.

What am I missing?

"Don't be fucking nice about it, Gray. It's a colossal ticking bomb we need to discuss," Ryker grunts, making my spine stiffen and my defenses rise as I glare right back at him.

"What the fuck is your issue this morning, man?"

"You." He barely lets me even finish asking him before he blurts his response, and I'm sure I'm missing something because it's not often Ryker gets pissed like this, and for it to be aimed at me, that's never the case.

Shit.

"What the fuck, Ryker?"

"Oh, hell no, you don't get to Ryker me right now. At this moment, you're speaking to your Prez."

I hear Emmett clear his throat as I swing my legs over the side of the bed and face Ryker head-on. "Okay. What the fuck, *Prez*?" I repeat, using the title he wears, but that doesn't seem to improve the situation at all.

"Do you recall anything at all from last night?"

My brows furrow as I still find myself at a complete loss. "Skip to the fucking point. I feel like shit and I really don't have time for this."

Ryker steps closer, bracing his hands on his knees as he bends down a little so we're face-to-face. "You're lucky feeling like shit is all you're dealing with this morning." His tone is a smidge softer now, but the irritation is still very much present.

Sighing, I turn my attention to Gray and Emmett, hoping they'll get to the point instead of talking in circles like Ryker. Emmett steps forward until his knees are pressing against the foot of the bed.

"Ryker found you passed out on the garage floor last night with remnants of coke and empty bottles of beer surrounding you."

Fuck.

Did I not bring myself home last night? Who the fuck stripped me down to a tee and my boxers and put me to bed?

Shit. Shit. Shit.

Dropping my face into my hands, I feel a mixture of embarrassment and annoyance, with a slight topping of shame. But out of all of the feelings swirling inside of me, annoyance is what I'm most familiar with, so I instinctively start to cling to it.

I clear my throat, fighting past the pain radiating through

me as I shrug, offering them a bored glance in response. "Well, as you can see, I'm perfectly fine now. Thanks for your concern, but it's no longer needed."

"Fuck you, Axel," Ryker bites and starts to pace beside my bed.

"That's enough, Ryker. I know you're worked up, but you're not helping right now," Gray murmurs.

"Is this a joke?" Ryker swings his arms out to the side in agitation as Gray moves toward him.

"You know what time of year it is," Emmett murmurs, avoiding eye contact with me as he speaks, but I can still fucking hear him.

"It's *never* been this bad before." The pain and worry shining through Ryker's words now has me tensing even more. I can't deal with their feelings and emotions on top of my own, even if they are for me.

"Can you guys just get the fuck out?" I don't look at them as I grab the pain meds off the nightstand and down them with the bottle of water placed beside it. If I was a better man, I would thank them for leaving them here for me… Shit, I'd thank them for being here with me, period. But I'm not a better man, and I'm not about to start trying now.

"No. You can't carry on like this." Ryker looks at me like he's at a complete loss, but I'm already floating out to sea without a raft to save me and guide me back to dry land.

Standing from the bed, I step into my jeans that have been folded on top of my dresser, before slipping my feet into a fresh pair of socks and my boots. "Not without something to eat, I can't. You're fucking draining me," I grumble once I'm ready, pulling my cut on and reaching for the pack of cigarettes in the pocket.

"Axel…"

I hear the plea in my name as Gray calls out to me, but I'm really not in the fucking head space to handle any of them right now, today, or even this fucking year.

I slam my bedroom door shut harshly behind me, stepping out into the hallway at the exact same time the door across from me swings open, revealing the little whore Gray brought home from the Reapers.

With a towel draped over her arm and a small caddy filled with bathroom supplies, it's clear where she's heading, but the way she looks at me with instant concern in her eyes pisses me off. I offer her a deathly glare that has made grown-ass men piss themselves before, but her stance doesn't falter. Not wanting to give her a chance to open her damn mouth, I turn for the kitchen and leave her behind, making a mental note to reach out to Shift again, our tech expert, and see if he has found anything on her yet.

The second I step foot into the kitchen, my bad mood dissipates of its own accord as I find Gray's mom, Maggie, hovering over a pan of frying bacon. She glances over her shoulder, eyes finding mine instantly as a soft smile crosses her face.

"Everything okay, baby cakes?" she asks in that sweet motherly voice like she always does, and I grunt in response. The smile wavers on her face as she runs her eyes over me, and I shrug.

"Not today, it ain't."

"Uh-huh, isn't that the same response you give me every time I see you?" She quirks a brow at me before nodding to the coffee machine, and my feet are moving at her silent command before it even fully registers in my head.

I turn the machine on and grab two mugs before I glance at her again. "That's because every day I wake up and make the wrong decisions, Maggie. Now I'm just living with them and failing to see any kind of fucking light at the end of the tunnel."

I don't know what it is about this woman that makes my mouth move and my filter stop working, but she has a way of effortlessly pulling out your deepest and darkest truths. Maybe it's because I looked up to her with awe when we were kids, blown away by how she treated Gray and loved him so fiercely, or maybe it's because she loved the rest of us just as hard.

"Why does today feel extra gloomy then, hun?" She

waves her hand in my direction, like she's caressing my aura and trying to make it all go away as she's done many times before, and I force a tight smile to my face.

"Because it's my own doing as always, but this time, I haven't just pissed myself off," I admit.

"If someone is pissed at you, Axel, it's because they care." Her words hit me hard, the truth harsh and sharp as she says what I already know deep down.

"But what I can't decide, Maggie, is whether to keep on fucking pushing until they stop caring altogether so I don't have to worry about it anymore, or if I should figure my shit out."

"We both know the latter of those two will be the hardest but most worthwhile, baby cakes."

I nod, before turning my focus on the coffee once more. When I finally turn to look at her again, a coffee mug extended in her direction, she reaches a hand halfway toward me before stopping in her tracks and smiling sadly.

"Oh, Axel. I wish I could wrap you in my arms and wash all your worries away."

"Sometimes, I almost consider it," I reply, taking the bacon and eggs from her and moving to sit at the small table.

Without a word, she takes the seat across from me, tapping her finger on the table in front of me so I look at her. It's only when she has my attention does she speak.

"We're family first, Axel. Always. You're just as much my boy as Gray is. I'm not above renaming you with a color too." She winks at me, lightening the mood, giving me a fucking out from my twisted thoughts.

"Why didn't you pass these good genes on to your son? He could fucking use them."

She chuckles, then lifts her mug of coffee to her lips. "Because I had to save them all for myself to use on you."

THIRTEEN

Scarlett

I hurry into the bathroom across the hall, pressing my back against the door as I shut it behind me.

Fuck me.

Axel has the most intense gaze I've ever felt. There was a challenge flashing in his eyes, but I didn't back down, I never do. Although, I did manage to keep my mouth shut and that's most definitely a first. The second he stepped away, I decided I didn't want to give him a chance to turn around and give me shit, so I rushed in here as quickly as I could.

I make sure the door is locked behind me before I take in the small space. The white tiles on the wall and the sparkly black floor are clean, far fresher than anything at the Reapers', and it doesn't go unnoticed that the stainless steel faucets are shining too. This definitely has a woman's touch written all over it.

I take a look under the vanity and find a neatly folded blue towel, which I claim, before turning the shower on. Giving the water a second to heat up, I brush my teeth and wash my face. The bags under my eyes aren't going anywhere today, not after last night, but it's nothing a little bit of make-up can't fix.

Taking my t-shirt off, I hook it on the door handle before stepping under the spray of the shower, and I instantly relax. Tilting my face to the water, I let it wash away all of the stress I've accumulated over the last twelve hours.

Addiction is hard. The battles that man must be facing are consuming him so much that he can't see any other way of hiding from them. As much as I understand that, I've lived it once before, felt the pain and found no solace in the world. I can't go through that again. I won't.

The thought of leaving him to suffer alone makes my heart tighten in my chest and I think I might be sick.

Fuck.

Grabbing my shampoo from the caddy, I rake my fingers along my scalp harsher than is necessary, but the pain pulls me from the spiraling thoughts overwhelming me. One saving grace is I got to see him standing on two feet moments ago, and that eases some of the anxiety that threatens to consume me.

If that had been my mom, she wouldn't have left her

bed until night came around, and even then, it would only be to repeat the process all over again.

Maybe there's hope for him yet.

Once my hair is clean and my body smells like shea butter, I flick the water off and wrap the plush towel around me. The mirror is fogged up as I step out of the shower, and I'm thankful I don't have to glance at my reflection right now with so many emotions buzzing through me.

I don't bump into anyone as I head back to my room, where I toy over what to wear today, but eventually settle on a pair of high-rise skinny jeans and a Metallica t-shirt that I tuck into the waistband. Braiding my damp hair back off my face, I glance at my cell phone to check the time, and I'm surprised to see it's almost midday.

My stomach grumbles in time with the realization, so I step into my combat boots, tuck my cell phone into my pocket and head for the kitchen. I pray with every step I take that I'll find the room empty, but as I get to the open doorway, I find a woman standing in front of the refrigerator.

Her bleach-blonde hair is clipped up high and her make-up is light, making her lips shine and her eyes sparkle. She's wearing a long orange maxi-dress and looks like she should be relaxing on a beach somewhere.

Whatever she was doing is halted as she senses my arrival, and any thoughts of animosity or bitchiness that I expected evaporate when she smiles at me.

Closing the refrigerator door, she whirls around with two bottles of water in her hand and places them on the table. "Hi, you must be Scarlett, right? I heard we had a new girl."

Apparently news travels fast, although this is technically my second day here. How does it feel like an eternity and no time at all at the same time?

Clearing my throat, I nod. "Yeah, that's me." I remain by the door, not really sure what I should do with myself.

"I'm Maggie, Gray's mom, but also the bossy bitch that organizes the food, get-togethers and all of the fun," she explains.

Gray's mom?

Looking closer at her, I can see it in her blue eyes, the same sparkle of mischief lurking there, and I relax a little in her presence.

"It's nice to meet you," I mutter, lacing my fingers together in front of me as she cocks a brow.

"Wow, manners too, huh?"

My nose wrinkles as I tilt my head at her. "That's the second time someone has commented on me being nice or polite since I got here." The statement blurts out before I can stop myself, but she just chuckles at me and moves toward the oven.

"So you met Emily, too."

I glance around me, as if searching for cameras or some shit, but come up empty. "How did you know that?"

The laugh that passes her lips this time is darker, less humorous, and more irritated than anything.

"Because the Ruthless Bitches are just that, bitches. Especially to other women, so a conversation like this doesn't happen, even with me."

"So I'm learning," I mutter, offering a tight smile.

"Oh, honey, don't let them get you down. There's more to the club than them. Like the barbecue I'm throwing this afternoon." A smile spreads across her face at the mention of it. "You're going to come and help, right? Enjoy yourself a little and maybe meet some of the old ladies who are also much nicer than the bitches," she pushes as she nods at me eagerly.

"Uhhhh…" I glance around the room, looking for an excuse, but I come up empty. "I'm really not sure if that's a good idea," I finally manage, and she instantly scoffs at me as she starts putting together a plate of food. She doesn't utter a word until there's a plate loaded with sausages, bacon, and eggs.

Did she borrow that oven off Mary Poppins or something? Where did all this food come from?

"Come." She waves for me to take a seat at the table, and I wait until she's comfortable in hers before I take the spot across from her. To my surprise, it's *me* she puts the plate of food in front of. "Eat."

Fucking hell.

I know exactly where Gray got those one word commands from; they just seem to use them in different ways. Thankfully.

When she offers me a fork, I take it and murmur my thanks before digging in. I may have eaten pizza with Gray last night, but after the dicking he gave me and the shit with Axel, I'm famished.

When I'm almost finished, Maggie clears her throat and smiles wide at me. "So, can you cook?"

"I can," I reply with a nod, leaning more toward helping her now that she's fed me, and I have a feeling that was her plan all along.

"Then I'm definitely calling on you for help."

Pushing my plate to the side, I return a smile with a rare one of my own. "After feeding me so good, I can't say no now, can I?"

She winks, extending her hand across the table. "You're catching on."

Her hand is warm in mine as I shake it, before reaching for the bottle of water closest to me. "I'm going to like you."

"Oh, it seems my two favorite ladies have met. Good."

Gray appears beside us and leans down to press a kiss to his mom's forehead. My heart swells as I watch her reaction, glowing at his touch, and I can tell there's a special bond between them.

"Are you telling me I've got competition for being your number one?" Maggie says with a grin, and I immediately shake my head.

Gray stands tall, bracing his hands on his mom's chair as he looks at me with a hint of mischief in his eyes. I glare at him so hard, but it doesn't seem to register. "I haven't tasted her cooking yet, Ma, so the battle is on and the winner is yet to be decided."

"Please tell me Scarlett is your girl, Gray. Make me a happy woman," she gushes.

"No!" I shout, far louder than was necessary, but the heat creeping up my neck and into my cheeks is a definite sign that I'm overwhelmed. "Nope, I'm no one's girl, Maggie. Don't you encourage him, he's bad enough as it is," I grumble, rising from the table and taking my dishes to the sink.

All I get is a chuckle in response, and that makes me even more concerned. I don't need anyone getting ideas. I'm not staying. Absolutely not.

"So, you want to kill some time and play a few video games with me? Unless, you know, your *one* friend is online instead."

I turn to glare at Gray again, before sighing at him. "I'm actually helping your mom with—"

"Oh, don't you worry about me. I don't need your assistance for a couple of hours yet," Maggie interjects, and when I blink, I let my lids remain closed for an extra second as I try not to let the pair of them sweep me off my feet.

I've gone from lurking in the shadows and avoiding everyone at all costs at the Reapers to receiving far more attention than I'm used to here. I was supposed to be blending in and this really doesn't feel like it.

Shit.

"Then I'm down for a game or two."

Gray ruffles his mom's hair as he kisses her cheek, before waving for me to follow him. I offer Maggie a small wave as I leave, walking across the hall and falling into the same spot I had last night.

As he sets everything up, my cell vibrates with a message from Kronkz; my *one* friend.

Fuck.

Swiping my thumb across the screen, I get rid of the notification as I place my cell face down on the arm of the sofa.

"Anyone exciting?" Gray asks, nodding at the device as he takes the spot beside me and hands me a controller.

I avoid his gaze as I look at the screen. "I have one friend, remember? I don't *do* exciting."

"That's not how I remember last night at all," he

replies, his voice growing darker as I turn to glance at him.

I swallow the lump in my throat as he watches me with hooded eyes. It's on the tip of my tongue to beg him to give me a live-action replay, the memory so vivid in my mind my thighs clench together with need. But the moment is instantly shattered as the sound of a door slamming into a wall makes me jerk in my seat.

My senses are on alert as I struggle to breathe, coming face-to-face with Axel, as he stands next to the vibrating door with his arms folded across his chest.

Noises like that fuck with my head, encouraging me to take a trip down memory lane, so I have to bite the inside of my cheek to fight against it.

"Why can't we find shit on you?"

The usual burning sensation of a trigger creeps up my spine. I know he's talking to me, and I should have been more prepared for this moment, but fuck. I was too damn distracted.

"Ax, man, calm down. What's your fucking problem?"

Gray places his arm behind me on the sofa, but I don't lean into his hold, my body too stiff to move an inch.

"Stay out of this, Gray." Axel walks around to stand in front of the television, his stance not changing as he glares at me.

Taking a deep breath, I try to calm my racing heart, but fail miserably. "Sorry? Am I supposed to know what you're talking about?"

"Fuck you. I knew there was something fishy about you the second you got here," he grunts, and his anger pisses me off, which has a weird way of grounding me in the moment. "Our tech guy ran every check possible against a Miss Scarlett Reeves and guess what he came up with? Fucking. Nothing."

"I don't know what you want me to say. I've done nothing but be honest with you since I got here, and I didn't come here of my own accord if you recall." I try to deflect, but it does nothing to slacken his tense jaw.

"Yeah, about everything but your fucking name."

"I don't know what checks you're talking about. All the people that could confirm who I am are dead because of you, so I don't know what you want me to do about that. Are these checks something you do to every whore you invite in?"

He takes a step toward me, hands balling into fists at my side as his nostrils flare. "No, but we don't get every whore from the fucking Reapers, who come in here talking shit about the Devil's Brutes," he bites, but I just roll my eyes at him, acting way more relaxed than I actually am.

When he doesn't proceed with more bullshit, I turn my gaze back to his as I shrug my shoulders. "I don't know what else you want me to say."

"What school did you go to?"

"I was homeschooled, asshole," I grumble in response, but that doesn't deter him.

"How old are you?"

"Isn't it a little fucking late for that question?" I hiss, rising to my feet as he comes to a stop in front of me so we're almost toe to toe.

"How. Old. Are. You?" The muscles in his neck bunch as he flicks his gaze between Gray and me.

"I'll be twenty-four on March twenty-first."

He definitely doesn't appreciate my sass as he squints even harder at me. "You don't fucking look twenty-three."

Throwing my hands up in the air, I glance at Gray who remains in his spot with his fingers wrapped around his controller. The confusion in his eyes tells me this isn't normal behavior for Axel, but it's also not his place to step in.

Not that I would want him to anyway. That would likely piss me off more.

"Tell me who your parents are." It's not a question, a request, or anything remotely resembling the politeness you see in common decency.

Nope. It's a demand. But he's shit out of luck.

"I don't know," I reply with another shrug, and he scoffs at me as Gray rises at my side.

"But you said your mom…" Gray's words trail off as his brows knit, and I'm starting to get a fucking headache from all of the stress.

Pinching the bridge of my nose, I take a deep breath. "She wasn't my biological mom, she was just…"

I trail off, hating to repeat the same speech over and over again.

"She was what?" Axel grunts, getting straight to the point again.

"She was a club whore, okay?" The room falls quiet for a moment. Gray winces at my words as Axel continues to drill holes into my skull. "And where is she now?"

I glance from Gray, to Axel, and back to Gray again before I answer. "She's dead."

"Of course she is, and what did the fucking whore die from?" Axel grinds, lowering his head so we're eye to eye, and it makes my chest tighten with anger and pain.

"Overdose."

Gray inhales; a reminder of last night likely flashing through his mind, but it doesn't affect Axel in any way, shape or form.

I'm the villain here, the target for his tongue-lashing, and he won't see shit past that at this moment.

"Are we done here? I wasn't expecting a trip down memory lane today and it's fucking exhausting to say the least." I fake a yawn, taking a step back so I can fucking breathe, but the beast of a man doesn't relent, edging closer.

"I'm not fucking done with you. I have questions and

you're going to answer them."

This time, it's my turn to scoff as I plant my hands on my hips. "So you can dish it out but you can't take it?"

"There's nothing to know about me." He's so sure in his words, irritating me even more that I don't give a shit about what the guys said last night, he's pissed me off too much now.

Cutting the distance between us, I wag my finger in the air, but before I can open my mouth, Gray's hand is wrapping around my wrist as my name falls from his lips. "Scar."

It's a warning, one I heed, but the interaction obviously doesn't skip past Axel.

"Why is he saying that, why the fuck are you saying that?" His anger is clear in his heated gaze, but I slip my wrist from Gray's hold and point the tip of my finger in Axel's face, making sure to not actually touch him.

"You want to bring up my past, my history, that I want nothing to do with. You don't seem like the kind of guy who would appreciate the same." I know I'm saying utter bullshit, trying to cover up what I was about to say, but it surprisingly works better than I expect when he storms toward the window without a backward glance.

"Fuck you," he bites out, but I don't reply until I'm near the door, needing as much distance as possible from him.

"Thanks, but I like my men a little more fucking stable."

I let the door slam shut in my wake, storming toward my room as I pray the angry motherfucker doesn't follow me. Because despite the anger in his demeanor, the knowledge that this man is relying on drugs, and can't see past the end of his own fucking nose, my body is tingling with his close proximity. Just like it does near Gray, and last night with Ryker.

I don't know what the fuck is wrong with me, but I need to get over it, and fast.

FOURTEEN

Scarlett

I stare at the ceiling, completely lost in my thoughts as a murder investigation podcast plays from my cell. I'm barely listening, but it's enough to keep me grounded and not spiraling down the path of my past.

If that fucker gets a hold of me, I'll be drowned in darkness with no end in sight. I've clawed myself out of that deep, dark hole too many times to count already, and I won't succumb to it anymore.

Axel got under my skin, there's no denying it. Gray, on the other hand, watched it unfold without knowing what to fucking say.

Am I surprised he checked on me? Yeah. Am I shocked he got nothing? No. But that doesn't fucking help me out in this situation I am trapped in.

It seems the Ruthless Brothers are more trouble than I was prepared for, but even more than that, I have a feeling

I'm not going to get the chance to leave on my own either. Not now that Axel has painted a target on my head, even if it is only him hunting me down. For now.

A small rap of knuckles against my door pulls my attention, but it doesn't magically pull me from my bad mood.

"Fuck off," I grumble, loud enough for them to hear as I continue to lie on my bed.

"And I thought you weren't a Ruthless Bitch."

Emily?

I'm up off the bed in a flash and darting toward the door before I can even take a breath. Swinging it open, I find her smirking at me with her arms folded over her chest and her hip cocked.

"I had a feeling that would get you to open it," she says as she brushes past me and steps into my room without an invitation, but it doesn't bother me.

"I mean, you could have just said 'hey, Scar, it's me, Emily,' and I would've opened it." I close the door and turn to face her with my eyebrow raised, but she waves her hand at me dismissively.

"Please, where would the fun have been in that?" She doesn't wait for a response as she spins on the spot, taking in my temporary room, and I use the moment to take in this crazy girl.

Her blonde hair is in a ponytail, her glasses fixed in

place, framing her heart-shaped face perfectly, while she wears a simple white ribbed-tee and high-waisted jeans. She's cute. Far too fucking cute for a place like this, which explains why Emmett seems to want to keep her as far away from here as possible.

He could work harder at it, I'm sure. She doesn't need to be tainted by all of this.

When she comes full circle, her eyes meeting mine, something shines in them, like she knows exactly what I'm thinking, and there's more to her than her innocence. A sign that she's already tainted on the inside.

"Fuck, please tell me you're not wearing that to the barbecue. Maggie will send you back in here to change so fast you won't even feel the breeze on your face." Her words pull me from my head as I glance at my band tee and jeans.

"What's wrong with what I'm wearing?" I grumble, completely caught off guard by her approach. I've never had someone question what I'm wearing before. I've never had someone seek me out. A girl at least. I've never really had... friends? Is that what this is?

"Oh, nothing's wrong with it. It's just…"

"It's just what?" Her hand is poised in my direction, her lips parted like she's trying to find the politest words, but nothing comes out. "You're almost wearing the same thing as I am," I add, pointing in her direction, and she rolls her eyes.

"Please, that's only because my asshole of a brother doesn't allow me to wear anything else."

"Do you need me to beat him up for you? Because I definitely can," I state, taking a step toward her, and she shakes her head as a smirk spreads across her lips.

"Nope, not today at least, but I'll definitely keep that in mind." I offer a small nod in response before she turns to scan my room again. "Where are your clothes?"

"Why?"

"Scar…" She quirks a brow at me, and I sigh, waving down at the open duffel bag that's laid out at the bottom of my bed. "You haven't put anything away?"

"That would imply I'm staying," I answer quickly and honestly, and this time, it's her who frowns.

"You're not staying?"

"The verdict is still out," I mumble, attempting to soften the blow. I don't know why her feelings matter to me, but I don't really want to get attached to people and leave them in the dust. That's happened to me before, and it sucks.

"Well, let's make sure you have a good time tonight. Then you might be more inclined to stay," she replies with a wink, before rummaging through my bag and pulling the clothes out.

She goes through it all, my tops, my pants, even my

fucking underwear, until she settles on the clothes that dangle from her hands. "We can make this work."

I look at each item, then back to her as I shake my head. "I'm already wearing those jeans, just in a different color," I state.

"Oh, they're not staying as jeans. If you give me ten minutes, I can either turn these into a pair of frayed shorts or a mini skirt. Which would you prefer?"

I gape at her for a moment, and the look in her eyes tells me there's no option C with this, so I go back and forth between shorts and a skirt. The idea of easy access after last night runs through my mind, but after the shit with Axel today, I'm sure that's now off the table.

Still… It might be fun.

"Skirt," I answer, and she squeals, bouncing on the spot before she tosses the cropped top in my direction.

"Perfect, put this on and I'll be back in ten. Get your make-up out for me too," she orders, dashing from the room before I can even piece together a sentence in response.

Deciding to just go with it, I take off my Metallica tee and slip into the strappy one Emily chose, before spreading my make-up out on the bed.

It's literally ten minutes on the dot that she waltzes back into the room with my jeans in multiple pieces, but the one that matters the most makes my eyes widen. Fuck, that's smaller than I thought it was going to be, but the prideful grin on her face has me reaching out for it.

"Do you want me to turn around to give you some privacy?" she offers, and I shake my head.

"Are you joking? You're going to see just as much when I've got it on anyway," I joke, shimmying out of my jeans and stepping into my new skirt. It falls just below my ass, covering more than I actually expected, and Emily claps. "Where did you learn to do this?"

"I'm studying fashion at college."

"Good, because you're freaking awesome at it," I state, making her smile grow before she turns her attention to the make-up on the bed.

"Let's get your make-up done before Maggie comes looking for us."

Without a word, I take a seat on the bed, letting her do her thing as she applies everything. I could have easily done it myself, but something tells me she doesn't get moments like this very often, and truthfully, neither do I.

Once she's done, she offers me a small compact mirror. "What do you think?"

I take it from her hand, twisting my face from side to side as I look at my reflection. How the fuck has she used the exact same stuff that I do on a daily basis, but comes out with results like this?

"Please tell me cosmetology is your minor or something because this is some next level shit." She preens under my praise.

"Stop, it's the base I had to use that makes it magic." I shake my head at her for brushing off my compliment, but I don't push, knowing full well it can make some people uncomfortable.

"Are we ready?"

"Yes, let's go. Maybe I can sneak a beer without Emmett looking if we get out there soon enough," she fake-whispers, before opening the door and stepping out into the hallway.

It's official; this girl is a fucking whirlwind.

Realizing I don't have anything on my feet, I search for the used sandals I slipped into my bag before I left the Reapers. They don't go perfectly with the outfit, but I guess they'll go better than my combat boots, which are the only alternative.

I follow after her and find her waiting at the inner door that leads into the bar area. When we step into the space, the usual hustle and bustle is nonexistent, but there's plenty of noise coming from outside. Emily leads the way, and uncertainty slowly starts to get the better of me as we step out into the late evening air.

There are people everywhere. Men in cuts occupy the yard, while women and children fill the picnic benches, and the Ruthless Bitches huddle around the trees in the distance. The space isn't huge, but everyone is here, together, and it instantly feels like… a family.

My gaze zeros in on the four men sitting at a bench separate from everyone else. Ryker seems to be glaring at Axel, who is picking at the label on his bottle of beer. While Gray hollers to his mom, and Emmett sits with his arms folded over his chest, eyes scanning the crowd.

I see the moment he spots Emily, and he rises to his feet, heading in our direction. "Ah, fuck," she mumbles under her breath, offering me an apologetic smile as he comes to a stop in front of us.

"Where have you been?" His words are blunt, but nowhere near as gruff as they were the other day, so I stay silent and let it play out before me.

"I was with Scarlett."

His eyes flick to me, narrowing, as he purses his lips. "You're supposed to fucking tell me if you see my sister."

"And how am I supposed to do that? Through telepathy? I don't have your number, and I didn't realize it would be an issue. I didn't get the memo in the short time I've been here," I grumble, standing off with him.

To my surprise though, he doesn't argue back. Instead, he turns on his heel and marches back to his friends.

"Wow," Emily breathes once he's far enough away, and I turn to glance at her.

"What?"

"Nothing, I've just… never seen anyone put my brother

in his place so easily before. It's impressive."

Before I can offer a response, my name is called out. Maggie waves me over to where she has the tables laid out with food. Emily sticks with me as we cut through the crowd. I sense a few eyes on us, but nothing that makes me feel uncomfortable.

"Hey, you made it," Maggie murmurs as I come to a stop beside her, wrapping her arm around my shoulders as she gives me a side-hug. I stiffen slightly in her hold, but she doesn't utter a word about it as she takes a step back.

Clearing my throat, I point at Emily. "Someone didn't really give me much choice."

The two of them high five before Maggie looks back at me. "Please, she's my secret weapon around here."

I smirk at them before glancing around at everyone again. It's bizarre as fuck how it barely feels like an MC right now. The barbecue burning in the distance, mixed with the chatter from everyone present and the casualness that has everyone relaxed just screams family. Normalcy. Or what I would imagine it is from what I've seen in the movies and tv shows I used to watch.

Everyone knows everyone, but there isn't constant bickering or arguing. There's no tension stifling the group. They may be in their own little cliques but they're still all present.

"Are you sure I should be here?" I finally ask, turning

back to them. "Everyone knows everyone and I feel like I'm overstepping," I add.

The scoff I get in response from both makes a bubble of laughter burst from my lips. "We're not taking no for an answer, Scarlett. I invite who I like, and even Ryker wouldn't overrule me," Maggie states, pointing toward the Prez, and I follow her gaze, only to find all four of them looking in our direction.

Fuck.

Turning my back to them, I rub my hands together and attempt to redirect the conversation. "Tell me what you want help with, that will make me feel better."

That snaps them both into action as Maggie flips the steaks on the barbecue and Emily leads me back inside to help prep a potato salad and a few other garnishes to go with everything. It's distracting and exactly what I need. Taking each item outside, we add them to the table of food, including some of the other things Maggie had prepared earlier and stored in the fridge.

By the time all the food is ready, the sun has set and some big overhead lights have been turned on as the chatter from everyone grows louder.

"Girls, get something to eat before I tell the men it's good to go because it will be devoured in seconds," she says, taking a plate for herself and loading it up with what she wants.

Emily does the same, and I follow suit, reaching for the mac and cheese, chicken wings, mini pulled pork sliders, fried pickles, and potato salad. Those are the things that have been calling to me while we were organizing. There's more I could try and grab later if there's anything left, but those are the essentials I need for my survival right now.

"Ma, are my burnt ends and mac and cheese done?" Gray hollers as he approaches the table, and Maggie smiles at her son.

"You know they are. Now tell the rest of these assholes here to eat up," she states, before waving for me to follow her.

"Ruthless Brothers!" Gray shouts at the top of his lungs, turning the entire yard into silence. "Grub's up, motherfuckers! But let the women and children go first."

Cheers ring out as everyone gets up, and I stick beside Maggie and Emily. When they take a seat at a table, I do the same, not realizing until it's too late that they've sat at the one table I was hoping to avoid.

Theirs.

Emily takes the spot between Maggie and I, leaving me open as the guys grab their food. Trepidation overwhelms my senses as I try to eat quickly before they get back, but I fail miserably.

A plate is put down beside me, and I take a deep breath before I look to see who pulled the short straw, only to find

Emmett. He doesn't utter a word as he drops down into his seat, Gray taking the spot beside him as Ryker and Axel complete the circle.

Thankfully, silence graces the table as we eat. Luring me into a false sense of comfort.

"Emmett, do you like my make-up skills I've been learning?" Emily asks, and my spine stiffens instantly.

Fuck.

As if he wasn't sure what she meant, she grips my chin and tilts my head to her brother.

"How does her sweetness and innocence allow her to get away with so much shit?" I grumble, not even fighting out of her hold, and Emmett scoffs.

"You fucking tell me."

At least there's something we can agree on.

"Hey, you didn't answer my question, Em."

Emmett rolls his eyes at his sister before looking at me again. "You did a great job of putting all of the sass Scarlett has on the inside, on the outside."

My lips purse as I try not to laugh at him. He offers me a wink, and Maggie chuckles from the other side of me.

"Are you looking at my sweet cheeks?" Gray asks, pulling my gaze to his as he grins wickedly, and my eyes quickly narrow at him. I don't know what his fucking game is here, but it's messing with my head.

"Are you his sweet cheeks?" Emmett asks, bracing his

hand on the back of my seat and my body warms from his close proximity.

"Not that I recall, no." My voice is far more breathy than I care to admit, but the moment is broken by Ryker.

"She ain't a Ruthless Bitch yet either."

I look over at him, but as usual, he gives nothing away, leaving me even more confused.

"My friend," Gray starts, waiting until everyone at the table is looking at him before he shrugs. "If you felt her pussy, you would understand."

I choke on thin air as my face heats. He did not just fucking say that in front of his mom. His. Mom. My face falls into my hands as the table rings out with laughter, and when I finally peer through my fingers to glance at Maggie, I find her laughing harder than anyone else.

I have no idea what I've walked into here, but I almost... like it?

Hands grab my waist in the next moment as I'm lifted out of my seat for the briefest second and placed in someone's lap. I didn't move far enough for it to be anyone other than Emmett, and when I drop my hands, it's the hot blond Viking.

I don't fight to stand up, surprised and aroused too much to think for myself as I simply look at him. His gaze remains locked on mine as he places his hand on my thigh, and I tense beneath his touch as my core tightens.

Fuck.

Running my tongue over my bottom lip, I don't know what the next move is, what it's expected to be, but I can't turn and look at Emily right now. I can't let her see the need in my eyes at her brother's touch.

I'm so screwed.

Emmett's fingers trail higher up my thigh, and I move my hand to his shoulder in preparation. For what, I don't know, but whatever it is, it doesn't come.

Two gunshots ring out in the air, startling the whole club as screams sound out, and a chuckle I would know anywhere echoes around us.

"What a perfect fucking get-together. Did my invite get lost in the mail?"

I don't turn to look, my eyes focused on Emmett's hand that is now tightly clamped down on my thigh. There will be bruises from his grip in the morning, I know it.

"Who the fuck are you?" Axel asks, and my eyes fall closed, already knowing the answer.

"We're the fucking Devil's Brutes."

FIFTEEN

Ryker

I glare at the motherfucker introducing himself to the club as the guy beside him points his gun in the air and fires two more shots into the night's sky. I'm positive he knows the first two shots they let off got everyone's attention, an extra two wasn't necessary, even by my standards. All it achieves is further sobs and cries of panic from the women and children, and the smirk on his face tells me the asshole feeds off it.

Clenching my hands in my lap, I glance around the table for a brief moment, looking at my three closest brothers. Axel's nostrils are flared and his hand twitches at his waist, ready to grab his own weapon in retaliation. Gray presses the palms of his hands onto the table, ready to launch himself up and into action. While Emmett's fingers look like they're piercing Scarlett's skin where he touches her, his eyes ablaze with anger as the sweet Reaper temptress keeps her head bowed.

She might be the biggest mystery I've ever laid my eyes on, but she got one thing right. The Devil's Brutes are going to be a problem.

I take my time turning my attention back to the unexpected guests that hover to my right. This is the first time we've been threatened on our property since I've become Prez. The one I'll always remember, especially since it's only been a few days. I need to handle this accordingly, because there's no way in hell I'm going to let other clubs think it's a good idea to bring shit like this to our door.

No. Fucking. Way.

But when it comes to our club, there's one priority that has always remained the same, and it won't be changing on my watch. Flicking my gaze to Maggie's, I see the worry in her eyes. "Take the women and children inside." My voice is clipped. She nods in response, before I turn back to the assholes interrupting our good time.

The motherfucker standing dead center wears the badge of Prez, so I settle my gaze on him. One leader to another. Maggie and Emily rise from their seats at my command, but the second Maggie takes one step toward the rest of the club, the fucker with his gun still poised in the air brings it down and aims it at Emily.

"I didn't say anybody could fucking move."

The sound of him turning the barrel of the gun echoes in my ears as Emily's eyes widen. In a complete blur, I don't even get a chance to look at Emmett to see his reaction, Scarlett launches from his lap and places herself between the weapon and its target.

"Redirect that gun before I fucking ruin you," Emmett bites, his eyes burning into the fool thinking he can get away with that kind of action.

Scarlett bunches closer to Emily, facing her head-on so they're eye to eye as she mouths something to her soothingly, but I can't make it out.

"You might have walked in here guns blazing, but this is our territory and I don't allow our family to witness the darkness we sow." My words are like thunder, my veins thrumming with rage as I force myself to remain seated. "Now drop the fucking gun." I don't look at the man holding the weapon though; I direct my order to their Prez.

His eyes burn into mine for the briefest of moments before he nods and the cunt beside him does as he's fucking told. Scarlett must sense the shift because she glances at me out of the corner of her eye, waiting for my signal before she takes off toward the club door in a hurry, dragging Emily along with her.

Emmett's jaw tightens with fury as he refrains from checking on his sister. His eyes are glued to the fucker waving his gun as I continue to assess our family. Or more specifically, as I continue to track Scarlett's movements.

The second she pushes Emily into the clubhouse, she spins back on her heels and races to help Maggie pull everyone inside. She soothes the crying children, offers support to the women swiping at their tears, and even helps carry an inconsolable Ruthie inside.

She's definitely more experienced with fuckers like this than most of the old ladies and Ruthless Bitches here. All except Maggie. She's been through more shit than I care to admit, but between them, they follow through on my order and clear the yard of anyone that isn't a Ruthless Brother.

As Maggie steps inside, Scarlett hangs back, hand firmly wrapped around the door handle as she looks back over her shoulder at me. She seems uncertain, of what I'm not entirely sure, but when I nod in her direction, she releases a heavy breath and steps inside, slamming the door shut behind her.

The moment the door stops rattling from the force of her swing, Emmett stands from his seat with his gun poised and ready, and I watch knowingly as he pulls the trigger three times in quick succession.

They're all aimed at the same man, the one I knew wouldn't leave the compound alive, who chose to aim his gun at the wrong fucking woman.

"What the fuck?" Their Prez bites, glancing at his

sergeant at arms in surprise as Emmett casually retakes his seat. Every other man standing behind him raises their gun in our direction, but none of us move.

"Don't ever step on our property waving guns around and firing shots when there are old ladies and children around. More importantly, don't ever make the mistake of aiming your weapon at one of them. You can see what the outcome will be."

He glances at the lifeless body beside him, his teeth bared as anger boils beneath the surface. "You've just wasted a perfectly good man," he hisses, turning his attention back to me as I shrug.

"A good man wouldn't do that shit," Axel says from beside me, lighting up a cigarette.

The leader of the Devil's Brutes wipes his hand over his mouth as he lowers his chin to his chest before he looks up at me again. "You're making me even fucking angrier, and believe me when I say I was already in the mood for blood before I got here."

Silence descends around us for a moment, my men filling the remaining tables out here, ready and waiting for my next order as Gray releases a scoff, breaking the stillness surrounding us.

"You still haven't explained who the fuck you are. The Devil's Brutes? What the fuck is that? I've never even heard of you." My men bite back their laughter at Gray's usual ability to stir shit up with his brashness, and I have to take a deep breath when I see he's fucking succeeding.

Standing taller, their Prez takes a step forward, placing his hand on the butt of his gun at his waist. "I'm about to be your worst fucking nightmare."

"And why is that?" I ask, quirking a brow at him as he shakes his head in annoyance.

"Because you took something very important to me."

"Which was...?" Gray encourages when he doesn't immediately explain what he fucking wants.

"Don't play fucking stupid with me. You took out the Ice Reapers and that was a bad move on your part."

Before I can open my mouth, Emmett beats me to it. "Oh shit, I heard there was a big explosion out there on their compound. Were there any survivors?"

The man before us pinches the bridge of his nose in annoyance, before pointing his hand in our direction. "You fucking know there weren't. You made damn sure of that."

Axel sighs beside me, flicking the ash from his cigarette at his feet.

"We don't know shit."

"Oh, I can fucking tell you don't know shit, which is exactly why I'm here to catch you up to speed." His smirk darkens as he digs into his own pocket to retrieve a cigar, and I internally roll my eyes. Is this a fucking pissing contest based on the size of what they're smoking?

Fuck. Me.

"I wasn't aware we needed bringing up to speed on anything. Especially when we had no knowledge you existed until you barged in," I state, trying to get to the actual fucking point.

"You messed around with more than you know. Plans had been made, deals had been agreed to, and you've caused a lot of trouble for yourselves." He takes a deep drag of his cigar. Gray raps his knuckles on the table.

"You're still not getting to the point," he grumbles, his eyebrows raising to his hairline in exaggeration, which seems to piss this guy off more.

"You're about two seconds from having a bullet in your skull, motherfucker." His gun is out of his belt in the next breath, but he cleverly doesn't aim it at anyone. Yet. But that does nothing to deter Gray. Nothing ever does.

"Please keep threatening me, you're making my dick hard."

Axel chuckles beside me, echoing the same noise coming from the rest of our men as our new enemy sends another warning shot into the air.

What is it with these fuckers making their presence known? It's getting on my goddamn nerves.

"We had a deal with the Ice Reapers, guns for cash, a debt that now falls to you," he bites out and his men inch closer behind him.

"Nothing falls to us because I don't know what the fuck you're talking about," I say with a scoff, reaching for my beer on the table and taking a swig. He's really starting to get on my nerves.

"*Everything* falls to you. Besides, we had a deal with the previous Prez of your dumb fucking club too, and we expect you to uphold that as well."

What?

"What deal might that have been?" Emmett asks as confusion floods my veins. He has to be lying. Our previous Prez may have been a cunt, but shit, he wouldn't have a secret deal… would he?

Shit. Of course he fucking would. This is the kind of mess we were trying to dig into already in relation to my father's death. Did these guys have involvement in that too?

Fuck.

"The deal where we get ten percent of each and every one of your drug runs."

Silence rings out around us, irritation bubbling in my veins as I sneer at him. "Like fuck are you getting a single cent from us."

"Oh, I am, Ryker Holden. I'm getting exactly what I want. And on top of that, you now owe me fifty fucking rifles to replace the ones lost in the explosion."

Rising to my feet, I shake off my cut and turn to face

him so we're toe to toe. "Are you not hearing me? I said you're not getting any money. Not a damn cent," I reiterate, but he doesn't absorb the information, so I clarify myself. "It's almost cute that you think you can stroll in here and make demands, thinking I'm going to take them. That's not how we operate. Now you have ten seconds to get off our compound before you learn exactly why we're called the Ruthless Brothers."

It's on the tip of my fucking tongue to start counting him down, but to my surprise, he takes a step back and places his gun away. "Mark my words, Ryker, you're going to want to obey me, it's the safest path that all the clever little boys take." I shake my head at him dismissively, but before I can decline, he nods his head toward the clubhouse. "Was that pretty little Scarlett Reeves I saw earlier? I'm sure it was. I wouldn't forget a sweet cunt like that anytime soon. Why don't you ask her about me? She knows far too well what is expected and what happens when you don't follow through." My body tenses at his insinuation, making my heart beat faster for reasons I can't even explain. "So, you've got seven days to get me what I want or it'll be *you* learning how we got the name the Devil's Brutes."

SIXTEEN

Scarlett

The door barely slams shut before Emily is standing toe to toe with me, wagging her finger in my face as another gunshot sounds outside. My spine stiffens from the telltale ringing that vibrates in my ears, but when I don't hear all hell break loose from the Ruthless Brother's, I know it was a different gun that was shot this time.

"What the fuck was that?" Emily blurts the moment the door slams shut.

"What was what?" My hands flex at my sides, my body on high alert from the arrival of the fucking Brutes, and I hate the fact that I'm practically forced to hide in here instead of watching what's going on outside.

"Don't ever fucking put yourself purposely in front of a gun again," Emily hisses, jabbing her finger into my chest, and I let her. Which is completely the opposite to my usual reaction to someone being too close to me.

Instead, I roll my eyes at her. "A simple 'thank you, Scarlett' would work just fine."

Emily scoffs in response, throwing her arms out to the side in disbelief before they settle on her hips. "No, screw that. I'm too much of a delicate soul to live forever with the knowledge that you died because of me."

I sigh, quirking a brow at her. "Were you the one pulling the trigger?"

"No."

"Then it can't have been because of you," I state, knowing full well that wasn't what she meant, just as she tries to explain the fact.

"You know what I mean, Scarlett, that's—"

"Girls, you can be mad at each other later, but right now, I need your help with everyone else." Maggie's voice filters through the fog that invisibly settled around the two of us, and I turn to glance at the rest of the people in the room.

Fear and tension are palpable in the air, the worry traveling from one person to another as uncertainty drags everyone down. The kids are cradled in their mothers' arms while the Ruthless Bitches sniffle among themselves.

Maggie's right, they're useless in this state. We need to protect them.

"Coming," I murmur, turning back to Emily as I offer her a small smile, and she instantly wraps me in her arms tightly.

A beat passes before she whispers in my ear, "Thank you, Scarlett."

I just hold her tighter for a moment longer, before stepping back and moving into action.

"What are we doing right now? My girls don't need to be around this." My attention is drawn to the woman in the center of the bar area, twin girls clinging to her as she desperately seeks a solution.

Sometimes I wonder how these women end up with a biker to begin with. They know exactly what they're signing up for and yet they crumble at the first hurdle.

I don't say that of course, instead I roll my shoulders back and step further into the room. "Is it possible to get everyone through the back entrance and around to the vehicles without being detected?" I ask, before my eyes settle back on the mom with the twins.

"It's possible, but the second we start an engine, they'll know."

Fuck.

Searching the room again, my eyes fall to the safest place in the entire building. I consider whether I should start spouting orders or not, but when no one else steps up to the plate, I take a deep breath and move toward the double doors that intimidated me when I first arrived.

"We need everybody—old ladies, children included—to get comfortable in the Church."

Chattering picks up as a few of the Moms nod at me and start to make their way toward the open doors without any hesitation.

"Who the fuck gave you the right to give orders?" Molly snaps with her arms folded over her chest. Mascara stains her cheeks, her eyes are red and blotchy, but the snarl on her lips remains the same.

"Where were you when *she* was protecting our own, Molly?" The question comes from an irritated Maggie, and before a slack-jawed Molly can mumble anything in response, Ruthie steps up from beside her with a soft smile.

"I'll help with the kids," she murmurs, moving toward me. Her hand brushes my arm as she continues, "Thanks for helping me out there, Scarlett."

I'm left staring wide-eyed after her as Molly hisses from her spot. "You can't lock us in there. If those fuckers try to burn us down or something, we'll have no way out."

Irritatingly, she has a point.

"We won't lock the doors, we'll guard them."

"Guard them?" Her scoff annoys the fuck out of me, so I decide responding to her needs to be someone else's job.

"Maggie," I holler, noting the side-eye she gives me before she turns her attention to the pain in my ass.

"What she said," is all she has to offer, and I smirk before Emily appears at my side with a frown tainting her forehead.

"No, you get in with us." Her words are softly spoken, a heartfelt sentiment tingling through my veins as I shake my head at her despite the fact that she's worrying for my safety.

"I've spent all of my life hiding. Now isn't the time for that, not for me at least."

I sense the protest on her lips, but before she can verbalize them, the sound of the door swinging open behind me gains everyone's attention.

Old ladies sag in relief as they see their men step into the room, while the Ruthless Bitches start wailing again. What those whores won't do for some needy attention. It's exhausting.

Turning on the spot, my eyes instantly clash with Ryker's as he clears his throat and forces a smile to his lips. "They're gone. Pack up your old ladies and kids and go home," he announces, dividing the men as some take care of their families, while the others head straight for the bar.

Deciding that means I can slip back into my room, I take the opportunity. I need a fucking minute of calm to get past the fact that the Brutes have made their presence known.

Fuck.

I barely take two steps when Gray calls out my name, rooting me to the spot. "Not you, Scarlett. Church. Now."

My nostrils flare at being publicly summoned, my eyebrows pinching at the order, but despite my irritation, I get on with it. The quicker I deal with their bullshit, the quicker I can get to handling my own.

Turning for the Church doors, I hear Emily's voice over the chatter of the crowd. "Why do you guys have an issue with her, Emmett? She…"

Her words trail off as I turn to glance at her at the same time Emmett envelops her in his arms, squeezing her tight, and she melts in his hold. Her eyes find mine as she tilts her head to the side, listening to him murmur in her ear as I continue toward the room. A moment passes before she's nodding along with her brother and being escorted away by Euro, leaving Emmett to follow after Ryker, Gray, and Axel.

"Hey, Prez, do you need us for this?"

"No, Duffer, you keep an eye on everything outside and man the bar for me."

I glance over my shoulder to see who Duffer is, finding him nodding eagerly in acknowledgment as he sits at the bar with an older man beside him. Once I step through the double doors leading into Church, the atmosphere instantly changes as Ryker shuts the doors behind him.

I assess each of the four men before me. Not one of them is giving me anything to go off of as they each find their spots at the table and drop into their seats. I don't need telling this time as I make my way to the other end of the table and sit as far away as possible.

When none of them instantly begin to talk, I sigh, giving them an exasperated look. "Am I supposed to know what this is about?"

"Yes." Axel glares at me, fingers steepling on the table top as his jaw tightens.

"Well, I don't."

A beat passes, then another, and another, before Gray clears his throat from his spot beside Emmett. "You warned us about the Devil's Brutes and when we don't listen, they suddenly show up... Is that your doing?"

I scoff at the absurdity falling from his mouth as I shake my head in disbelief. "If there is one thing you should hear me on when I speak, it's the fact that I would never, *ever*, reach out to a single member of the Devil's Brutes, even if my life depended on it. Especially Kincaid." The taste of his name on my tongue is like acid as a shiver runs down my spine.

"I'm assuming that's the prez," Ryker states, and I nod.

"He knew who you were," Emmett adds, leaning back in his seat as he drags his eyes over my face.

"Believe me, I'm very aware that he knows who I am. It saddens me every fucking day that he's still breathing." I instantly wince at myself for letting my feelings show so effortlessly, and it doesn't go unnoticed by the Ruthless Brothers.

"What does that mean?"

"It's nothing to worry about," I reply, shrugging the stress from my shoulders, before I lace my fingers together in my lap.

"Was he a regular?" Axel grunts.

"What's it to you?" I bite out.

"Look, you're supposed to be helping us right now," Ryker interjects, and I roll my eyes.

"Then ask me questions which are of use to the club." My response makes them pause, before Ryker nods and braces his arms on the table between us.

"Okay, how long were the Reapers in bed with the Brutes?"

"Two years, maybe three," I reply instantly, but it seems my openness doesn't offer them any reassurance.

"Did they run guns for them?"

"Yes."

"Were they close?"

"Very. People regard Kincaid in two ways; he's either a threat or a God. The Reapers practically made a shrine for him, believing he would lead them to greatness, when all he ever offered was a glimpse of hell."

Gray tilts his head to the side as he observes me, while Emmett's frown deepens.

"Is there any other information you can give us on them?" Axel mutters, not looking directly at me as he concedes slightly, revealing that he does in fact need my help.

I almost consider making a point of it, but that would only reconfirm to him that I'm a bitch. So instead, I sit tall in my seat and sigh. "Like I told you before, these men act like they rule the world. We're all outlaws here, from the members of any motorcycle club, to the prospects, right down to the whores, old ladies and their children. But they somehow manage to take it to another level with little effort on their end. They don't care who they tread on. They take what they want, when they want, and however they want, without waiting for permission from a single soul."

Ryker clears his throat. "He told me that the President of the Ruthless Brothers, my predecessor, had a deal in place with him where he took a percentage of our operations. Could that be true?"

I'm nodding before he's even finished speaking. "Anyone within a fifty-mile radius of that man and his followers pays him something."

"And when you don't pay?" Gray asks, nostrils flared with anger at the truth I'm giving them, truth that muddies their own doorstep.

"He takes," I answer honestly as my body trembles with the memories threatening to barricade me in my mind, leaving me to lose my strength and wither away.

"He takes what?" This time, the question comes from Ryker, and I focus on his green eyes for a moment, grounding myself in the present so I don't succumb to the pain I've hidden away.

"Whatever he wants. The lives of the men he considers a threat, their women, their whores… their children."

"Fuck," Axel grunts, slamming his palm on the table, and I jolt at the sudden movement.

"Why did I expect this to be harder than that?" Emmett asks, and it takes me a second to realize he's looking at me.

"What?" I toy with the end of my skirt nervously as I try to process what he's talking about.

"Why are you so forthcoming?"

"I was a club whore. My loyalty lies with me." My statement isn't entirely true, but my loyalty does lie with me. Always. It's the only way to survive this dark and twisted world.

"We will have to bring this information to the table in the morning. I need the night to think. This is our legacy, our club, and our future. We won't fall at the first hurdle, and not at the mistakes of the men who falsely led us before." Axel, Emmett, and Gray all nod in agreement with their Prez as I rise from my seat, hoping this means I can get out of here.

There's no gavel hitting the wood to draw the meeting

to an end since this isn't all that official tonight, so when Emmett turns toward me instead of heading for the door, I'm frozen in place.

When he's within arm's reach, he grabs my waist, lifting me into the air and catching me by surprise.

"What's going on?" I ask, the panic noticeable in my tone as he holds me so we're face to face.

"You deserve a reward for being so cooperative."

What the fuck does that mean?

"So cooperative?" I repeat, confusion getting the better of me as he bands one arm tighter around my waist, keeping me pinned to him, while the other strokes down my face softly, making me shiver.

"And for protecting my sister without hesitation," he adds.

"I didn't do that for you," I breathe, my brain malfunctioning with him this close as he grins at me. His hand drops from my face and trails up my thigh. My core clenches as goosebumps pebble over my skin.

"That's exactly why you earned my appreciation."

SEVENTEEN

Emmett

My body has been thrumming for her since I pulled her into my lap. My mind consumed with her from the second she lifted from her seat and placed herself between Emily and the loaded gun.

A. Fucking. Loaded. Gun. Pointed. At. My. Sister.

When I felt her heat leave my lap, I expected her to run with fear, but she surprised me. Without question, she protected the one thing that matters most to me in this world. Shit, my father was in the crowd somewhere too, but he didn't rush to his daughter's aid, not like she did.

I want to slam my cock inside of her on the table in the middle of Church. I want to show her just how grateful I am despite the fact that we don't truly know anything about her. Axel would hate it, but I don't care. Not when she acted so selflessly. That's enough for me. My respect for her has grown tenfold.

She wraps her legs around my waist and tightens her arms around my neck. She's blocking my view of the room but replacing it with the most beautiful alternative. Her tits are begging to be nipped at, and once I get us out of here, I'll get my taste.

She's a mystery, and my interest is piqued. She stirs something inside of me that I can't explain, but all it does is lure me closer to her.

I shuffle around the table and blindly find the door handle before tilting my head to glance back at Ryker, who remains in his seat. I nod toward Axel, making sure he knows someone needs to keep a fucking eye on him tonight, and it's clearly *not* going to be me. The swift raise of his chin tells me he's got the situation in hand, so I step into the bar area without a backward glance.

I'm almost surprised that Gray isn't pouting that I'm carrying her away from him, but he must sense the need I feel for her, and he's not giving me any shit for a change.

When I step out into the crowd with Scarlett in my arms, a round of cheers sound out around us, along with the soft muffling of Scarlett chuckling.

"Are we *finally* going to have this girl complete the rite of passage now?"

Peeking over Scarlett's shoulder, I march straight toward our destination. There's no way in hell my appreciation fuck is turning into something else. I don't mind an audience, fuck, if anything I love one, but not these fuckers.

Pushing through the door that leads to the private quarters, the music dulls and the chatter fades into the background as I make my way down the hall. My hands flex on the globes of her ass as her thighs clench around me. She's already so responsive and we haven't even done anything yet.

My teeth sink into my bottom lip as excitement creeps up my spine. Kicking my bedroom door open, I spin on the spot as I step over the threshold, before slamming it shut and pinning her body against it.

Her breath hitches as her pupils dilate and her lips part.

Hot. As. Fuck.

Our chests heave in sync, desire coursing through my veins as I get lost in her stunning blue eyes.

"Tell me what you like?"

Her eyebrows quirk at my question, and I push my chest against hers, needing to be as close as possible.

"Does it matter?" Her question doesn't match the hope in her tone or the way her eyes track my lips instead of meeting my gaze. She's as intoxicated as I am.

"Of course it fucking does," I grunt, dropping her down an inch so she can feel the outline of my dick press against her core. "If I was just going to take what I wanted, I would have fucked you in the Church. I'm *trying* to be civilized,"

I add with a grin as her fingers move to my neck.

"I feel like I'm supposed to trust the person I tell those things to," she answers with an unspoken question in her eyes that I can't understand or piece together, so I shrug.

"Tell me anyway."

My response seems to pass whatever test she was holding me accountable for as she wets her lips and leans closer. "Gray asked me the same thing last night. I was just making sure you fucking me hadn't become hot gossip."

A grin spreads across my face as she explains. "The running commentary I got came from Ryker, but whatever happened after you left the bar, Gray has kept to himself." What's the point in lying? What I heard was hot as hell. I wouldn't expect anything else though, not when it was Ryker describing it to me. He's usually the least fazed by the Ruthless Brothers and the Bitches fucking in the bar, but last night, he was caught up in her allure.

"I asked him to fuck me into the mattress, hard and fast, just how I wanted it."

My cock juts in her direction at the thought of it, and I thrust lightly so she knows exactly what she's doing to me. "Is that what you want now?"

"No." Her eyes widen with that one small word that falls from her lips. "Nothing gets me wetter than choking on dick," she adds, her cheeks flushing as she admits it out loud, and I chuckle.

"Ryker *may* have mentioned that." Mentioned it? Fuck, he had my dick straining from the mere fucking description he gave. "So, after I've choked you with my cock, what do you want?" I ask, moving closer so my nose brushes against hers and our breaths mingle.

"I don't care, I just want you to consume me."

"Consume you?" My voice is raspy, deeper, and needier as she swipes her tongue out and drags it along my lips.

"All of me."

Our lips collide in the next second. Who erased the remaining distance between us, I can't be certain. Our tongues tangle as her fingers find their way into my hair, making me groan.

My hands clench around the globes of her ass, likely leaving bruises in their wake. We break apart, struggling to fill our lungs. Her throat bobs as she gulps heavily, and I grin.

"You still want this?"

"More than my next breath."

My grin spreads wider as I lean forward and trail my nose along her throat, before settling my lips against her ear. "Then get on your knees and take my cock like a good girl."

She groans in response as I lower her feet to the floor, and she doesn't hesitate in dropping to her knees with her back pressed against the door as I widen my stance. Before

I can reach for my belt, she's unbuckling my jeans and pulling the material down just enough to slip her hands inside my boxers.

My cock grows harder as she reveals my length, preening under her greedy gaze as she gapes at my favorite feature.

"Holy fuck." Her words are barely more than a whisper, but I don't miss them.

"There's more than enough to fill that beautiful mouth of yours. Are you ready?" I'm sure she thinks I'm being a cocky fucker, but I know my length and girth are not the norm. I'm bigger and thicker than any man here; a fact that can put women off sometimes, but not her.

Shit, her tongue sweeps across her lips as her eyes fill with hunger. Hunger for me.

"I'm not even sure it's going to fit," she mumbles, continuing to stare at my dick. "It's the hottest and most tempting fucking popsicle I've ever seen."

Fuck.

Is she trying to make me come from her appreciation alone? I thought I was supposed to be showing her gratitude, not the other way around.

"Are you ready for me?" I ask, still in awe of how she greedily stares at my dick.

"Even if it's the death of me, I'm not going to refuse," she replies with a smirk on her lips as I move the tip of my cock to brush against her lips.

Her breathing is labored, and she groans, at simply licking the tip of my dick.

Her tongue peeks out, testing the weight of my cock. I expect her to nervously lick and suck at the head, building up courage, but once again, she catches me off guard.

Her fingers grab the open ends of my jeans, pulling me closer as she takes me to the back of her throat in one swift move. "Fuck." The curse slips from my lips without warning as she swallows around the end of me, the vibrations of her groaning making me tingle with need.

Retreating, I think I take a deeper breath than her before she takes me further into her mouth again, tightening the suction of her lips as she moans. She groans as I gasp, taking me an extra inch each time until there's nothing left to take.

Wow.

Just fucking wow.

I've heard of the unicorns that love to suck dick, but never have I met one like this.

I almost sob when she releases my cock from her mouth, sitting a little straighter against the door behind her as she peers up at me through her lashes with her mouth wide. *Fuck.* Ryker swore to me that she practically came alive in front of Gray when she encouraged him to fuck her mouth, and I can't fathom how this could possibly get any better.

"Pat my thigh if you want me to stop," I mumble, inching forward as I line my cock up with her lips once more. I thrust into her mouth lightly at first, but the instant bite of her teeth against my sensitive skin, paired with the glare in her eyes, tells me that's not good enough.

Dead.

I'm dead.

I want it written on my headstone that I died from a blow job. I want every fucker to know the magic this woman wields.

Pulling out, I slam straight back in hard and fast. She swallows me instead of gagging. Her eyes are damp with unshed tears, and it makes my hips snap harder and faster, making the door rattle behind her.

She pierces her nails at the back of my legs, and my knees buckle. I'm going to fucking come.

Tearing away from her mouth, I wrap my hand in her hair to keep her against the door, panting for breath as I stare at my cock glistening from her touch.

"Please."

My dick juts at the plea from her lips, but I shake my head. "You're about to bring this to an end quicker than I want," I admit, then tug up for her to rise to her feet. Crouching so we're face to face, I rest my forehead against hers as I still struggle to catch my breath. "God, if anyone is on the other side of that door right now, they'll be able to hear exactly what you're doing to me." Her cheeks flush deeper as her pupils grow even wider. "I wonder what you'll sound like when I take your pussy, Scarlett."

"Come and find out."

Taking a step back, I look her over from head to toe. Her denim skirt now sits around her waist, revealing her black panties. Before I even consider what I'm doing, I reach forward and tear the fabric in two so I can get a good look at her pretty pink pussy.

The material falls to the ground as I repeat the same motion to the cropped top she's wearing. Her hair is wild from my hold, her perky tits dancing with every breath she takes as her skirt holds position at her hips.

She's a fucking wet dream.

I don't know where to touch her first. Every inch of her body pleads for me to feel her, use her, please her.

We groan as I cup her pussy, my fingers tracing the moisture clinging to her center as my palm grinds against her clit. She's wet as fuck and it's all for me.

"Oh God," she cries out as I thrust two fingers deep into her pussy, matching the same force she wanted in her mouth and her sensitive walls clench around me.

"I want to feel you come on my hand, drip down my wrist, and cover me in your scent," I grunt, my nostrils flaring as need courses through me from head to toe, and her pussy squeezes my fingers even tighter. "Seems like you want that too, Scarlett. Are you going to obey and be a good girl?" I purr, leaning in close so my lips gloss over hers as she nods eagerly in response.

Adding a third finger, I drop to my knees, swiping my tongue between her folds as I get more brutal with every thrust of my fingers. Her palms slap against the wood on either side of her as her groans get louder and louder, and when I sink my teeth into the sensitive flesh of her taut nub, she falls apart in my hands.

"Holy fuck, holy fuck. Holy fuck," she chants as her back arches up off the door, gripping my hair, as wave after wave of her orgasm crashes through her. I drag out my movements and extend the pleasure for as long as possible.

Her shoulders slump as she looks at me with hooded eyes, her jaw slack as she tries to focus through the sex-induced cloud floating around her. I don't know what she expects from me next, but it's not the fourth finger I insert into her core.

Even though I think I have the upper hand, I'm mistaken, because she repeats one word that's like music to my ears. "Please."

When I remove my fingers from her pussy, her lips part in disappointment, but it doesn't last long as I take a step back and shake out of my cut and t-shirt, before removing my boots and losing the remaining clothes that stand between us.

The stain on her lips is smeared, her make-up doing nothing to hide the flushed and blotchy skin beneath as she stares at me with raw need burning in her eyes. She shimmies out of the denim skirt, and I catch a glimpse of her orgasm trailing down her legs. The beast inside of me wants to step forward and run my tongue over it, but I know I'll come the second it touches my lips.

I move to take a step toward her, and she lifts her hand to pause me. It takes all my strength to stop, but when she opens her mouth, it's fucking worth it. "Cut. Put your cut on. I want Emmett, the Ruthless Brother's VP, fucking me."

Pre-cum drips from the end of my cock, weeping with fucking joy as I slowly slip the leather back over my shoulders, reaching into the pocket to retrieve a condom while I'm there.

"Just like this?" I ask, prowling toward her, and she nods.

"Just. Like. That."

Tearing at the condom packet, I slowly drag the latex down my length, and she watches my every move. Perspiration clings to every inch of her skin as she steps toward me, placing her hand on my chest as she nudges me backward.

"I know I mentioned you doing whatever you want

with me, but this might be the only time you let me see your cock and I need to know what it feels like to ride you."

Collapsing back on the bed, she leaves me fucking speechless as she climbs into my lap and lines up my dick with her entrance. Her fingers spread across my chest as she uses me to gain her balance, before slowly sinking down onto my length.

Her eyes roll back in her head as she cries out with pure joy. "Holy fuck," she mumbles, swirling her hips slightly as she works to take me all the way in. Dragging the walls of her pussy up my dick, I moan at the loss of heat, before she slams back down onto me faster this time.

I've found heaven. I've fucking found it.

I let her repeat the motion two more times. Her body trembles with desire. I grab her waist and spin us on the bed. Her fingers instantly sink into the sheets, excitement dancing in her eyes as she widens her thighs.

Grabbing her hips, I tilt her slightly so I have the perfect angle, before I thrust hard and deep into her pussy. Her moan is long and sensual. "Harder. Please. Harder," she begs.

Doing as she asks, I go harder and faster, the force touching brutal as she practically sings. She releases the sheets with one hand, then strokes her hand down her chest as she teases a trail to her clit.

My cock plunges inside of her as her delicate fingers ghost over her needy bud. No pinching, no flicking, no harsh touch. Just a soft swipe in comparison to the harshness of my rhythm, and she screams at the top of her lungs, exploding at the seams. It's impossible to survive the tightening of her pussy around my cock, and with my next breath, she triggers my orgasm. It starts at my toes, swirling up my legs and burning my spine before I grunt, my movements becoming slower and shallower as I come with her.

"Holy fuck," we say in sync. A soft, airy chuckle passes both our lips.

She looks like an angel tangled in my sheets with a heaving chest and I know, in this moment, that this definitely won't be the last time.

Amidst all of the awe and ecstasy as she took my cock, I didn't get the luxury of tasting her tits. And I *have* to have a taste of them.

EIGHTEEN

Scarlett

The body behind me provides warmth to my skin. Morning fog clouds my thoughts as I come to my senses.

Lips feather over my cheeks, my forehead, my eyes, all the way down to my chin.

If I fell asleep tangled in the sheets with Emmett and he's cocooning me with his body from behind, then who the fuck is kissing me?

Squinting, I peer out of one eye to find Gray lazing beside me, a wide grin on his face as he continues to dot a few more kisses over my skin, before propping himself on his elbow.

"What are you doing?" My voice is groggy from sleep as I force both eyes open.

"Well, I called your name first, but that didn't seem to work at all, so I thought I would try other tactics to wake you." His blue eyes darken with mischief as he leans in once more and presses his lips to mine.

I'm disorientated as shit right now, especially with Emmett's hands at my waist and his dick nestled between my ass cheeks.

"Did you need me for something?" I'm not trying to be rude, but it sounds a little rough to my ears.

Gray slaps his palm against his chest, collapsing back like a wounded soldier as he rolls dramatically from side to side. I roll my eyes at his dramatics, and he eventually sighs, dropping the act.

"Can't a guy just search you out for no reason?"

"No, not usually." I murmur, shaking my head dismissively as he rolls his eyes at me.

"Now, who's being dramatic?"

Is he for real?

As if sensing my thoughts, the hand at my hip flexes against my skin before Emmett's gruff voice joins the conversation. "Ignore him, Scarlett. Gray doesn't know what dramatic looks like because he never looks in the fucking mirror to see it."

A grin spreads across my face as I bite back the chuckle bubbling beneath the surface, which only grows louder when Gray glares at me.

"So, anyway, last night was fun," he says with a smile, like everything prior to this moment didn't happen.

"Which part?" I ask, my thoughts completely confused with what is actually going on right now.

"You know, when guns were being fired. I mean, Emmett had the most fun dropping the asshole waving his gun around, but I still enjoyed it," Gray explains with a shrug.

"Of course you did," I mumble, shifting my position slightly so I can push the hair back off my face, but both Emmett and Gray make it difficult for me to move at all. The sheet is at least pinned under my arm so my breasts aren't spilling out, but something tells me that might not be the case for much longer. The thought alone makes my core clench.

I should be exhausted. Between the pair of them, my muscles ache in places I didn't even know I had them, yet my body still wants more.

"Something has been playing on my mind though," Gray adds, pausing my thoughts as I blink up at him. The wrinkle between his brows and the softening of his eyes tell me I'm not going to like where this is going.

"What?" Emmett asks, curious as to what his brother is talking about while I would rather sink through the mattress and land in hell than find out.

"Some of the things Kincaid said, mixed with what you said last night, makes me wonder..." His words trail off as though he's trying to carefully find the right ones, but the tightening in my chest and the thundering of my heartbeat has already begun. I have to act quickly if I want him to shut the fuck up, and I do. I really do. This is way too heavy for me when I've only just opened my eyes.

Reaching my hand up, I grip his neck, considering whether he'll stop if I press my lips to his right now. But as I inch closer, something else catches my attention.

"Did someone bite the bottom of your fucking ear off?" The words spill from my lips before I can formulate an actual sentence, and I cringe at myself, but to my surprise, Gray grins proudly beside me.

How did I not notice this before?

"Yes, yes, they did."

With wide eyes, I tilt my head around so I can look to Emmett for confirmation, and he lazily nods at me.

"How the fuck did that even happen?" The second I ask, I know I have him distracted, but it doesn't ease the tension that's already risen inside of me.

"You've started it now, Scarlett," Emmett grumbles from behind me, running his nose up the length of my throat as I shiver in his hold.

"Shush, our girl wants to know, so I have to tell her," Gray retorts with an eye roll, and I smirk.

"You don't, you really fucking don't," Emmett mutters, his lips against my skin, and I bite back a moan. Gray leans forward, kissing my lips for the briefest second, heat in his eyes as Emmett caresses me.

I'm more than happy for us all to be distracted for the moment, but Gray continues with his story, "So, I was selected to represent the Ruthless Brothers in an underground fight." Emmett clears his throat, making Gray sigh. "Fine, we were all pitted against another club, but I went out there guns blazing metaphorically, flashing these bad boys." He flexes his biceps as he wiggles his eyebrows and I giggle at his antics. "Anyway, I KO'd that motherfucker in the second round. It would have been sooner, but Axel made me promise to drag it out a little bit, put on a show for the crowd and all that."

"So the opponent bit your ear?" I ask, eyes wide at the enthusiasm coming from him, but he shakes his head.

"No, it happened after that."

"He just wanted to make sure you knew how good he was with his hands, Scar," Emmett breathes against my ear just as Gray trails a hand down my arm.

Fuck.

It definitely doesn't help that I can feel Emmett's cock swelling behind me too. They're leaving me dizzy as I struggle to remain focused on Gray's story.

"Afterward, we were in the bar area and some girl leaned in close to whisper in my ear."

I gasp, unsure whether it's annoyance over the mention of another woman or the fact in general.

"A fucking girl did that?" *Show me the bitch right now and I will slaughter her with my bare fucking hands.*

"Would you stop interrupting?" The pointed look he offers makes me slam my lips shut. He still rolls his eyes at me like he expects me to interrupt again, but now I'm way too conscious of it so it won't happen again.

"Then get to the point, asshole," Emmett says from behind me, and I have to sink my teeth into my bottom lip to stop myself from laughing.

Gray's stare quickly turns to a glare at Emmett, before his eyes become animated once more. "Just as her lips pressed against my skin, some fucking savage swiped at my other ear."

What the fuck?

"Who?"

The smirk growing on his lips gives me the sense that I'm about to be either shocked or pissed at what he's about to say next.

"It was Axel."

"Axel," I repeat with a frown tainting my forehead, and he nods in confirmation. "Why the fuck would he do that?"

"I think he was mad about the fact that I didn't listen to him. When he said to last more than the first round, he didn't mean I should K.O. my opponent within the first three breaths of the second round."

How is he okay about this? The whole bottom half of

his earlobe is just… gone.

"How the hell are you still friends with him?"

Gray's eyes widen at me as he shakes his head once. "Friends? Fuck no. That man's my brother through and through. Besides, I lost the club a lot of fucking money that night; half an ear is nothing in comparison to what else could have happened," he explains with a shrug as I gape at him. "Now you think I'm even cooler, don't you?" He winks at me as I scramble to find a single word to say in response, but come up empty.

"You've left her speechless, Gray. We're going to need to find her voice again." Emmett's hands travel up my waist beneath the sheets, making me shiver. Gray's eyes track the movement as a wicked grin spreads across his lips.

"She makes the prettiest fucking noises, man," he mumbles in response, his tongue glossing over his bottom lip as he looks up at me through hooded eyes.

"And the flush that creeps up her neck and takes over her cheeks…" Emmett adds, making the heat travel over my skin in the exact way he mentions.

Fuck.

How am I supposed to survive them? Have I finally met my fate? Is this how I die?

Gray's mouth is poised above mine as Emmett's lips trace over my shoulder. I can barely catch my breath, high on their proximity and the possibility that hangs in the air.

"Fuckers, let's go."

I have to blink three times before I realize that wasn't Emmett or Gray talking, and I pout the second Gray rolls off the bed, nodding toward the door.

"You have the worst fucking timing, Prez," he grumbles, not hiding the fact that he's rearranging himself in his jeans. Following his line of sight, I find Ryker leaning against the doorframe with an amused grin on his lips.

"We've got errands to run. You can play with your new toy when we get back," he states before sauntering down the hallway.

New toy? New. Fucking. Toy?

That asshole!

Any hope that they won't race after him is diminished the moment the thought enters my head because I know where I am. To a biker, nothing comes above the Prez's orders. Not a whore, not an old lady, not even the temptation of a threesome.

I roll to my back when Emmett steps from the bed, butt naked with his blond hair loose around his shoulders.

"Fucking cockblocking asshole," I mumble, my hands balling into fists as I hit the sheets with a huff.

"Oh, feisty," Gray says with a wink from the doorway, and I snap my teeth at him, which only makes his grin grow wider. "You're hot as hell when you're mad, sweet cheeks. Save a little bit of this anger for later, yeah?"

He doesn't wait around for a response, following Ryker before I can even think of a reply. I tilt my head back to Emmett, only to find him completely dressed now with his hair pulled back into a bun at the back of his head.

"He can have your anger, Scarlett, because I'm claiming all of your cries."

The door slams shut behind him. I went from the hottest, most tempting moment of my life one second to a very fucking sour mood in record time.

They can demand my anger and my cries, but all those motherfuckers are going to get is a smirk on my lips and the scent of me on Emmett's sheets from taking care of myself when they couldn't.

Take that, you Ruthless fucking bastards.

RUTHLESS BROTHERS MC

NINETEEN

Gray

I adjust my dick as the strain against my jeans throbs like a motherfucker when I walk away from Scarlett sprawled out in my friend's bed. I hate to tease and leave, but when the boss gives you orders, you listen. Ryker might be one of my closest friends, but he's now my Prez and that takes precedence over everything else. Even hot pussy.

Emmett grunts as we move into the bar area, seemingly just as disappointed as I am as he strokes his hand over his beard. "Should have locked your door, man. Then we would know where she is when we get home." I smirk, and he glances at me out of the corner of his eye, but doesn't utter a word as he continues toward the door.

It seems he's just as intrigued by her as I am. She's so fucking refreshing, somehow mysterious, yet blindly innocent and tempting all at once. The grin on my lips stretches just thinking about Emmett not trying to block me from her and my dick strains even harder at the thought of sharing her.

Fuck.

If we've got errands to run, I need to get my head in the game. I almost consider sneaking into the bathroom quickly to take care of myself, but something tells me it wouldn't ease the tension radiating from my cock.

I prowl through the bar, letting Emmett lead the way. *Get your fucking head in the game, Gray.*

He props the door open for me and the second I catch it with my hand, I lift my head high, forgetting that my cock is raging in my pants and the woman tangled in the sheets. Instead, I scan my eyes over the men gathered at Ryker's order.

Our Prez and Axel are standing beside their Harleys, talking to each other as Euro, Eric, and Duffer roll their motorcycles out of the garage. Emmett's dad nods in our direction as we pass, before we quickly join them with our own rides.

As the new Treasurer, my rank and riding position shifts dramatically, placing me third in line after Ryker and Emmett. Lifting my leg over the seat of my black-on-black motorcycle, I secure my helmet in place as I balance the weight of the machine between my thighs.

Ryker pats Axel on the shoulder and they separate. Axel lights a cigarette and makes his way to the back of the formation. As the new sergeant at arms, he will bring up the rear, which will work perfectly for him since he doesn't like to have to keep in line among the pack. From behind, he can set his own pace and distance from us.

Concerned, I glance back at him. His sunglasses are firmly in place so I can't read his eyes, which allows the memory of the other night to bombard me. The worry of a repeat flashing in my mind.

Ryker clears his throat, and I shake the concern from my shoulders. Axel won't accept help until he's willing to help himself, so for now, I can only focus on the task at hand.

"We're collecting a shipment from the Newport yard today. With everything that happened last night with the Devil's Brutes, we're not going to organize on-site. Instead, we're going to separate and dispatch from our three other locations around Jasperville." Everyone nods in understanding, pleased with the extra precautions after the mess that came from last night. "Euro, you're with Emmett and Gray. Duffer, you're going with me and the prospects to the red house, while Axel will go with Eric to the green house. Keep your wits about you," he adds, then turns to sit on his bike.

Revving my engine, I relax onto the leather seat as my bike vibrates between my thighs. This is exactly the drive I needed to clear my fucking head of that tempting pussy.

Ryker starts moving, and everyone rolls out.

I glance back over my shoulder before I drive off the compound, nodding at Eric behind me, and it reminds me that he won't have that spot forever. Not when Shift finally gets back. I'm hopeful he'll be back from our Northern chapter sooner rather than later, but it's still not certain. He's the craziest tech guy I've ever met, and when they were dealing with some security issues with the rival gangs, he offered up his services. That was almost four weeks ago, so I don't know what has him so distracted, but it surely doesn't take this long to fix.

He must be doing okay if Axel reached out to him to do a background check on Scarlett; another fact which completely blows my mind. Axel never concerns himself with any of the Ruthless Bitches, so why start now? Sure, she came from the Reapers, but that was my doing.

Annoyed that my train of thought is circling back to her, I focus on the road ahead, letting the sun beat down on me. The wind whips against my face and my cut flaps with the speed, my knuckles tightening around the handlebars as we weave through traffic.

I've been on the Newport run for over twelve months now, so I don't even have to think about where I'm going as I drive there on autopilot.

The first shipment of the month, like this one, is always the largest, with AK40s and shotguns being the heavy carriers, while the second delivery is mainly handguns. So today is more work and more distribution, but it will be worth it when we're swimming in money within the next twenty-four hours.

Ryker slows up ahead as he nears the gates of the shipment yard and the rest of us do the same as we pass through the gates. As we get near the containers, we split up, parking in twos in a few different spots so we don't draw too much attention. I'm not sure how it makes all that much difference since the security system will show us all arriving together anyway, but it's a rule that's been in place for as long as I can remember.

I kick the stand down on my bike three containers away with Euro at my side, shut off the engine, then we head to the left toward the cream container. Axel and Emmett are already standing at the double doors, unlocking the padlock as we get there, while Ryker hangs back with Eric.

It's weird as fuck doing this with new roles, watching Emmett step effortlessly into Ryker's shoes as he stands back and observes. I'm sure it's going to be a huge shift for him, but one completely worthwhile for the club.

Axel throws the lock through the air and Euro catches it beside me with a small grunt as Emmett starts to open the doors. Prospects line the exterior of the group, facing away from the goods as they act as protection.

My fingers flex at my sides, ready to start loading up

the storage on my bike, when Emmett's grunt stops me in place. "What the fuck?"

"Shit." The curse falls from Axel's mouth with a bite, and I rush to see what's going on before Ryker can even move a step.

My brows furrow as I stare at the single wooden container placed in the middle of the space.

"One? Why's there only one?" I ask.

"It's a setup," Ryker breathes, the words barely passing his lips before a gunshot rings out, followed swiftly by a grunt from one of the prospects as they fall to the ground.

I glance around the area and come up blank as someone grabs onto my cut from behind, moving me to safety down the side of the container.

Tilting my head, I turn to see Eric releasing his hold on me as he pulls his gun from his holster, and I do the same. When another gunshot doesn't follow, concern and confusion burns through my veins, making me take the safety off.

I rest my back against the metal, preparing myself, when an explosion sounds, lifting me off my feet and hurling me in the air until I smash into the huge container across from me and slump to the floor.

Plumes of black smoke engulf me, like waves that keep on crashing. Dizziness attempts to pull me from the present as I gingerly lift my hand to my face, only to find blood coating the tips of my fingers.

"Ambush!" Axel yells from fuck knows where as I blindly search for my gun on the ground beside me.

Once I feel the metal in my hands, I stagger to my feet, coughing and spluttering in search of Eric. I find his feet first, a few yards away from me, and it's only when I get closer that I see the rest of him as he lies coughing and gasping for breath.

"Help them, Gray. I'll still be here," he grunts, hissing through the pain as blood drips down the side of his temple.

I blink down at him a few times before I finally turn around, processing his words and seeing them through. Using the container that caught my fall, I stumble to the end as flickers of orange and red break through the thick smoke. It stands in place of our container, nothing remains but the metal torn into hundreds of pieces.

Blood runs down my eyes, blurring my vision, and I attempt to wipe it away with my t-shirt so I can focus better. Fast paced footsteps sound from behind me, coming up on my left, and I know with certainty that it won't be one of our men moving so quickly after being caught off guard like this.

Taking a deep breath, I roll my shoulders back, wincing at the pain in my muscles, before pointing my gun in that direction. My eyes zero in on the branded cut first—Devil's Brutes—before I do as I was trained to do; and pull the trigger.

Without a silencer, the noise vibrates around us, but all I truly hear is the sound of the bullet meeting flesh as he takes his last breath, slumping to the ground, his blood starting to pool around him.

"Motherfuckers!" someone calls out, the voice unfamiliar.

As the flames grow, the smoke rises, offering me a better view of what is actually happening around me. Ryker is hovering over a lifeless body, blood dripping from the back of his head and his hands as he tries to catch his breath. Axel goes to pull his trigger on a Brute storming toward him with a blade in his hands, but it catches, confirming there's no bullets left in the chamber.

Fuck.

I move to raise my own weapon in their direction, but Axel launches himself at the enemy, using his brute force and strength to disarm them. I'm sure I hear his skull crack, even from this distance, as Axel continues to lay into him, over and over again, until all that remains is a pile of flesh and bones at his feet.

Another gunshot rings out around us, pulling my attention from Axel's busted knuckles and sneering face.

"Over here, it's Emmett," Euro hollers, and my feet are following his voice before I can even process it. He's two containers away on the other side of the explosion. A member of the Devil's Brutes has pinned him down. A knife handle sticks out of Emmett's thigh.

Holy shit.

Euro struggles to breathe as this asshole strangles him against the container. He's done enough damage; I'm not losing one of our guys at his hands.

Aiming my gun in his direction, I hesitate for the briefest of moments as I consider my accuracy with how close he is to Euro. Then… I pull the trigger. Blood splatters across Euro's face as the Brute drops to the floor.

If it were under different circumstances, right now I'd be beating myself up over doubting myself for even the smallest moment, but the amusement is short-lived as Emmett grunts, trying to pull the blade from his thigh, and it quickly brings me back to the present.

"Fuck, don't mess with that, Emmett," I rush, dropping to my knees beside him as adrenaline runs through my veins.

"I'm fine, it's just fucking stings," he grunts, sweat beading at his temples, blood staining his jeans.

"I'm sure it does, but let's get you out of here before we start messing around with it, yeah?"

He doesn't have a chance to defy me as Ryker rushes to my side, hand on my shoulder as he glances at his close friend and VP. "We're all clear. There's no more of them, they're gone, along with the guns. But I've got Hare on his way over now with a van. Don't touch that fucking wound until we get back."

Relief washes through me, only lasting a moment at the knowledge that we're no longer under attack, but I know that doesn't mean the shit we're in is even close to being done with. If we thought them appearing last night was inconvenient, this is something else entirely.

It's the end of one battle but the beginning of a war. The moment you have to decide whether you drop into defense or strike with offense, but there hasn't been any pre-game video tapes here. No heads-up on who we're up against. Just carnage. But the Brutes underestimate us if they think we'll just sit and take it without retribution.

Emmett's safety and well-being is paramount at this moment, we won't react as rashly as we did with the Reapers, they'll be expecting that. With every breath I take, I become stronger, angrier, and more merciless.

Let the enemy burn bright as we rise from the ashes of today and rain hell down on their souls.

We're filled with rage.

We're ready to riot.

We're as ruthless as ever.

TWENTY

Scarlett

Frustrated and unsatisfied, I climb off the bed with a huff. Emmett's sheets slip from my naked body as I search out my clothes.

I was sandwiched between two hot men.

Two. Hot. Men.

It's not something I've ever really considered before, not until Ryker wrapped his lips around my nipple as I leaned forward to take the weight of Gray's cock on my tongue. *Now* it's all I can think about.

Yet I'm completely alone with no one but myself for entertainment, and suddenly, it's just not good enough. I wasn't a virgin before I got here, far from it, but one thing is for certain… I have never chosen to sleep with a biker. I've tried so hard to keep my sex life as far away from club life as possible, until I found myself here.

This… this is addicting, intoxicating, and all I crave.

Finding my discarded clothes in a messy heap, I recall my cropped top being torn to shreds. One of Emmett's white t-shirts hangs over the chair in the corner.

It falls to mid-thigh on me as I pull it over my head, then clean up the room and make the bed. Taking my tattered clothes, I ball them up in my arms and grab my cell phone from the nightstand.

A new message flashes through from Trig, the only contact I have in my cell, and I remember he messaged me yesterday too.

Fuck.

Sweeping my gaze over both messages, I gulp, glancing around the room like someone can see me, before quickly typing a response out.

Scarlett:

I'm tied up at the minute. When I'm free for work again,
I'll let you know.

Now isn't the time for me to be earning more money, I'm trying to keep a low profile. It's not the first time I've told him to put me on hold and it certainly won't be the last, so it won't be an issue.

I pause at the door, taking a deep breath as I reach for the handle and step out into the hallway. I'm ready to make a mad dash back to my room, but I don't get two steps into the hall before a gasp from my left halts my movements.

Glancing out of the corner of my eye, I cringe at the sight of Emily. "Of course you did," she says with a scoff, leaving me unsure as to how she's feeling right now, but sneaking out of her brother's room is enough explanation as it is.

I clear my throat, turning to face her. "Uhh… Am I supposed to say I'm sorry?" I ask, my eyebrows pinching in confusion since I've never found myself in this situation before.

She cocks her hip. "Do you want to say you're sorry?"

I shake my head. "I'm not going to mean it if I do," I admit.

"Then don't say it." The shrug she offers in response still leaves me fucking confused. I can read someone's body language if I think they're a threat. I can tell if someone is flirting with me. But shit, ask me to understand a woman's thoughts and compare them to her actions and I'm screwed.

Shuffling from foot to foot, I hate how awkward I feel. A sensation I haven't felt before. "Is this going to make things weird for us?"

"Do you care?"

"Kind of?" The truth slips from my lips without caution, but ends up sounding like a question.

"What does 'kind of' mean?" Emily's hands drop to

her sides, the pinch between her brows lifting as I scramble to try and find the right words.

"I don't know. I just… don't feel the need to want to scratch your eyeballs out for being annoying as hell. Most girls make me feel like that, and you don't… so that means something to me, I guess."

Silence swirls around us for what feels like an eternity before she smiles. "Well, that means something to me too."

My eyebrows lift in surprise. "Good."

"Good," she replies, like it really is that simple.

Gripping the clothes in my arms tighter, I clear my throat again and point to my door. "So, can I go and get changed now?"

Emily releases a little chuckle as she waves her hand at me. "Yeah, shower too. I can't spend time with you if you're just going to smell like my brother. I'll be in the kitchen with Maggie." The light-heartedness to her tone tells me all I need to know, and I turn for my door instantly, but pause when I grasp my handle.

"Does Emmett know you're here?"

"Holy fuck, he dicked you good, huh? Passed on all of that worry he has and left it in you while he's away." Her head falls back and a full-on belly laugh ripples through her. "Don't worry, he knows. His favorite prospect is following me everywhere as usual," she explains, and I nod dumbly.

"Noted. I'll be five minutes."

I turn for the door, desperate to get changed, but her words reach my ears anyway. "It's going to take longer than that to wipe the grin off your face, Scarlett." I can hear the mirth in her voice, the humor at my expense as I slam my lips shut, unsure how I've been grinning since I stepped into the hallway.

The blush that creeps over my cheeks tells me so, making me hide my face as I quickly rush into my room and slam the door behind me.

I'm so fucked. So truly fucked, I have a feeling I'm going to pass on to the other side with cum leaking out of me.

I step into the kitchen with my hair twisted up into a damp bun, black yoga pants, a worn Marvel t-shirt. It's the little comforts I benefit from, and this is one of them. A minute without having to worry about what I'm wearing or attempting to impress someone, whether I actually want to or not.

Maggie and Emily are dicing vegetables and salad ingredients on the table top, while a guy sits with his feet propped up on the table. I step closer, eyeing his cut, and hating once again that the Ruthless Brothers choose to not have their names on their leather. It would make my life a hell of a lot easier if they did.

Prospect is stitched in white thread, and I assume it's the guy Emily mentioned earlier, which makes me assess him deeper. His blond hair almost grazes over his collarbone, tucked behind his ear to reveal his sharp jawline. He's not as bulky as some of the other guys here, but the way he holds himself, even in this relaxed position, tells me there's more than meets the eye with him.

"You must be Scarlett," he states, announcing my arrival as he drops his boots to the floor but keeps his eyes fixed on me.

"And you are…"

"Duffer." A knowing grin spreads across his face, and before I can stop myself, I repeat it back to him.

"Duffer?"

"Yeah."

"Do I want to know?"

"You really don't," Emily mutters as Maggie smirks and the prospect's grin grows wider.

"It's because I have two boys under the age of two, and two women carrying two girls in their last trimester." And just in case he thinks I'm not catching on, he adds, "I spend far too much time getting everyone pregnant."

I step back on instinct, like him merely saying it could be contagious. "On purpose?"

Maggie and Emily laugh louder from their spot as I take in the enigma before me. "Nope. I just have that strong jizz going on, I guess. I even wore a condom with one of them," he says with a shrug.

"I mean at least the thought was there, I guess," I mumble, at a complete loss for other words as the women cackle in the corner.

"You're too much, Duffer." Maggie wipes the tears from her eyes as she fights back her laughter. "But that's enough of your awful storytelling for now. Go and give us women some peace and quiet for a bit," she adds, waving her hand at him dismissively.

He glances around at the three of us for a second, before his eyes settle back on me. "Okay, but only because Scarlett's here." He rises to his feet without another word, but I point my finger at him before he can get past me.

"Because I'm here?" *What the fuck does that mean?*

"Yup." Duffer nods like it all simply makes sense. "Emmett's orders. Emily is safe with you." He shrugs for good measure, before slipping past me and leaving the conversation at that.

Safe with me? How can he be sure she's safe with me?

But more importantly, why the fuck does that make my heart race with a feeling I can't quite decipher? Hope, appreciation, respect? Shit, I think I might be better off going back to my room and getting lost in another crime

243

podcast so I don't have to deal with my own thoughts, but it's as if Maggie senses my uncertainty.

"Scarlett, be a doll and help marinate that meat, would you? It's warm outside and I love any excuse to get the barbecue going. Especially after those assholes spoiled our fun last night."

How was it only last night that the Devil's Brutes showed up and caused havoc? If Emmett killed the guy firing the gun, then that means their sergeant at arms is dead. Good riddance. I fucking hated that guy, but it means they're not done with us yet. Or the Ruthless Brothers more specifically. Maybe I need to figure out a way to not be here when they return.

My throat thickens, my ability to speak narrowing at the memory of the Brutes, of Kincaid, so I quickly nod and fall into step at the worktop to keep my mind distracted. I'm not going to be making some kind of grand escape today, not that I'm even sure I'm trapped here.

There are three bowls with marinades already prepared, so I go about adding the meats and covering them before reaching for another bowl and putting together my favorite seasoning. A good helping of cajun seasoning, garlic powder, paprika, a pinch of cinnamon and sugar, before finishing it off with salt, pepper, and olive oil. Neither Maggie or Emily seems to mind as I layer the bowl with chicken thighs and coat the meat all over. After covering it up like the rest, I rinse my hands at the sink.

It's only when I'm done that I realize we've been working in complete silence. Maggie wasn't kicking him out of the room for a gossip, it was for exactly what she said, and it makes me like her even more.

"Is there anything else you want me to do, or do you want me to carry the meat out to the grill?" I ask, and Maggie smiles as she finishes mixing together a chargrilled corn and tomato salad.

"We'll all help, then we can come back for these bits too. I told Hope, Euro's old lady, to bring the kids by later. She'll tell a few of the other moms too, so no food will go to waste."

"Like the brothers themselves couldn't inhale it all anyway," Emily says with an eye roll.

"You can't give these guys too much of a good thing or their asses will take it for granted."

Grabbing the closest two bowls, I head for the bar area, still grinning at Maggie's words. The moment I step into the bar area, I sense eyes on me and find the Ruthless Bitches huddled around one of the booths, all staring in my direction.

Molly scoffs and I'm ready for whatever bullshit is about to spill from her mouth, but the double doors to the clubhouse swing open forcefully as men start shouting. I freeze in place, overwhelmed by the sudden intrusion of noise and panic as feet stomp and names are called.

I blink twice, confirming that it's Ruthless Brothers' cuts they're wearing, but it's not until I find Gray through the crowd that I calm down a little. His blond hair is in disarray, his palms bloody and his jeans stained, but what holds me captive is the panicked look in his bright blue eyes.

"Scarlett, we need you. Come with me."

His words make my heart race ten times faster, the calmness I felt drift over me moments ago disappearing as he points over his shoulder to where Ryker and Axel help Emmett inside. It's like my eyes are a beacon for the problem, finding a crimson stained t-shirt wrapped around a wound on his thigh as Axel tries to keep pressure on it.

"What the fuck happened?" Those four words from Emily's mouth hold so much fear and pain that it makes my heart seize. Before I can utter a word in response, Gray calls my name again.

"Scarlett. Now."

They're charging through the bar area, heading for the back rooms without another word as I turn and pass off the two bowls in my hand without seeing who even takes them. The second my hands are free, I'm reaching for Emily at my side, her jaw still slack since she spoke those four words. She's as white as a ghost, panic and shock taking over.

"Let me see what's going on, okay? Stay here with Duffer. If it's bad, he won't want you to see him like that," I murmur. She nods, and I seek Duffer through the chaos. He's at my side in seconds, draping his arm around Emily and guiding her toward the nearest stool.

"Eyes on her at all times, Duffer," I order, like I even have a place or voice to do just that, but he turns to me with determination in his eyes as he nods.

"Yes, ma'am."

I don't stick around to correct him, not wanting to be called ma'am at twenty-three, but that's an argument for another day.

Rushing to follow after them, I practically claw my way through the men doing the same. I race to the end of the hall just as they're turning into Emmett's room and I've never been more relieved to have made a bed and cleaned up after myself until this moment.

Just as I reach the threshold, a hand blurs my vision as it comes down and blocks me from going any further. "Why the fuck are you coming in here?"

Axel.

His sunglasses hide his eyes and his true expression from me. His long brown hair is loose today, framing his face and making him almost seem gentle, but the sneer on his lips tells a different story.

"Not now, Ax. We need her help with Emmett." To my

surprise, it's Ryker who bites out the words, but they do the trick and Axel drops his arm with a grunt.

"Whatever, just make it fucking happen."

I internally roll my eyes at him, not sure why Gray called me in here. "What is it you're expecting from me?" I say, slipping through the last few people to stop at Gray's side.

Worry fills his eyes, and he pulls me by the waist, closer to him. "After the other night, something tells me you're helpful in times of crisis, even ones like this." His words are a whisper against my ear as I glance from Emmett's leg back to Gray. "Please, Scar. If you can help him with this, then I need you to, he needs you to, *we* need you to. Otherwise, I'll call in someone who can."

It's not even a request; he's pleading with me.

Fuck.

Fuck. Fuck. Fuck. Fuck. Fuck.

Swiping my hand down my face, I exhale heavily before stepping out of his hold.

"If you want my help, I need at least half of you to get the fuck out." There's no fucking around in my tone, no question in my demand.

"You can all fuck off," Emmett bites, eyes fixed on me, and Ryker shakes his head, but before he can protest, Emmett pushes on, "Give me a fucking minute, Prez. I'm in good hands. Wait outside of the door if you need to, but she isn't going to be able to concentrate with all this."

Ryker looks at his friend helplessly as I move around to him, but my gaze is locked on Emmett's. "Are you sure about that? These hands might not be as awesome as you think they are," I say with a small smile, trying to lighten the mood.

"Without a doubt." The certainty in Emmett's voice rattles my bones, but more so, it has Ryker hollering for everyone to get the fuck out with him.

My pulse thunders in my ears for what feels like an eternity as someone thrusts a huge first-aid kit in my hands, and then everyone disappears. When the door clicks shut behind the final person, I release the breath I didn't realize I was holding.

Inching closer, I notice a bottle of scotch on the nightstand beside him. "It seems someone thinks you need to take the edge off." I nod at the liquor and then open the kit to see what I'm dealing with. Gauzes, needles, thread, cleaning alcohol, and even a pair of forceps and a scalpel.

"I don't need it," he grunts in response as I roll my shoulders back and peel away the blood-stained t-shirt covering his wound. The gash is instantly recognizable as a knife wound. The jagged edges and the size make it clear there was no gun involved.

"You sure?"

He doesn't respond, so when I glance up, he just quirks

his brow and I don't bother to ask again.

"Who pulled the knife out?" I ask, attempting to distract him with conversation as I check around the wound before sterilizing it. The hiss that comes from between his clenched teeth makes my nose wrinkle apologetically as I work as gently and efficiently as I can.

"Me, on the way here."

It takes a moment for me to realize what he's saying after the long pause from my question, leaving me to blink up at him in surprise.

"You're crazy."

"I know."

Shaking my head at him, I try to calm the slight tremble in my hands as I rub my lips together nervously. "Do you have music on your cell? I need something to relax me."

He nods, then pulls his cell phone from his cut pocket and unlocks it for me. A grin stretches my lips despite the current circumstances. "You're a Swifty, huh? I never would have guessed it."

I click shuffle on the playlist that is open, and Taylor Swift's voice meets my ears with her latest hit.

I expect him to get embarrassed or get upset, but he shrugs. "I only listen to it because Emily dragged me to one of her concerts. It's a good memory, a core one, that I don't ever want to forget."

Well, that explains it.

"Yeah, yeah, whatever," I mumble and focus back on the task at hand. I methodically clean the area, noting the lack of blood which means a major artery hasn't been cut, so I prepare the needle and thread.

"Hold this in place for me, please." I hand him a few pieces of gauze to keep the wound clean as I steady the needle and thread the cotton through the small hole. For once in my life, it doesn't take me an eternity to do it, the thread going through the needle on the first try.

Glancing up at Emmett, I seek for a reassuring nod before I start piercing his skin, but my eyes catch on his bare chest. Was I blind last night? Or too distracted with him fucking me into oblivion? I recall telling him to keep the cut on while he fucked me, but surely, I would have noticed the huge scar running down his chest. The puckered skin marking him in a way I've only seen once before.

I focus on the stitching as he moves his hand away from the area, but I still can't stop myself from asking. "Your heart?"

After a few moments, he shifts and responds, "Yeah."

Keeping my eyes downcast as I sew his wound shut, I push, eager for more. "How old were you?"

"Too young to really remember." His words are short but not clipped, clearly not mad to be talking about it, but the fact that he has an everlasting scar and no memory of it must be crazy.

"I can't even imagine." My words are a feeble attempt at comfort? I don't even know. As I finish off the last few stitches, I clear my throat. "Is everything okay with it now?"

"I assume so. I haven't been to the hospital since I was fourteen."

Fourteen? Isn't this something they would continue to check forever? Tying off the end of the thread, I take the gauze from his hands and cover the wound before I finally meet his gaze.

"Are you willing to put your life at risk like that? For yourself? For your loved ones?" My words are surprisingly soft, attempting to be non-judgmental.

"I put my life at risk every time I put my cut on."

I scoff this time, unable to hide the level of unimpressed that I am. It's wrong to be coming at an injured man like this, but I've never been the best at social cues.

"Your cut is for honor, for blood, for heritage. Not taking care of your heart is irresponsible and selfish. You have a sister who believes you hung the fucking moon."

I toss everything back into the first-aid box with more force than necessary, making myself even more annoyed at my own actions. Emmett grips my wrist, waiting for me to meet his gaze.

"Are you saying you care, Scarlett?"

I bristle at his insinuation, rising from the bed in a

flurry. "Of course not." My cheeks heat, calling out on my bluff. "You're all done. I'll check on it again tomorrow. If there's nothing else…" I head for the door.

"Scarlett, I…"

I don't hear another word as I step out into the hallway, slamming the door shut behind me with a curse. My irritation increases as Gray, Ryker, and Axel stare at me inquisitively, but I can't deal with them right now.

Pointing my thumb over my shoulder, I step away, half-wishing I had grabbed the bottle of scotch for myself.

"He's all yours."

TWENTY ONE

Scarlett

Stepping into the bar area, I search for my target, but she's nowhere to be found in here either. I rub my lips together, irritated by the nervous action as I sweep the room once more with no luck.

Emmett.

He's got to be somewhere. No one answered when I knocked on his door a moment ago, but surely, he hasn't gone too far. Not with an injured leg.

I fidget, my nerves attempting to get the better of me again, but I've let them take hold for too long as it is. It's taken me longer than I care to admit to build up the courage to go in search of him since I stormed off like a sullen child yesterday. But despite my thoughts and opinions, along with my inability to shut my damn mouth, his injury needs to be checked.

If someone else is taking care of it, that's fine, then I

won't feel guilty for not checking in sooner. .

Rolling my shoulders back, I hold my head high as I sense the Ruthless Bitches' attention turn my way. I'm surprised there are as many people in here as there are since it's only noon, but MCs can start as early as they want, I guess. Besides, if I stay in my room for a moment longer, I may claw my eyes out by going crazy.

I fight the urge to fiddle with the hem of my oversized Led Zeppelin tee, acutely aware that I'm only wearing panties underneath, but I originally planned to dash across the hallway and back. Now there's a fucking audience, and as much as they might piss me off, I won't back down under their gaze.

Heading through the bar area barefoot, I discreetly watch where I'm stepping as I move as quickly as I can. The stares from the Ruthless Bitches intensify as I get closer to them, but I keep my focus locked on the door.

"Fucking whore." I internally roll my eyes at Molly's comment clearly aimed at me. She won't get the satisfaction of a reaction from me. Not today. Not when there's other shit going on. She's inconsequential in the grand scheme of things.

The general chatter of the room drowns her out as I near the door, my hand ready to knock, but before I can touch the wood and escape into the garden, a tingle rises up my spine, but it's too late for me to react.

Hands shove at my forearm, making me stumble to the right as I nearly trip over my own feet, throwing my arms out to the sides to keep my balance.

What. The. Fuck?!

My hair drapes over my right shoulder as I glance back to confirm which bitch touched me, only to find Molly standing with her hands planted on her hips and a malicious smile spread across her face.

Aware of the silence in the room now, I stand and stare down the bitch that keeps on trying to get a rise out of me. "Are you done?" I spit out, my nostrils flaring with anger as my breath stutters in my chest.

It's not like it was at the Reapers, I have to remember that. I'm a whore here. Just like she said I was. There aren't certain things in place to keep me protected from her wrath, but that also means there's nothing keeping me from putting my hands on her.

"I won't be done until you get your shit and get out of *my* fucking club," she snaps, tossing her hair over her shoulder dramatically as the remaining Ruthless Bitches murmur behind her. Sounds of agreement ring in my ears.

I'm failing to see what the fuck I've actually done wrong. We're all here for the same reason, for shelter, protection, a place to hide out from the rest of the world. They're all here, what's the difference with me?

Sighing, I quirk a brow at her. "I wasn't aware this was

your club."

"It's more mine than it is yours, so if you don't get your shit and get out of my house, I'll make you regret it." She takes measured steps toward me with each word that falls from her mouth.

"I'm assuming your threats usually work, but I really couldn't give a shit." My nails stab into my palms, holding back the desire to throat-punch this bitch. My response doesn't appease her though, not like I expected it to even touch the surface, but when she raises her hands to shove at me again, my restraint is tarnished.

In a flurry of movements, I whip my hand in her direction, my fingers clamping around her throat as I thrust her body into the wall beside the door. Her eyes almost bulge out as I loom in her personal space, a sneer tainting my lips as my heart races like crazy in my chest.

"I don't care who you think you are, I don't care that you're trying to scare me, shit, I don't care if you actually get what you want and force me to leave," I whisper against the shell of her ear, unable to control the anger and annoyance storming in my veins. "It's *you* that should care about who *I* am. *You* that should be worried about what *I'm* capable of. And *you* that needs to watch your back because I don't take too kindly to people touching me without my permission."

My chest heaves with every breath I take, my body

vibrating with the need to pound my fist into her face as she looks at me with glassy eyes.

"What's going on in here?" Maggie asks from the middle of the room with a cloth thrown over her shoulder and her arms folded over her chest. Her gaze flicks between Molly and I, waiting for someone to give her a response, but my tongue is like lead in my mouth.

I blink once, twice, letting the angry haze clear in my mind as I finally manage to summon words to my lips. "Nothing. Nothing at all." The tension is still evident in my voice, my hand still wrapped around her throat as my fingers flex along her skin. It takes a deep breath and another slow blink before I can retract my hand and take a small step back. Clearing my throat, I keep my gaze fixed on Molly as I speak. "Maggie, have you seen Emmett?"

Molly's gaze sharpens on mine as she lifts her hand to her neck, lips pressed in a thin line.

"He's out in the garage with the others. They said not to be interrupted, unless it was you."

I almost sprain my neck at how fast I whip my head around to look at her. There's a knowing glint in her eyes and a flicker of a smirk at the corner of her lips. She's either making that extra shit up about them only being interrupted by me, or she's enjoying the reality of it far too much. Either way, I need to put some distance between Molly and I before I change my fucking mind.

Nodding at Maggie, I shoulder-pass Molly before I step out into the warm heat. The slight breeze tickles my t-shirt around my thighs, distracting me from my rage.

Regretting not even throwing on a pair of shoes, I pick up my pace toward the garage when I hear my name being called from behind me.

"Scarlett?" A prospect heads toward me with a box in his hands. "Are you heading toward the garage?"

I nod. My nose wrinkles in confusion as he comes to a stop and extends the box to me. "Could you take this delivery with you? It's got Prez's name on it, but I don't want to interrupt since we were warned not to."

"So, why are you giving it to me?"

I don't even finish asking the question before he's thrusting the package at me while rolling his eyes, then turning and walking away. I almost call him back before Maggie's words come to mind again. Apparently it wasn't a lie, then.

No one can interrupt them but me? I don't like the sound of that. If they wanted me, why didn't they just come find me?

Leaning my forehead on the box, I take a deep breath in an attempt to calm myself and stop my mind from going crazy. If they wanted me for something, they *would* have come to get me. That's not what this is, or it's not their usual course of action, but it still doesn't allow the uneasy feeling to leave my chest.

Reluctantly, I cut the remaining distance toward the garage and find the four of them talking among themselves with a Harley Davidson between them.

Gray is on the floor with his back against a large red toolbox, grease coating his fingers as he grins at whatever Axel is saying. He is talking animatedly with a cigarette hanging from his lips and his t-shirt long forgotten. His brown hair falls in waves down his muscled back, and if I didn't know the asshole that body belonged to, I would definitely store it away for my fantasies, but alas, he's a dick.

Distracting myself from asshole-ish men, I steer my gaze from Axel to Ryker as he spins a wrench in his hands, his dark hair swept back off his face and his white tee filthy.

Finally, my attention moves to Emmett, who is in a chair in a pair of shorts with the same bandage from yesterday still wrapped around his thigh. He seems in good spirits despite the circumstances, but the smile quickly drops from his face as he locks eyes with me.

Great.

I'm too distracted by the emotion in his eyes that I can't quite decipher, to notice when Gray appears in front of me and takes the box from my hands. "Oh, thanks," I murmur, earning myself a wink. He walks over to Ryker.

"What's this?" Gray asks, placing it on the tool box.

"I don't know. A prospect gave it to me when I was heading over here and said it had just been delivered with Ryker's name on."

"Why the fuck would they hand it to you?" Axel grunts, taking a long drag of his cigarette as his eyes rake over me from head to toe.

I almost consider whether he's actually related to Molly, since they both get under my skin in the worst way possible. I bite back the snark from my tongue and shrug, but it's Ryker who responds.

"Because I said if anyone but Scarlett approaches, they will take a bullet to the fucking knee." Ryker doesn't look up as he speaks, too intrigued with the box in front of him.

"And why *are* you out here?" Axel pushes.

Ask me to defend myself, I can do that. Ask me to keep my head down and survive, I can do that too. But ask me to show any level of care, concern, or remorse for words spoken, then shit, I'm at a loss.

My eyes flash to Emmett. "I don't know, I just wanted to make sure the wound was healing okay and wasn't starting to get infected because it hadn't been cleaned and changed," I ramble, hating so many words falling from my mouth. "But if someone else has already seen to it, then I'm all good," I add.

"Oh, he needs you to check it, sweet cheeks. But since you two had some heated words, he didn't have the balls to come ask. Did you, Emmett?"

The telltale prickling along my cheeks annoys me more than anything as he offers a tight smile. His lips part, but whatever he was about to say is interrupted as Ryker curses under his breath, gaining everyone's attention as he stares angrily into the box.

"What's up?" Axel prowls toward him, his anger toward me forgotten as he approaches Ryker, who slowly dips his hand into the box, retrieving a piece of paper and a gun.

"Fuck," Emmett, Gray, and Axel all grunt in unison as they look at the gun in Ryker's hands, but I have no idea what the issue is, until he turns the slip of paper over to reveal a familiar symbol.

"Courtesy of the Devil's Brutes," he grunts, his eyes darkening as he scrunches the note up in frustration.

When they came barreling into the compound yesterday, I didn't ask a single question, instead focusing on making sure Emmett was okay. It wasn't until later that night when I slipped into the kitchen that I heard the rumors of what had happened. What the Brutes had done.

So if I put two and two together, I know the gun in Ryker's hand is one that should have been there yesterday, but the Brutes had taken it. Kincaid and his men love nothing more than showboating and theatrics, they love the game of it all, but what twists my gut is knowing this is only just the beginning.

The rage dripping from each of the men increases with every passing second, but none more so than Ryker. The muscles in his neck are bunched together, the veins in his arms protruding as he strains them, his jaw grinding so tight he could cut glass.

Angry men really shouldn't be so fucking hot. They should be a warning, a giant red flag for me to run and hide. Yet they lure me closer and make my thighs clench, simply from being in their presence.

"Fuck." Ryker's outburst is louder this time, his fist slamming down on the metal toolbox.

"Ryker, brother, you need to clear your head, lose the rage and frustration, so we can figure out the next step together. As a club."

My eyebrows raise at the softer tone of Axel's voice as he soothes his friend, but he doesn't consider taking another step toward him.

"I haven't got time to forget all of this and clear my mind, Ax. These fucking guys show up like this, making demands from the second they step foot onto my property." Ryker rakes his fingers through his hair, gripping the ends tightly before suddenly grabbing the box and swiping it off the toolbox.

Guns clatter to the ground with his anger, while some hurtle toward the motorcycle behind him. My feet are carrying me before I even process I'm moving, protecting the motorcycle from any potential damage.

"What the fuck, Ryker? Throw shit in anger, get mad at the shitstorm the Devil's Brutes are brewing, but don't pull that shit near a motorcycle that did nothing at all." My nostrils flare as my chest heaves, my anger from earlier transforming into annoyance at his ignorance of the beautiful bike now standing between us.

Fuck, I miss my baby, and here he is, wreaking havoc on one so carelessly.

"You don't know shit about my bike," Axel says with a scoff, folding his arms over his chest as he moves to stand beside Ryker.

I try so fucking hard to not bite back against the stereotype I know he's thinking. "I would be a fool not to know anything about a Harley Davidson Sportster S, woman or not."

Axel rolls his eyes at me as he tosses the butt of his cigarette outside of the garage. "Please, you don't know sh—"

"Production of the first Harley Davidson Sportster started in 1957. This looks like the latest S model which started being manufactured this year. It's got the revolutionary max 1250 T liquid-cooled powertrain engine with double overhead camshafts and variable valve timing. Along with the new high exhaust mount and digitalized instrumentation. It's a beauty. It's just a shame that you opted for the bright billiard blue as opposed to the gray haze because that coloring is so fucking fire, I'd likely come on the spot just looking at it. You pulled me away from the Reapers in such a haste that my baby is still there. I would give anything to clean it up good and just be in its damn presence."

Silence greets me as I look up from the bike to the Ruthless Brothers looking back at me. The tingle over my cheeks intensifies as it creeps all over my face, undoubtedly making me red as hell as all four of them gape at me in surprise. Axel included.

I almost want to be smug, but if I even so much as smirk too hard at him right now, he won't take me seriously, and when it comes to bikes, that's all I am.

Gray clears his throat, breaking the deathly silence clinging to us as he nods in my direction. "I think you have your distraction, Ryker."

Gray's grin widens, and Emmett rearranges his dick through his shorts. While Axel stares at me long and hard.

"What?" I finally ask, when none of them turn away from me, but it's only when my eyes settle on Ryker that he answers.

"You."

TWENTY TWO

Ryker

My teeth grind together, my hands flexing at my sides. I can't take my eyes off her, transfixed with the hollow of her neck and the quick flutters of her pulse. When I can finally draw my gaze to hers, she holds me captive, her piercing blue eyes shining as she stares deep into my soul.

My heart thumps in my chest, my cock pulsing in my pants as she stands taller, not frightened by my approach. I don't stop until we're toe to toe, and only then do I release the breath lodged in my throat.

"Everyone out. Unless you want to watch."

Scarlett's eyes widen as she gapes up at me, her pebbled nipples brushing against my cut as she practically pants. She was more than responsive the night she initiated herself as a Ruthless Bitch, but it's something else entirely when it's aimed at you.

"Do I get a say?" She drags her tongue over her bottom lip as the corner of my mouth lifts with a smirk.

"I'm not into non-consent, Scarlett. I only fuck when there's some level of chemistry. I don't touch the Bitches, the whores, none of them. The body language they give off doesn't stir my dick to life, but the way I'm reading your body right now, tells me you're just as eager as I am."

"Am I supposed to believe that?" A scoff falls from her lips as she quirks a brow at me, but I simply shrug in response.

"I don't give a shit what you do or don't believe. I only care about right now." Lifting my hand, I glide my fingers down her cheek, sweeping down her neck, before skimming over her peaked nipples through her t-shirt.

Her jaw slackens, but before she can speak Axel coughs and lights his cigarette. "Find me later and I'll help figure this shit out." I don't lift my gaze to watch him leave, too absorbed by the woman before me.

"Are we sharing or…" Gray's words trail off, a hint of hope in his voice, but I shake my head.

"No."

"Fuck," he grunts in response.

"Fine, I'll be busy jizzing in the shower over the image of those pretty tits hiding beneath that t-shirt." Scarlett's cheeks turn red as she flushes at his words.

I turn to look at Emmett. "Last warning," I offer, and a

grin spreads across his face.

"I'm good."

I knew he fucking would be. He loves a show.

"Last chance, Scarlett," I murmur as I turn back to her, the rest of the world fading into darkness as just the two of us stand together.

She runs her tongue over her bottom lip as she lifts her hands between us, her fingers skimming over the edge of my cut, before she grips it tightly with both hands and drags me close. Her full lush lips are on mine in the next second, my hands at her waist as we crash together.

Fuck.

I expect her kisses to be delicate, but after the first brush of our mouths, she rakes her teeth over my bottom lip and makes me groan.

Needing her closer in whatever way I can, I grab the back of her thighs and lift her into the air. Her legs wrap around my waist, her arms around my neck as our tongues battle for control.

Her skin is so soft and silky against my palm. I inch higher until the globes of her ass are in my hands. It takes a second for my brain to realize that she's not wearing any panties, nothing in between us as she moans into my mouth, letting me swallow her pleasure for myself.

Tearing my lips from her when I can't take it anymore, I glance around the garage, unable to focus or process where anything is, like it's all new to me. Eyeing the red tall tool box near Emmett, I carry her toward it before placing her down on the cool metal top.

Her legs spread further, encouraging me closer as she grips the neckline of my tee.

She's not pliant like she was for Gray. She's taking from me just as much as I'm taking from her. A match I'm desperate for at this moment.

Sweeping her tongue over her bottom lip, she observes me through hooded eyes as I capture her nipple between my teeth.

"Ah, fuck." Her words make my cock flex in my pants, desperate to get to her, but I want to draw this out longer. Tease her until she can't take it anymore, then maybe take some more.

My world is practically crumbling around me. I've barely been the Prez for a matter of days and there's already trouble knocking at our door, injuring my men and wreaking havoc on our operations. But my brain can't process all of that and find a solid course of action in response while I'm seething over it. I'll act on instinct, just like I did with the Reapers.

I can't do that again.

I need to lose myself in something else so I can regain control.

I need to lose myself in her.

Releasing her nipple from my mouth, I grab her hips and tilt her into the perfect position so I can see her pretty pussy glisten between her thighs. Raising her top around her hips, I bite back a groan as I reach out and drag my fingertip through her folds.

She shivers intensely at the soft touch, her hands slamming onto the toolbox as she tries to maintain her balance.

"Did you taste her, Emmett?" I ask, not looking in his direction as her breath hitches. She might blush at us talking about her, but I know it turns her on. The way her thighs tremble and her pulse quickens as her pupils dilate gives her away.

"Fuck, man. I didn't. My cock got too hungry for her for my tongue to even get a chance," Emmett grunts.

I keep my eyes locked on hers as I lower myself so I'm in line with her pussy, making sure to watch her reaction as I swipe my tongue from her entrance to her clit.

"Holy shit," she pants when I twirl my tongue around her clit, her thighs tempting to clamp shut as I tease two fingers at her core.

"Be warned though, brother, her pussy is hot as fuck."

Emmett's words make Scarlett's pink cheeks redden. I lap at her clit, the tight nub begging for attention as I thrust my fingers deep inside her, swirling them against her walls until I settle on her G-spot.

Emmett's right. Her pussy is like liquid fire to the touch. Enticing and needy all at once, making my cock plead to have a feel.

Scarlett's hips start to roll, riding my hand with need as I drag my teeth over her clit. Her breath comes in short, sharp pants as she scrambles for her next breath.

"Please. Oh my god, please," she chants, her pussy clenching around my fingers as her hands find my hair, her hips grinding the best she can in this position.

I know the moment she finds exactly what she's looking for as she slams down on my fingers, my lips locked around her clit, while she grinds up against my mouth.

"Yes, yes, yes!" Her chants are like music to my ears, making my dick strain against the waistband of my jeans as her juices trail down my fingers.

When she's wrung out, completely spent from her orgasm, I slip my hand from between her thighs and stand tall once more. I wait until I have her attention again before I bring my wet fingers to my lips and taste her sweetness.

If I thought her eyes were blown before, they don't compare to now. Her pupils nearly spread so wide that no blue remains.

"How does she taste?" I don't respond to Emmett's question as I reach for Scarlett's hand instead.

I make sure she can hold her balance as I bring her fingers to my lips first, kissing each one of them before

I slowly skim them over her folds. Her gaze darkens as I nudge two of her fingers in with mine, coating us both in her essence.

I fail to restrain myself, slipping from her core too quickly as I offer her hand out to Emmett.

"Come taste for yourself."

The scrape of his chair tells me he's moving. "His leg, he shouldn't—"

"It's worth it," I cut her off. Emmett comes to a stop beside us. I hold her wrist out for him, and when his hand engulfs hers, ready to feast on her, I bring my finger to her mouth.

He groans beside me at the same time I trace her lips with her climax and her tongue peeks out to take a taste.

Shit.

That's hot as fuck.

Without warning, she takes my finger into her mouth, sucking it dry before releasing it with a pop.

"The sweetest thing I've ever fucking tasted," Emmett grumbles, and I couldn't agree more. "Now take her pussy and join the dark side, brother. It's like an addiction watching her fall apart, and I want to see it happen again. Around your cock."

He doesn't say another word as he finds his way back to his chair, leaving me to stare at Scarlett as she grabs the hem of her t-shirt and pulls it over her head. She's completely naked before me, unfazed by her surroundings.

She's confident in her skin, confident with what she wants, and it only makes *me* want her more.

Slipping my hand into my wallet, I pull out a condom. Her lips sink into her bottom lip as she watches my every move. "Don't I get a taste of you too?"

Her question makes Emmett chuckle, and I know I'm clearly missing out on something, but I shake my head. "Not yet. This is about you."

I don't know why I say that, whether it's because I love hearing her moans or because focusing on her is helping to keep me distracted, but shit, I mean it.

I lower my jeans just enough to have room, before rolling the condom down my length. She's a little higher than I would prefer on the toolbox, so I start scanning for alternatives. The second I see what I want, I'm moving into action.

When I grab her waist, she squeals in surprise. Giving her a little spin, I place her down on her feet. Her hands are on my shoulders as she looks up at me, and it feels like my world stops.

Fucking is just that—fucking. But she makes me more present in the moment than I've ever been before. Heightening my senses and creating a bigger need inside of me.

"If you love the bike so much, I'm going to fuck you

over it."

I grab her arms and turn her so she's facing it, my chest to her back as her hands move to the leather seat. She's so fucking stunning, bare for me beside Axel's bike, but I know she'll look even hotter draped over it.

Before I can guide her into the position I want, she inches closer, resting her stomach across the seat. "Please."

Fuck. Me.

No whisper has ever sounded sweeter, no plea ever hotter.

My hands fall to her hips as she blindly searches out my dick with her pussy, rising up onto her tiptoes to get closer.

Without any further encouragement, I line my cock with her entrance and slam inside her. Heat engulfs me as I see stars, basking in her warmth. Her cries are like a prayer to my ears.

"That's it, Ryker, she likes it rough, but don't knock the bike over." Emmett's statement makes my cock thrust deeper inside her. I'm desperate for my release and for her pussy to squeeze my cock, milking me for all that I am.

Retreating, I pull out until the tip barely remains, then I slam into her harder as she clings to the bike for stability. When her moans get deeper, more sensual, my body takes over, thrusting into her relentlessly as our bodies heat and sweat clings to my temples.

I tighten my right hand on her hip, then I reach for her hair with my left, wrapping it around my knuckles to tilt her head back, fucking her without restraint as she cries out for more. As her pitch gets louder and her breathing becomes more jagged, I know she's close.

"Please, Ryker. Please."

Releasing her hair, I wrap my arm around her waist and pull her back so she's against my chest, before grabbing her leg and placing it on the seat of the bike. Emmett has the perfect view of her pussy now as I bend my knees slightly and thrust up into her, somehow getting deeper from this angle.

With one hand capturing her tits, just like I did the other night, and the other tapping at her clit, it only takes four more thrusts before she's coming around my dick, chanting my name in ecstasy.

The way her pussy squeezes my dick leaves me no choice but to follow after her, my orgasm ripping through my body, causing chaos in my veins as I ride out each wave.

It feels like an eternity before I manage to catch my breath, her body slumped in my hold as I cling to her. Glancing over her shoulder, I catch sight of Emmett wiping at his dick with a cloth, and I know he enjoyed the show too.

Scarlett leans her head back against my shoulder before

stiffening in my arms. "Does that make me a Ruthless Bitch now?" she asks, uncertainty in her voice with a hint of disappointment, but before I can respond, Emmett beats me to it.

"Never."

She sags in my arms once more as I meet his gaze. Did we have an audience? Yes. But there is no way in hell I'm making her fair game for everyone. Not a chance in hell.

I don't know what it is about her. I can't put my finger on it.

All I know is fucking usually clears my head, but all it's done is leave me even more consumed by her.

RUTHLESS BROTHERS MC

TWENTY THREE

Gray

Fucking my hand definitely doesn't compare to fucking Scarlett Reeves. I'm almost embarrassed that I thought it would be satisfying enough to get me through the day, but knowing Ryker is out there, tasting and teasing what I'm desperate for, dulled the experience.

She isn't a bitch and she doesn't cause drama simply by opening her mouth, enjoying the mess it creates, plus she sprouted off information about Axel's Harley like a pro. She's a complete fucking mystery. We don't get girls like that around here. Ever.

Hearing her mention her own motorcycle has me coming up with a plan. One that's going to get me closer to her, and I know it will be worth it.

Not that I have feelings for her, I refuse to have feelings for anyone. I just want to see her face light up again. The way it only does when she talks about bikes.

Fuck.

Sweeping my hair back off my face, I head for the door. If I stay in here any longer, I'll start thinking about my emotions, and I'm not facing that today.

The hallway is quiet as I move to my room, but it's a surprise to see Axel sitting at the foot of my bed when I push my door open.

"What's up, man?"

He sighs as he rubs his hand on his thighs. "While they're out there getting their dicks wet, we need to be thinking about how to handle this shit with the Brutes."

"I'd rather be out there getting my dick wet too," I grumble, searching out some fresh clothes.

Axel scoffs, shaking his head at me like he's not surprised to hear me say that, but it still pisses him off. "Get dressed, Gray. Your dick won't shrivel up and die if it's kept in your pants for a bit longer. Besides, I'm sure Scarlett will be ready to take you too in an hour or so."

My defenses rise as I glare at my brother. "Don't keep aiming all your anger and stress at her, man. She hasn't done shit to you."

He quirks a brow. The way he glances away from me tells me he knows what I mean.

"Whatever, let's focus on what's actually important, shall we…"

"Yeah, like the enemy," I grumble, reluctant to agree

with him.

"I didn't say she wasn't the enemy."

He's not looking at my face, but that's because he knows I'm not going to be impressed with him saying that shit again. I take a deep breath instead of responding though. I know he's going through a lot at the minute, his drug use is out of control and his traumas are creeping out of the woodwork to devour him as the anniversary looms.

"I don't know who the fuck these Devil's Brutes think they are, but we are *not* going to just roll over and play nice with them."

He nods, anger flashing in his eyes. "They showed up at our compound, firing weapons and acting like they were above us. Then they stole our weapons, attacked our men, and injured Emmett. It can't be a coincidence that it all started at the same time *she* showed up."

My brows furrow for a second as I try to process what he's talking about, before I realize he's referring to Scarlett. Again.

"Axel, I don't know what your problem is, but I think all of that has more to do with the fact that she came here after we tore up the Ice Reapers' compound. That was our doing, man, our actions, not hers." His jaw tightens with every word I say, but I don't back down to make him feel better. He needs to see past whatever issue he has with her and focus on the bigger picture. "Besides, it was me that brought her here, not her inflicting herself on us."

"Why would you lead the enemy straight through our doors, Gray?"

I drop my towel and reach for my boxers. He's fucking with my head. I don't want to defend her, but I don't want this energy to remain in the air because it's fucking with my good time.

"I didn't bring the enemy through our doors, Ax, I brought pussy. If you weren't so obsessed with tying up women so they couldn't touch you, you might be able to enjoy her too," I mutter, stepping one leg into my boxers when movement through the open door catches my eyes.

Messy hair, crinkled top, dilated pupils, and cheeks as pink as her pussy.

It's a well-fucked Scarlett.

Fuck.

"Miss me, sweet cheeks?"

She whirls to a stop to look at me, her eyes traveling from me to Axel, then back to me. Or more importantly, my dick.

"I feel like it could have been me that was missing out," she purrs, teeth sinking into her bottom lip as her eyes somehow manage to darken even more with heat.

I know what she's insinuating, the gleam at her lips and the slight tilt of her eyebrows tells me enough, but before I can even summon a half decent response, Axel beats me to it.

"I wish. Gray gives head like a champ, but I've got bigger shit to be dealing with right now. We don't all drown ourselves in pussy to help us keep our heads on straight."

I don't miss how she clenches her hands at her sides. "That… is hot as fuck," she breathes, completely bypassing the jab that also fell from Axel's mouth. "But you're an asshole, so don't say shit like that to me and give me a lady boner because you don't fucking deserve it."

It's my turn to gape at her in surprise as she spins on the spot, slipping into her room and slamming the door shut behind her. It's Axel's snicker that pulls me from my hot daydream, and I pull up my boxers, failing to cover my stiff dick in the process.

"What the fuck, Ax? You can't say shit like that."

"Like what? I wasn't lying." The challenge in his eyes is fierce, a smirk tilting the corner of his mouth as I glare at him.

"I didn't say you were, but now I have to live up to those words of being a champ, and I don't need that level of pressure, whether it's a dick on my tongue or a clit." I throw my hands out wide, exasperated.

I know it beats him being in a shit mood, but fuck, not at my expense.

"No, now you have to focus on everything else that actually affects the club and not some club whore."

My glare doesn't soften as I slip a t-shirt over my head. "Fine, call a meeting. Get Shift on the phone too so we can have all the men on deck."

Axel nods as he stands from my bed, heading for the door before he pauses, a knowing smirk growing even wider on his face. "You've got ten minutes to take care of your raging cock and then your ass better be in your seat."

He doesn't give me a chance to respond, but I don't need one. Ten minutes isn't that long, and I need to make the most of it.

Axel raises a brow at me as I drop into my seat at the Church with a second to spare, but I ignore him and his shit-teasing as Ryker throws down one of the guns from earlier on the table. The room falls silent, clearly feeling Ryker's temper rising as he leans forward, planting his palms on the wood.

"Courtesy of the Brutes."

"Fuck." A chorus of sighs flutter around the room, everyone understanding what Ryker's saying as he glares down at the weapon.

"Fuck is right, but it isn't going to give us the answers to the problems we're facing," he grunts, slamming his fist on the table before dropping down into his seat. "We know the chaos they've caused in such a short space of time, so I'm not going to waste my breath repeating it, but this needs to end."

"I had a chat with Merl, Prez, and he confirmed he was somewhat aware of these bastards leaving a trail of carnage in their wake. They make a lot of noise if shit doesn't go their way and it's generally deadly to the other party." Shift's voice filters through the cell phone in Emmett's hand. Fuck, if Merl, the Prez of our Northern chapter, is aware of them, then why the fuck aren't we?

"Could we really have been paying him off?" I ask, looking around the table before settling my eyes on Ryker.

"Who fucking knows, but we aren't any longer. I refuse to. We don't survive as a club by lying on our backs and letting any man shove his dick into our mouths while we plead to be fucked with a baseball bat." I shiver at the thought but I get the point. "We survive as a club by making a stand, believing in our charter, believing in our bylaws, and defending our family like it's our birthright."

A few hoots holler around the table in agreement, my own blood bubbling in my veins as I nod along with them.

"Shift, do you think you can access any surveillance that may be of use to us to get a better sense of the whole picture?" Emmett asks, his nostrils flaring with the anger he's bottling up.

"I will see what I can do. No guarantees from up here,

but I've told Merl I can help out here until the end of the week before I make my way home. From there, I will be able to hopefully access more if necessary."

"For now, we need boots on the ground, make use of our prospects and see what the word on the street is. Especially since they seem so pissed about the Reapers," Axel adds, and my chest soars with excitement.

It's hilarious these fuckers think they can tear us down so easily. We may have looked weak before, with Banner in control, but now, with the weight of the club on Ryker's shoulders, I know he won't give up without a fight. Even if it means the club is burned to the ground, I will happily fall with it. But that's never going to happen.

This is our family, our home, and we have a lot of lives to protect.

"Maybe if we were paying them before it was done to keep us safe, maybe we were already doing the right thing." My gaze slides to Becker, an old-timer like Eric who sits beside him with a glare on his face. I tilt my head, assessing him, but it doesn't seem to be a case of him knowing about this all along, more a worry and concern for the club.

Ryker rises from his seat, jaw tight and shoulders tense as he twirls the gavel in his hand. He takes the time to look each and every one of us in the eyes, before he settles his stare in Becker's direction.

"We're not safe under the reign of someone else, and that's exactly what that would be. We would be making ourselves sitting ducks, pawns to break at their leisure. If that's how you want your Prez to act, then elect another one, because it sure as shit won't be me." I love, respect, and feel triumph for the man before me, I always have, but it's in this moment I see him as the leader he was truly born to be. "All in favor of refusing to pay the Brutes?"

"Aye." My agreement is lost in the sea of confirmations from every member at the table, Becker included, before the gavel hits the wood, sealing tight the oath of our brotherhood.

Let the war begin.

TWENTY FOUR

Scarlett

I close my eyes as the monotone voice filters from my cell phone, going into detail on the latest case that is being investigated on the murder podcast I'm listening to. It's hauntingly fascinating how people and authorities dissect the killer's actions, piece together the puzzle they left behind and find the answer.

My hair is damp from the shower I took, knowing the coast was clear as everyone had been called to the Church. I decided on a pair of combat pants and a white tank top to relax in as I avoid the world.

Every time I step from this room, something happens. From some bullshit with the Devil's Brutes to getting shit from Axel or the Ruthless Bitches. Occasionally, I might be lucky and get a great orgasm or two, but either way, it feels like drama at this stage and I'd rather avoid it as much as possible.

My mind wanders to the visual Axel hinted at earlier. The thought of Gray on his knees for him... My core clenches at the idea of it. It didn't look like he was joking and Gray didn't rush to correct him, which only excites me more.

Fuck.

I had to leave them in that moment, because even though my body was completely spent from Ryker's touch and Emmett's gaze, they were bringing me back to life all over again.

Maybe Axel is right, maybe I am a whore. I've never acted like this in my entire life. Making sure to keep my legs closed at the Reapers, and only finding solace in the odd guy here and there on a night out.

No one has ever asked me deep questions, or been interested in my wants and desires, but here I am, giving it to them on a plate. If that makes me a whore, then sign me up, because I've never felt more empowered in my life.

If anyone from the Ice Reapers saw me now, they wouldn't believe it, and that leaves me even more exhilarated. The only issue that remains is where I align myself with the Ruthless Brothers or the Devil's Brutes.

They're dangerous. A darkness I thought I had managed to escape, but I should have heeded my own warning when I first mentioned them to the brothers.

Startled by my thoughts, my eyes blink open at the

sound of my bedroom door swinging open. The panic that instantly bubbles to the surface quickly dies when I see it's Emily in the doorway.

"Don't fucking do that, you scared the shit out of me," I grumble, not moving from my spot on the bed as I try to calm my breathing. If she notices my discomfort, she doesn't mention it as she moves to take a seat beside me, leaving the door open for Duffer to come in too.

My eyebrows pinch for a moment as I stare at him. This is the first time there's been a guy in my room since I got here and he's most definitely not one of the ones I would be excited about. He also doesn't feel like a threat though, so I opt to let him stay without kicking up a fuss.

If Emmett trusts him with Emily, he must be safe enough to be around without being a raging asshole. I hope.

"I've been looking for you, but I didn't think you would be hiding away in here when it's so nice outside," she states, quirking her brow at me in exaggeration. She's wearing a pale blue crewneck sweater and a pair of ripped jeans, no hint of skin revealing that it is actually warm outside, but I don't call her out on it.

"With deep and dark intent, the killer used acid to burn the remains in the bathtub…"

"What the fuck are you listening to?" Duffer asks, leaning against the chest of drawers with his arms folded across his chest.

"It's just a podcast," I mumble, reaching for my cell phone and switching it off.

"It sounds to me like you were getting ideas and storing them away for a later date," he replies with a grin, waggling his eyebrows at me suggestively, and I smirk.

"You wouldn't believe the shit I've learned from these things, but you can try me if you like."

His smile quickly drops and his Adam's apple bobs, making my smile grow wider. "I'm good. Thanks." His short and clipped response makes Emily chuckle beside me, lighting the room around us, and I quickly laugh along with her.

"Are you going to come out of your cave and say hi? Maggie was asking where you are."

I'd really rather not deal with the Ruthless Bitches and Axel right now, but I can't say that out loud. Not when I'm supposed to be a whore and want all of that shit. Although, I don't think Emily or Maggie see me in that light at all.

I'm good at many things, but it's apparent that pretending to be an entirely different person is beyond my reach. I can be myself, that's it. This altered version of me, the sex and all, is still me, just a newer, improved version that I didn't even know was possible.

It seems no longer having my wings clipped by the Ice Reapers is giving me a chance to grow. Imagine what it would feel like without the looming weight of any MC altogether?

Do I still want that? I think so, but then I look at Emily and Maggie and I'm blown away with how they've accepted me so effortlessly.

"Fine, I can show my face for a little while," I say as I move to sit up on the bed, while Emily claps excitedly.

"Thank God you didn't make me beg and plead like a hot mess."

She gives nothing away, so I glance at Duffer who must be able to read the question in my eyes. "She's only allowed in the bar area if you're there with me too."

My head rears back in surprise as I frown, looking back at my friend. "What did you do before I got here?"

"I wasn't allowed to go." She shrugs like it's no big deal, but if that was the case, then she wouldn't be this excited about it.

"Emmett likes to overprotect you, huh," I state as I step into my combat boots and zip them up, and she nods in response.

"That's an understatement. Ever since Mom died..." She clears her throat, tucking a loose lock of hair behind her ears as she shakes her head. "He always felt like our dad could have done more, so he takes it upon himself to safeguard me from anything and everything. That even includes slipping on the pavement," she adds with a roll of her eyes, trying to lighten the mood the best she can.

Shit. I didn't consider that their mom had passed. I haven't considered a lot of things since I got here. Simply brushing the surface and not digging any deeper out of fear of falling too hard. But I was more than happy to give him a hard time over his fucking heart like that was any of my business.

Shit.

If anyone knows how to fuck something up, it's me.

"I wish there had been someone there to protect me, Em. There never was and there never will be someone in my life who loves me that fiercely. It's hard to try and not take it for granted, especially when he might leave you feeling caged in sometimes, but unconditional love like that is worth fighting for." She gulps, wetting her lips as I offer her a tight smile. This is getting heavier than I can handle. "Anyway, let's make the most of it before he changes his mind." I link my arm through hers and head for the door before she can object, but she seamlessly falls into step beside me.

Duffer rushes around us before we get to the end of the hallway so he can hold the door to the bar open for us. I murmur my thanks as I bite back a groan at how busy it is tonight. Despite my best efforts, my gaze instantly moves to the Prez's booth where I find Ryker, Axel, Emmett, and Gray seated with a few Ruthless Bitches hovering around the table, but none of them are actually offered a seat.

I can't deny the smugness that I feel, but also the raging desire to waltz over there and step between them. As if they're mine to want, mine to have, mine to claim.

Shit, maybe I do need a drink to get out of my own head for a while.

"What do you guys want to drink? I'll go to the bar while you find us somewhere to sit," I offer, shaking my head at Duffer as he opens his mouth to object.

"Emmett said we can sit with them if we want. I feel like I want to be near him since he's injured, so I can annoy him with some sisterly love, but if you're not okay with that…" Her words trail off as I turn my shaking head to her.

"That's good with me. I'll meet you there."

She smiles wide before rhyming off the name of an alcohol-free cocktail she wants, while Duffer asks for a soda. Taking off in a different direction than them, I make my way through the crowd of people in cuts or skimpy outfits, before I brace my arms on the bar.

Glancing up and down, I search for Maggie, only to find her knee-deep in orders and a little rushed off her feet. Patting the bar, I move to the end, rounding the wooden top and fall into step with her.

"Who's next?" I call out, placing my hands on my hips as I look out at the crowd. Maggie glances my way but she doesn't tell me to piss off or anything so I hold my position.

"Two coronas." No please or thank you, but I don't expect anything different. Reaching into the fridge, I flick off the bottle tops and stuff a lime wedge into the top before handing them over, and then moving onto the next order.

I spend almost twenty minutes running down the line, with Maggie taking one end and me the other. There are a few guys in here without cuts tonight. It's weird that MCs are my sanctuary, yet I want to escape, and seeing guys without any cuts at all leaves me even more uneasy. But the Prez and VP are present so they must be okay with them being here.

"Girl, you're my queen in shining armor right now. Thank you," Maggie says when the line dies down and there's no one waiting.

Wiping my hands on a towel, I smile at her. "It's no problem. Although I did only sneak over to get a drink for Emily, Duffer, and me, but this was fun."

"I'll remember that when I'm sinking again because Lord knows I can't get any help from the Bitches," she grumbles, nodding in their direction. They're all over by the door except the three still hovering around the Prez's table.

If they're not helping out, then what the fuck are they actually doing here? That's not how I was raised for things to be done. I don't ask though, it's really not my place.

"If you need me, just give me a shout," I reply, getting two sodas before quickly mixing the fresh juices for Emily's drink.

With my hands full, I make my way to the end of the bar and around to where the crowd is when the music cuts off and commanding shouts bounce around the room.

"Jasperville County Sheriff's Department, hands in the air where I can see them or I'll be taking more men than I'm actually here to collect."

My bones turn to jelly, my heart crashing against my chest as I struggle to breathe. The two bottles and the glass in my hands slip from my grip, shattering at my feet, but the noise goes unnoticed among the riot sounding around me.

Stumbling backward, my hip hits the bar, and I use it to brace myself as the crowd moves around me, desperate to escape the law.

This is it. It's coming. My time is fucking done.

Someone bumps into me, and I slump to the floor in fear of being seen, before crawling on my hands and knees over the sticky wood flooring back behind the bar.

"You're not arresting anyone today, Petey."

I try to focus on Ryker's voice as he speaks to the sheriff, but he's barely audible over the ringing of my pulse in my ears.

"I have a warrant for the arrest of Emmett Brockman and Robert Lopez, aka Euro." A hint of relief washes over me when I don't hear my name called out, but it doesn't stop the panic from vibrating through my body.

Fear holds me in place, even though I want to step between the cops and Emmett, or at least shield Emily from the storm, I can't. I'm frozen in place with my knees bent and my arms banded tightly around them.

"What bullshit does your warrant say, Officer?" Axel grunts, but before the cop can respond, Emmett speaks.

"It's okay, brothers, you know the drill. I'll appease the cops, just as Euro will. We won't be there longer than an hour." His tone is certain, his voice unfazed as I hear the telltale sound of handcuffs being used. Each click of the metal increases the tightening in my chest and renders me useless.

The commotion seems to die down as footsteps retreat, and when the doors swing closed behind them, Ryker addresses the room, "If you're not a Ruthless Brother, get the fuck out. If you are, get your ass to the Church. Now."

What the hell is going on? Why is Emmett being arrested? I don't understand, but I also can't bring myself to stand up and find out.

Closing my eyes, I try to inhale deeply through my nose before exhaling from my mouth. It works a little as I continue to repeat the motion, but my anxiety and fear are sky-high right now. It's going to take more than this to bring it back down to a livable level.

"Gray, get Shift on the line, we're going to need our lawyer at the station before Emmett and Euro fucking get there. Eric and Becker, follow after them, we want as many eyes as possible," Ryker orders.

When I blink my eyes open, I can at least see a little clearer now compared to before, my vision more than just blurred shapes and colors. But I instantly regret it when a guy crouches in front of me, a sneer on his lips.

"Why the fuck were you hiding like that?" Axel glares at me, his hands fisted as he waits for an answer, but my tongue is like lead in my mouth.

I have nothing to offer him, no defense, no reason, nothing. I sure as shit am not giving him the truth. He doesn't deserve it. None of them do.

"I. Said. Why. Did. You. Hide. Like. That?"

My heart is in my throat as I take short, strangled breaths.

"Back off, Axel. She's panicked and in shock and you're not helping." Maggie's voice is like heaven to my ears, but as she inches closer and places her hand on my shoulder, I flinch at the touch. She moves back without another word, and Emily calls my name from a distance.

My eyes slam shut again, and I hate that I feel the trickle of a lone tear tracking down my face. But most of all, I hate that Axel is witnessing it.

"Take Emily to her brother's room for now. Scarlett will be there soon, she just needs a minute," Maggie murmurs, and I'm beyond thankful. I don't have the mental capacity to handle anything more than my own worries and fears, and if I see Emily, I'll want to take all her worries away.

Fingers push at my chin, tilting my head up, but I don't blink open my eyes until I hear Gray's voice. "Scar?"

My name, a soothing breath on his lips, pisses Axel off even more as he slams his fist into the unit behind him and the sound of shattering glass follows.

"Fuck off, Axel. You're not helping," Maggie shouts, louder this time, but he shakes his head in disbelief at her.

"Our brothers have been taken by the cops, and you're all here worrying about the woman that likely has something to do with it," he bites, and I scoff despite barely being able to breathe. "Do you know something?"

Although the panic and anxiousness within me is in full motion, the fear slowly starts to spiral into anger at his incessant pushing. "No," I bite, my breathing coming in bigger gulps now as my chest heaves with each breath.

This isn't who I am. I've worked so hard to be better, be stronger, be anything but helpless, yet here I sit, on the floor of another MC with my life under someone else's control.

"Then why hide?" Axel's feet shift apart as he folds his

arms over his chest, refusing to follow everyone else into the Church without an answer from me.

"Because that's what I've always been told to do, you fucking fool," I grit out, hands clenching into fists as my emotions make my blood boil. When his eyebrows furrow in confusion, it's my turn to sneer at him. "Childhood trauma doesn't just disappear." I almost add that it's not just him that has it, but I manage to refrain as he twists his lips in thought.

"Let her fucking be, Axel. We need to get everything under control for Emmett and Euro." Ryker appears in my peripheral vision, not glancing at me as he addresses his friend. It feels like an eternity passes before he rolls his shoulders back and then leaves with Ryker.

I sag with relief, hating the fact that he gets under my skin like that.

"Do you need anything?" Gray asks, moving to reach his hand out to me, but Maggie stops him before he can touch me.

"No. I need to be left alone or be given the chance to actually fucking leave." The words are through clenched teeth and it's Axel's voice from a small distance away that responds.

"You're not going anywhere when I know there's shit you're not telling us."

I feel like I'm going to explode. Every part of me

is ready to detonate at this moment. "Space it is, sweet cheeks," Gray breathes, looking at me solemnly once more before rising to his feet and following the others.

A sense of relief coats my skin, but I still feel clammy and drained.

Maybe the sheriff should have taken me in, maybe the darkness should. This pain was meant for me to feel, for me to survive, for me to be stronger, but holy fucking shit, that doesn't make it any easier to handle.

TWENTY FIVE

Emmett

My head thumps against the headrest as I slump in my seat. Inhaling, I smell the familiar scent of tobacco and coffee. This isn't my first time in the back of a cop car and I'm sure it won't be the last, but that doesn't take away from the fact that it's inconvenient as hell.

The door slams shut beside me, locking me in as I spy Euro being carted away in the other marked car parked next to me. These fuckers didn't read me my rights, didn't confirm why the fuck they're lifting me from the compound, or offer any other type of explanation.

Something isn't right, I can sense it. No matter how many times they've shown up at the compound unannounced, they've always grinned as they read out the charges with pride. That didn't happen this time, but it was pointless putting up a fight in there. Not in front of Emily.

The sheriff and another cop climb in up front, and

we're moving in the next moment. Lights and sirens blare as we exit the compound and take off into the night through Jasperville.

My hands flex, feeling the restraint of the handcuffs, while my leg burns where the wound is from being pulled from my seat and dragged away. Something tells me this is going to be a long-ass night. At least I won't be worrying about Emily's safety though. Not with Maggie, Duffer, and Scarlett there, they'll make sure she's okay. My father, however, will likely drown his sorrows in another bottle of bourbon rather than worry about someone else.

Sighing, my head hangs forward, my chin pressing to my chest.

"It feels like it's been a hot minute since we last saw you, Emmy." I tilt my eyes to the passenger seat without lifting my head, and I recognize him instantly. If I didn't know his face, the use of the nickname would have done it anyway.

Slowly lifting my head, I keep my eyes steady and my jaw relaxed. "Porter, it's been a while."

I went to school with this fucker. Last I knew, he went into the military, but it seems he's back in town now in a more permanent position. I didn't like the asshole then, so I certainly dislike him more now that he's in uniform.

"It's Deputy Hallman to you," he quips back, making me smirk at his smugness as I shrug, not correcting myself.

"Did you really think you could outrun the law like you have been doing?" he pushes, and I turn my attention to the window, watching the world drift by.

"Ah, don't want to talk about the bigger stuff, do we?" He chuckles as the sheriff grunts.

"Emmett was always the hound dog with nothing to say. Luckily for him, the boys in lock up tonight like 'em quiet." I try not to roll my eyes at him. It's like he lives to piss me off, attempting to get under my skin.

"I like watching them break when it takes a little more of a mental attack to bring them down." My eyes burn with the need to glare at Porter, his tone darkening as he takes on a more sadistic twist, but I refuse to give him the reaction he wants. We're not too far from the station, which means I don't have to put up with them for much longer. "Club compounds are grim to look at, Sheriff, you should have prepared me for the dive I was walking into," Porter adds.

I run my tongue along my teeth, taking a calming breath as the town lights fly by.

"If I had told you how bad it was, you wouldn't have aided us and we needed all hands on deck in case anyone tried to resist arrest," he replies, before coughing. It's the groggy sound that you get from smoking too much, the type that shreds at your lungs and throat as you fail to actually lift anything off your chest.

"I'll tell you what did catch my eye though," Porter

pushes, his voice raising as I feel his eyes burn into the side of my head. "A pretty little blonde. That wasn't little Emily there, was it? All grown and full of tits. Has she finally succumbed to the dark side and labeled herself a whore like your mother?"

"Shut. Your. Damn. Mouth," I spit, practically frothing at the mouth as I stare him down. I realize my mistake the moment he grins at me.

"There he is. There's the bad boy we wanted. I should make a note that it's family that gets under your skin. Or was it the reference to your whorish mother that did it?"

He must have called my mother a whore a thousand times in school and I never let it bother me. It's the mention of my sister that sends me over the edge. I knew I shouldn't have relented on her being allowed in the bar area.

"Maybe I should take little Emily for a spin myself, fuck her like I did your deadbeat mother. See if she begs for my dick just like she did."

My foot lifts before I can stop myself, hitting the back of his seat with force, but it does nothing to calm the burning anger inside of me. "Why don't you say that shit to me when I'm not in handcuffs, Porter? See how big and strong you think you are then," I bite, watching as he glares at me.

"I would consider that assault and threatening an officer, wouldn't you, Sheriff?" He doesn't tear his gaze from mine, a sneer touching his lips as the car comes to a stop.

"At least you'll have something real to put down on the report since you've brought me out here for some bullshit," I grunt, clenching my hands tightly behind my back.

I notice the building out of the front window, my feet able to carry me to lock up with my eyes closed if it was necessary, but instead I have to wait for these fuckers to get out of their seats and pull me from the car.

It's not surprising when it's the sheriff that opens my door and tugs on my arm. He's likely aware that if it was Porter standing there right now, I would headbutt the bastard into next week. Unfortunately, I'll have to save that for another time.

The sheriff leads me inside, Euro hot on my heels as he's brought in by two other cops, while the rest gather in the dark parking lot. Hopefully they're not going to drag their feet with whatever is going on here, I didn't have any patience before we left the compound. Now, after listening to Porter's bullshit, I've surpassed it.

Sheriff Hayes tugs on my cuffs, making me grit my teeth as the automatic doors open and we step inside. The receptionist is at her desk, I can't remember her name, Janet maybe? I'm not sure. She's on a call so she doesn't bother to lift her head as we trudge past. The dressing around my thigh is noticeable with the shorts I'm wearing, but that doesn't mean the sheriff slows his pace, if anything, we're moving faster than ever.

Fucker.

Riding through the pain, I'm almost relieved when I see the door that leads to the holding cell. Porter pushes open the door and the sheriff leads me inside as Euro is nudged through behind me. There are two cells, one on either side of the door, with a desk and seat at the other end of the room for whoever gets the short straw of having to watch us.

The cell to my left is unlocked and I'm walked inside, my handcuffs unlatched before the door is swiftly closed behind me. I glance over my shoulder to find they've actually put Euro in here too. He rubs at his wrists, a pinch to his brows as watches the officers file out of the room one at a time.

"What the fuck is all of this, VP? None of this makes sense, not without them reading our charges anyway."

I nod in understanding. "You're right, I don't know what this is."

"Why us though?"

All I can do is shrug in response. I don't have the answer to that either, so I don't make any effort to pretend to. All I do know is Ryker won't have us sitting here forever, he'll have plans in motion and we just have to ride it out.

Eyeing the metal bed frame that's bolted to the floor,

I stretch my leg a little before moving toward it. My ass barely touches the seat before the door is swung open again, but it's not the sheriff or Porter stepping back in. No. It's worse than that.

Their faces are unrecognizable, but the cuts that they're wearing are not.

Devil's Brutes.

Those motherfuckers.

The door locks behind them, the catch of the metal echoing around us as I watch the grins spread across both of their faces. One of them has brown hair and a scar down their left cheek, while the other is blond with piercing green eyes.

Without a word, Scarface dangles the key to our cell on his pointer finger, before he slowly slips it into the lock and lets the door swing open.

"I didn't realize we would be having visitors so soon into our stay. Did you bring any snacks with you?" I ask.

Not liking my sense of humor, the blond guy sneers at me as he kicks the door shut behind them. "The only gift we've brought you is your last breath." He pulls a switchblade from his pocket, flicking the knife out, and it shines under the light.

The cops have always refused to take payouts, and now I understand why. They wouldn't take it off the Ruthless Brothers because that would put them in conflict with the deal they had already made with another motorcycle club. The Devil's Brutes. But if they think they're going to drag me in here to meet my maker, then they're delusional.

Placing my hands on my knees, I rise to my feet, ignoring the throb in my thigh as I take the two steps necessary to come to a stop beside Euro. He doesn't look at me though, he's too busy staring at them with a mixture of anger and uncertainty in his eyes.

"The devil isn't calling for me yet." The bite in my tone is undeniable at the same time Blondie swings his arm out, attempting to come at me with the knife, but I manage to step back just in time. Lifting my foot high, I kick him in the gut, my thigh screaming at the feel of my stitches tearing as he stumbles back.

Grunts sound from Euro and Scarface, but I leave them to go at it while I stare at the man standing in my way. He quickly regains his balance, charging toward me with his arm swinging left to right, and I manage to catch him just in time and knock the weapon from his grasp, before smashing my fist into his face.

My knuckles vibrate from the force as his head rears back dramatically, blood instantly bursting from his nose as he swings his leg out and kicks me in my bad thigh.

Fuck.

My leg gives out, forcing me to my knees and making me hiss. Blondie scrambles to get his knife and I try to beat him to it, but he boots me in the face, sending me sideways as I struggle to see through the pain.

Lying on my side, I blink through the pain, working my jaw as I see the Brute heading toward me with determination in his every step. Swinging my leg out, I hit his shin and he cries out with intense agony.

Despite my own discomfort, I manage to get to my feet before he can come at me again as I feel the trickles of blood dancing along my skin, down my cheeks and chin, before landing on my cut.

He's going to pay for that.

I don't rear my right arm back before I throat-punch him, catching him completely by surprise as he staggers back, one hand around his neck while the other grips the blade. He's not going to stop coming for me until I'm dead… or he is.

Rolling my shoulders back, I sway on the balls of my feet as I assess him thoroughly this time. His nose is busted, his leg is likely throbbing, and his cheek is swelling. His hand flexes around the blade as he lifts it once more, but I'm done worrying about his weapon.

I drop my height, bending my knees as I charge toward him, not stopping until my shoulder hits his stomach and I barrel him into the bars of the cell with a grunt. A burning sensation drapes over my neck, and I know he's caught me with the blade along my skin. Not wanting to give him the chance to thrust it into my neck deeper, I swing my fists at him repeatedly.

Gut. Gut. Thigh. Face.

Gut. Gut. Neck. Chest.

Gut. Neck. Thigh. Face.

The blow knocks the air from him as he plasters his back against the bars. He came in here to take a life, to feed it to the devil, he just didn't realize it would be his.

He's barely holding on to the blade and it's far too easy for me to pry it from his hands. With the handle in my grip, I turn the blade in his direction and waste no time thrusting it into his gut. Once. Twice. Three times.

My chest heaves as he slumps to the floor, no longer a concern of mine as I wipe the blade off on his t-shirt and tuck it into his leather jacket.

"You tell the Reaper I'll be seeing him soon, just not today," I murmur, before turning to what is going on with Euro and the other Brute. Euro's arms are braced around his neck, a weak chokehold keeping him at bay as blood splatters across Euro's t-shirt.

I take one step toward them when the door opens and Porter steps into the room. The smirk that's on his face is short-lived as he pauses, taking in the sight before him. "You better clear your fucking men out of here before I continue to wreak havoc on this motherfucker as well."

TWENTY SIX

Scarlett

Swamped in my old Puddle of Mudd hoodie and a pair of baggy sweats, I curl my hands into the oversized sleeves as I shuffle to the kitchen. My face is hidden with the hood pulled up. Sleep wasn't my friend last night, neither were my racing thoughts. Drenched in a world of memories and fear as my chest constricted with every breath, I feel like death. Just like I do every time my anxiety gets a hold of me. My childhood reminding me very clearly that I am who I am today because of it.

With groggy eyes and a cloudy brain, I almost fall into Maggie, but her hands on my arms stop me. That's what I get for walking with my head down and not paying attention.

She runs her fingers over the edge of my hood, pushing it back a little as I lift my face. "I'm sorry," I murmur, the words spilling from my mouth in a whisper.

Her smile is soft as she keeps her fingers gently at my arms. "Well, now you can see better, so you'll know where you're going."

"Not for that... well, yeah for that, but also for last night."

I feel overwhelmed, embarrassed and completely mortified. No one ever sees. No one. At the Ice Reapers, I always hid away, never immersing myself in club life and the bar scene. If the cops showed up, I was silently rocking in my room, waiting for them to leave. It was never so public.

Maggie's eyes crinkle as her thumb rubs soothingly over my hoodie. "Honey, we all have demons. You can be mad, sad, happy, or anything in between, but don't ever be apologetic for the life that was dealt to you. We all keep our head above water as best as we can, but sometimes life sweeps the rug from under our feet and we're not prepared for it."

Unshed tears prick the back of my eyes, but I sink my nails into my palms, forcing them to stay at bay. Her words soothe my heart, but my head refuses to let me be vulnerable again.

Taking a deep breath, I nod at her. She takes a step back, giving me the space I need. "Coffee?"

Just like that she reads the signs and changes the subject. Where did this woman come from? And how the hell did such an angel find herself here of all places?

"Please."

She moves around the kitchen effortlessly as I move toward the table, standing behind a chair as I brace my hands on the back of it.

"We got word that Emmett is ready for release, so Gray and Ryker have gone to pick him up."

My heart races in my chest while I somehow feel a sense of relief wash over me. "Have they said what he was taken in for?"

She shakes her head, glancing back at me with a dark look on her face. "No. Which means something isn't right, but hopefully we'll get more information when he's home."

I nod, about to respond, when her gaze passes through me. A smile spreads across her face before I turn to see what has her attention, only to come face-to-face with Axel.

Fuck.

I really don't need him berating me again this morning. I can't fucking take it.

I'm surprised to see him not glaring at me like an asshole as he assesses me. His hair is tied in a bun, his eyes dark and tired, but there are no sunglasses for a change. I can see the torment swirling in his iris', burning the man repeatedly in front of me as he adjusts his cut over his plain black tee.

He remains quiet for a few seconds longer than I expect, so I turn back to the table, praying it stays that way when his voice cuts through the air. "I have something for you."

Phew.

He's not talking to me either. I can sip my coffee while Maggie takes a look at whatever he's talking about.

Pulling out the chair in front of me, I move to take a seat when Maggie clears her throat and murmurs my name. She's standing beside the table now with my coffee in hand, but she's nodding at the man behind me.

"What?"

"Axel has something for you."

It takes a second for the words to register in my brain, and I slowly turn to look at him. "Something for *me*?" I clarify as he nods once, short and sharp, and I scoff. "Is it a gravestone with my name on it or something because I'm going to be honest, I really don't want one."

Maggie chuckles at me like it's a joke, but I'm dead fucking serious. This man clearly doesn't like me, so him giving me anything is a major red flag. My life is definitely on the line.

He rolls his eyes at my dramatics, a move I'm sure he's done a hundred times before in my presence behind his sunglasses, but this time, I get to see the swirl for myself. "If I was going to kill you, I wouldn't give you anything for people to remember you by," he grunts, turning toward the door and waving for me to follow after him. "Come."

Fucking asshole. Is this a joke?

Maggie nods at me to follow after him. There's a knowing glint in her eyes, a pull I can't describe that has me taking my coffee mug and trailing after him. I step out of the kitchen to find him holding the door to the bar open, waiting for me.

I step through the space, taking longer than necessary as I make sure not to brush up against him. The memory of the night he was passed out replays in my mind and the words Gray said to me. It's for his trauma and my fucking sanity.

The second I'm through, he's heading for the main doors, long strides making it hard for me to keep up with my mug in my hands. "Asshole," I mumble, but he stops at the door, turning to face me with his brow quirked.

"What was that?"

My stomach clenches, hating that this motherfucker is calling me out. I might be lost in my own thoughts and feelings right now, but if he's going to kill me, I'm going to go down saying exactly what's on my mind. I don't stop until I'm standing right in front of him. "I said you're an—"

The rest of my sentence is lodged in my throat as my eyes skim past him and land on the piece of metal standing a few yards behind him. I shove my mug into his chest, not caring whether he catches it or not as I sprint, barefoot into the yard.

I can't breathe as I fall to my knees, my face pressing into the perfectly stitched leather that makes the seat on my bike.

My. Fucking. Motorcycle.

Mine.

How?

I run my fingers over the front wheel, still unable to truly comprehend what is right in front of me. Swallowing a handful of times, I manage to loosen the lump in my throat enough to croak out a few words. "Please tell me this isn't some kind of joke."

"I'm funny, but not that funny," Axel grumbles back, scrubbing a hand over his jaw. "Although, if I had known how dramatic you were going to be, I wouldn't have gone for it."

I look at him. Really look at him. He's staring at me intently, his jaw tight, hands stuffed in his pockets, and his forehead marred with frown lines. Yet the look in his eyes is… softer?

That can't be possible.

"Why?"

It takes him a moment to answer. "You were right last night. Trauma doesn't give a shit how or when it affects you. I still think you're shady as shit, but I thought you should at least have your bike here with you."

My heart soars, my cheek pressing into the leather as I take a deep breath. It's shitty as hell, but the truth remains the same; trauma knows trauma.

"Thank you. I can't tell you how—"

"You're right, you can't. Your dramatics are getting on my nerves."

There it is. The barrier back in place as he slips his glasses from his pocket and covers his eyes. Abrupt, short, and snarky, I shouldn't expect anything else from this man.

I rise from my crouched position and instinctively run my fingers over the handlebars. The rumble of an engine catches my attention as a pick-up truck comes to a stop a few feet away.

"Finally," Axel mutters, moving toward it just as the rear door opens and Gray steps out. Moments later, the doors to the front open too and Ryker climbs out with Emmett coming around the back of the truck.

I'm confused as fuck by the small gash over the bridge of his nose and the black eye that marks his face. Those sure as shit weren't there when he left last night, so what the fuck happened?

Before I can ask anything, Axel slaps his hand and they man-hug, murmuring among themselves as Gray moves to the other side of my bike.

"Who does this hot thing belong to?"

My mouth spreads into a wide smile as I beam. "Me."

He points at the bike, his brows knitted as he looks at me. "You?"

"Yeah. Axel brought it for me."

He whirls around, gaping at his friend who has his back turned to him. "When the fuck did you do that, Ax?"

"When you left." His grunt is unsurprising, just like the fact that he doesn't turn around to look at Gray either.

"You motherfucker!"

I frown at the annoyance on Gray's face as opposed to the humor I'm used to seeing. Why the fuck is he mad about it?

"What am I missing?" I fold my arms over my chest, trying to put two and two together but coming up empty.

"This fucker knew where we were stopping on the way back from town and I was pissed when we showed up to the remnants of the Ice Reapers' compound just now and found nothing there. Especially not the bike I was looking for."

Wait, what?

"Just let it rest, Gray. Your favorite flavor of the week got her prized possession back, be happy about it." Axel still doesn't look around, which only seems to piss Gray off more.

"But the good deed was for me to do, not you, asshole." Gray turns to me, annoyance in his eyes as he waves his hands at Axel, but I don't know what I'm supposed to say or do.

Ryker clears his throat, patting Emmett on the shoulder as he ushers him around to where I'm standing. "Emmett, go and relax. Sleep, fuck, whatever you want, and I'll take these two assholes inside and update everyone on what happened last night."

Axel moves toward the door without a backward glance as Gray stomps after him, still muttering under his breath about making shitty moves. Once Ryker has left as well, Emmett finally looks down, exhaustion darkening his eyes as he sighs.

"Keep me company?"

I lift my hand to his face, running my finger just under his bruised eye. He doesn't wince or pull away; he just continues to stare at me with his arms relaxed at his sides. "Sure."

I nod and take a step back, running my fingers over my seat one final time before heading to the door. Emmett is right behind me as I step inside.

"Have you broken through Axel's armor?" Emmett asks as we move into the hallway that leads to the private area, and I scoff as he opens his bedroom door.

"Please, it's a chink at most and even that feels like I'm over exaggerating," I reply, hovering at the entrance as he sits on his bed. Not wanting to discuss whatever the fuck just happened out there, I clear my throat. "Is Emily okay? I kind of got swamped by my own bullshit last night, so I was no use to her, but I've been worrying about her."

I expect him to be mad for some reason, but a tired smile touches the corner of his mouth. "She's in class, Duffer is watching her. She told me you had a lot going on last night and that I should come check on you when I got back."

Fucking Emily. When did they make friends like her?

"She should be worrying about you instead of me," I reply.

"Oh, she put my ass through the wringer for making her worry. I'm hoping that means she was worried about me, but who knows." He shrugs, a lightness to him that's only there when he's talking about his sister.

I smile softly in response as I nod at his bed. "Are you going to nap now or do you want me to take a look at your stitches?"

He shakes his head immediately, before running his hand over his beard. "Sleep isn't going to help me, and my stitches can wait. But I'm too tired to get my dick up too. So I can't do anything Ryker suggested ," he says with a smirk, and I chuckle softly.

"We can hang out for a bit," I offer, and he scoffs.

"I don't play video games, Scarlett."

"I wasn't saying you had to," I retort with a quirk of

my eyebrow. "So what do you do to unwind that doesn't involve sleeping or fucking?"

He rakes his teeth over his bottom lip as he glances down at the ink on his forearms. "You want to get a tattoo?" I ask, almost feeling dumb saying it so cautiously, and his smirk widens.

"No, well, yeah, but I also like to do them."

My eyes widen. "Are you saying you're good with a tattoo gun?"

He nods, his eyes raking over me from head to toe. I can read between the lines, I know what he's saying without saying it and it makes my heart race.

"I don't have any ink yet," I murmur, stepping further into the room, letting my hands fall to my sides as his eyes brighten.

"Even better."

***

"Are you sure this is the one you want?"

I roll my eyes at his repeated question. He's asked me this a million times and I'm fed up with repeating myself.

No, I haven't gotten a tattoo before, but that doesn't mean I haven't wanted one. Having him press the needle into my skin, marking it forever, will be the most freeing thing I will ever experience.

No rules. No opinions. No bullshit.

Just me, in my skin.

"If you don't turn that damn thing on and stab me with your gun, then I'll find someone else here who will." I raise my eyebrow at him in challenge. This may have started out as a way for him to decompress, but my heart is fucking set on it now and there's no way in hell I'm backing down.

"Like fuck," he grunts, shuffling in his seat so his legs are spread wide on either side of me as I sit on the chair he pulled in from the kitchen. He takes my wrist in his hand and slowly twists it from side to side, looking at the stencil that's on my skin ready for him to trace.

I asked him to freestyle it but he refused. In his words, 'There's no fucking way in hell I'm ruining your sweet porcelain skin with one wrong line out of place.' Seemingly, I trust his abilities more than he does, but I'm not going to argue with him.

"Do you want to listen to some music?" he offers and reaches for the tattoo gun.

"I'm good with Axel's music unless you want to hit me with some Swifty," I offer, grinning at him. The heavy metal music started playing about twenty minutes ago, and even through the closed bedroom door, it's still loud enough to be heard clearly in here.

"Swifty isn't the right music for inking you, Scarlett," Emmett murmurs with a scoff, before turning the tattoo gun on.

The sound of the needle kicking into action sends a shiver down my spine. It makes me feel nervous and exhilarated all at once. Emmett runs his calloused thumb over my skin, memorizing the stencil outline like it's not there to guide him, before he lowers the gun to my skin.

I don't know what I expect the first feeling to be like, but it's less harsh than my mind was making me believe. The needle is piercing my skin, outlining and marking a trail to remain forever. You would expect that to hurt like a bitch, but it's more of a soft hum grazing repeatedly over my flesh.

My shoulders relax as he continues, my eyes closing as I let the vibrations soothe me. Even though we're sitting in silence, it's distracting enough that I'm not lost in my own mind again. If anything, it lulls me into a restful state, forgetting the real world and the issues I'm facing right now.

I could tell them the truth, I could explain, but I don't want to. Not when they brought me here as a whore, and treat me like this instead. Like a fucking queen most of the time. Back at the Reapers, whores were treated like shit, but that's not the case here, not even for Molly and her tribe of Bitches.

I'm not respected any less and I'm not slurred at simply for breathing.

It hasn't been an act either. I've fucked who I've wanted to fuck, I've spent time with who I want to spend time with, and I've explored my own wants, needs, and desires more than I ever have.

"Are you asleep or daydreaming?" Emmett's voice cuts through my thoughts and I blink my eyes open.

"Daydreaming," I reply, not really sure it counts as daydreaming if I'm basking in the glow of my life right now, but I don't specify that.

The corner of his mouth tilts up in a smile as he nods at my arm. "The outline is done. Are you good for me to carry on and shade it in?"

Looking down at the black ink coating my skin, a buzz of excitement zaps through me. My cheeks ache from how wide I'm smiling as I nod eagerly. "Definitely color it in. Please."

I can't take my eyes off the black outline of a Harley Davidson at the top of my inner forearm. By the time he's done, there will be orange and yellow flames elegantly swirling from the back of it. It's perfect. But more so are the words underneath it that are etched forever in my skin.

Forever Free.

.

RUTHLESS BROTHERS MC

TWENTY SEVEN

Emmett

The second the needle pierces her skin, I want to defile every inch of the outline marked in blue looking back at me.

I want to wash it off and do it freestyle, just like she asked. It would be done a lot quicker than this.

I want to etch into her skin with every fiber of my being. One word. Just one.

A word I can't explain, a word that I've never used before when it comes to a woman, yet, here I am, warring with myself. After the bullshit that was last night, and the way my body calmed when I saw her in the yard with Axel earlier, I know it with certainty.

I can't do it.

I won't.

Not yet at least.

But the four letters are burned into my mind forever,

waiting desperately to be inked on her flesh.

Mine.

RUTHLESS BROTHERS MC

TWENTY EIGHT

Axel

Gray glares at me as we take our seats in the Church. The empty spot reserved for our VP is noticed, but we all know he's home and well, despite the bruising on his face. Gray needs to get the fuck over himself so we can focus on what actually matters here; the club and dealing with these fuckheads who have decided to become the bane of our existence.

"Is my son home?" Eric asks from the opposite end of the table, the bags under his eyes heavy and dark from a lack of sleep. It will likely have more to do with losing himself in a bottle yet again than pacing the floor with actual worry for his son, but out of all of the people here, I'm the last one who should judge.

"He is, but the details that come with his return leave more on our plate to handle," Ryker states, slouching back in his seat.

"Hit us with it, Prez," Briggs grunts from beside Eric, his hands balling into fists on the table top as he nods at Ryker. It makes me smile on the inside, even though I give nothing away on the outside. Knowing our brothers are ready to go into battle with little information as to why always fills my veins with adrenaline.

Smashing some skulls with my bare hands will take a load off my shoulders for sure.

"During the haze of the cops storming us last night, we didn't catch a real glimpse of the new deputy in town. Porter Hallman. He was a classmate of ours in high school. He was a no-good cunt then, and an even more inconvenient one now," Ryker spits.

I thought we had seen the back of that guy when he left to join the Army, but clearly I was wrong. I may have also been wrong to stay behind to get the damn bike for Scarlett because now I'm learning this information along with everyone else. It gives me no chance to react to the shit that went down last night, so I bottle it up.

"To add to that, when Emmett and Euro got put in the holding cells, the good old sheriff's department let in two Devil's Brutes members to try and slaughter them." Curses murmur around the room, anger getting the better of everyone as tension rises. "If you see Emmett, you'll notice he's sporting a black eye and a gash on his nose, a consolation prize for killing one of their men before they came for one of us instead."

"Thank fuck for that," Eric grunts, slamming his fist into the table.

"And Euro?"

"He's good, beaten too, but the new deputy decided to check in before either of them could make another example of the remaining Brute."

"Good, he can send a message back to them," I state, leaning forward to brace my forearms on the table as my brothers nod in agreement.

"They clearly see us as weak since the loss of our old Prez, but they don't realize how much we've grown from that movement, how much our backbone has strengthened despite the loss."

I nod along with Gray's assessment, knowing it couldn't have been put any better. With Ryker in charge, we're only going to be stronger than we ever have before, and they're going to need to learn that sooner rather than later.

"We need a response, an aggressive and measured retaliation that shows how our club now operates. There will be no more confusion over where our strengths lie." I shake my head, hearing my own words in my ears as I stare around the table. "You would have expected them to know that already with how we took out the Reapers," I add, annoyed as fuck.

"True, but to them it probably looked like a hasty

response. Which it was, we blew up the fucking clubhouse, leaving no surviving member of the Reapers on a whim," Gray states with a shrug. It looks like it doesn't make any sense to him either.

"Were there any rumors that the prospects picked up?" Ryker asks, turning the question to Briggs who is the unofficial prospect organizer.

"Nothing official, but there were a few guns on the streets that they weren't familiar with, and when they asked one of the guys about it, he was shifty as hell and ran off."

"They're threatening our men, our livelihood, and our fucking town. Enough is enough. We've given them far too much room to play with already." I can't hide my anger any further, my hands clenched on the table and the cords in my neck straining with every breath I take. "Someone has to pay, and it sure as hell isn't going to be one of us."

"This is exactly why you're our sergeant at arms, Axel. Between you and Ryker, we'll fucking follow." Briggs pats his chest, the vein at his temple throbbing with every breath.

They're ready. All of them. Eric included. There's a fire around this table that I haven't felt in a very long time, and with how everyone is looking at us, they know it too.

It's a new era, a new dawn, and a new enemy, but that won't make us falter.

Ryker rises from his seat, nodding, but I can tell he's

deep in thought for a moment before he finally settles his eyes on the gavel in front of him. "They'll likely know that Emmett and Euro are back now and that we have the full story. They'll be expecting the same response we gave the Reapers, but they're not going to get it. Rest up, we're going to place a few more feelers around town, and then we're going to strike. We just have to know where we're aiming first."

The gavel hits the wood, ending the discussion, not that there's anything left to be said, and everyone starts to disperse around us. I rock back in my seat, tapping my fingers on the table as the need to release some steam takes over me, but I instantly sense a glare coming from Gray. It's like he's had it on pause the entire time, instead of just getting over it.

I want to stand and walk away, but Gray's the kind of annoying asshole that will just follow me, which will only draw more attention our way, and I really can't deal with that right now. Instead, I maintain my spot as everyone leaves. I expect Ryker to go too, but instead he holds the door closed, folding his arms over his chest as he looks between us.

"You two need to get over whatever bullshit this is. The Devil's Brutes require our full attention and *not* my Brothers causing shit within the club."

"Please, everything was good until this asshole decided

to pull the rug from under me," Gray retorts with a pout, wagging his finger in my direction.

"Last night, after I fucking mouthed off at her for causing a scene, you basically ripped me a new asshole. So I decide to be the bigger man and get over myself and that's not good enough either." I cock a brow at him, my fingers itching for the cigarette packet in my pocket.

"You fucking did that by taking away the gift I was going to give her."

"Does it matter *who* gave it to her when she still got it in the end?" My chest tightens, annoyance creeping up my spine with every breath that passes, but he shakes his head at me like I'm the one not listening.

"How about the pair of you get a fucking grip? You weren't mad when Emmett fucked Scarlett, or shit, when I literally kicked you out of the garage to do the same. Did Axel step on your toes with the bike? Probably, but it's not worth this bullshit."

"The bike is more personal. The bike *means* something," Gray grinds out as I scoff.

"No, it doesn't."

"Yes, it does." Gray is quick to retort as Ryker shakes his head in disbelief at us.

"Do you actually hear yourselves?"

A knock sounds from the door, but none of us respond as we continue to stare each other down.

"I just don't understand why you would play me like that, man?" Gray sounds defeated, like I've pissed on his fries or something, but I can't comprehend why.

The knock sounds again, and despite Ryker blocking the door, it still manages to open. Maggie steps around him with her hands folded over her chest and a pinch to her eyebrows. "I don't know why you bothered shutting the door, everyone can fucking hear you."

I balk at that, scraping my chair back along the floor as I stand. "I'm not doing this."

Before I can get to Ryker, Gray's words hold me in place. "I'm feeling things. Things I can't really explain, and they all circle around her."

Fuck.

"We can't trust her, Gray."

"But we can give her a two-wheeled vehicle to escape with?" His retort is quick, annoyed, and snarky.

Clenching my hands at my sides, I consider how to respond in a way that doesn't make me look like even more of an asshole, but it's harder than it seems.

"The four of you will figure your shit out eventually," Maggie murmurs, her sweet voice slicing through the otherwise gruff air around us. "You each need your own time alone and with her."

"With her?" It's Ryker's turn to give her a questioning glance, but she simply brushes him off with a wave of her hand.

"Don't play dumb with me. Scarlett showed up here as everything was changing and has worked her way under your skin whether you like it or not." She ends her sentence looking directly at me, and I grunt.

"Whatever, I'm done. Tell her the bike was from you, I don't give a shit, and I'm sure she'll still let you fuck her tonight either way," I say, shouldering past Ryker before any of them can stop me. My fingers are clenched around my cigarette packet as I storm through the bar area toward the door, plucking a smoke from the packet, and the second I'm outside in the sunlight, I flick my lighter and watch the end burn.

I inhale deeply, hating my dependency on yet another vice that has sunken its claws into my flesh, but it doesn't stop me from taking another pull of the cigarette, followed all too quickly with another.

The door creaks behind me, and the sweet scent of cherries tells me who it is without turning around. "I don't need you saying shit like that to me. I don't have anyone under my skin, and certainly not *her*. She can't be trusted. There's something we don't know about her and that's all I'm interested in figuring out."

It takes a moment for her to respond as she comes to a stop beside me. "That's the nicest thing you've done for someone other than Gray, Ryker, or Emmett in years, after one of the shittiest things you've done," Maggie states, referring to last night, and I sigh.

"I gave her something that was important to her, just like mine is important to me. It's not an apology, and it's certainly not anything else either."

The rumble of a bike catches my attention, pulling my gaze toward the compound gates.

There's only one making its way toward us, but my defenses are still high after the past few weeks. It takes a couple of seconds, but I quickly come to recognize the cut he's wearing; a matching one to mine.

Despite everything that's just happened, a smile spreads across my face as I approach the Harley Davidson that's come to a stop in front of Maggie and me.

"Brother," I holler, our hands clasping as we slap each other on the back. "It feels like it's been an eternity."

"I'm glad to be home, Brother, where I'm needed. Set me to work and I'll do everything I can."

"Shift? Is that my boy? It's been forever," Maggie sings, filling the space I took moments ago as she wraps her arms tightly around his neck.

"I'm not saying I haven't missed you, but it's been like, what, four weeks? You guys exaggerate too much." The smirk on his face matches the humor in his voice, and it feels good to have him home.

"I'm cooking up a feast tonight for the return of our

Shift," Maggie declares, clapping her hands excitedly as she rushes back inside without a backward glance.

My cell phone vibrates in my pocket, but I ignore it for now, focusing on my friend that has been away for too long. "Is it as bad as it feels?" he asks, and I grimace.

"There's a feeling in my gut telling me we're missing something major. A key piece, but I can't pinpoint what it is. All I know is we need to figure it out so we can bury the Devil's Brutes with our bare hands."

"Count me in, Ax. I've been desperate to get my hands dirty since the moment I left."

TWENTY NINE

Scarlett

I still have my hood up over my head, covering my forehead as I glance at the length of my chest to where my arm is resting on my stomach.

There's ink on my skin.

Permanent fucking ink, and I'm obsessed with it. The way the orange and reds swirl at the back of the bike fills my soul with a new level of love I've never experienced with anything other than my Harley. Seeing the words 'Forever Free' fills me with joy.

This truly feels like a new me, the next stepping stone in my life, one I never thought I would get. But the panic from last night still simmers in my veins, reminding me that my life isn't completely free, not when my past continues to haunt me in the most ridiculous fucking ways.

My eyes are hooded, my brain and body exhausted from the lack of sleep I had last night, but I can't fall asleep yet. It's too early. If I fall asleep now, I won't be able to sleep tonight, and I can't bear the thought of being awake and alone at twilight hour.

I can't stand the darkness, the moment when everyone around you is sleeping, while the depths of hell claw at you. My chest grows tight just thinking about it, the itchy feeling that runs under the skin traveling down my arms.

Fuck.

Sitting on the bed, I rest my head in my hands and yawn.

I ducked out on Emmett once he finished my tattoo. One of the Ruthless Bitches knocked on his door and declared someone called Shift was home, and that Maggie was setting up a barbecue for him. Emmett was ecstatic, but I don't have that level of enthusiasm to put on a fake smile and pretend like I give a shit. Although, how I'm feeling right now, locked in my head, could be worse than the fake shit, so maybe I need to re-evaluate.

A knock on my bedroom door startles me as it creeks open without warning, making my back stiffen at the intrusion, until I see Emily's face in the opening. Relief washes over me. My racing heart begins to slow, and I quirk a brow at her.

"Aren't I supposed to respond to the knock *before* you come in?"

Emily scoffs as she edges the door open wider, rolling

her eyes at me and stepping into the room. "Not when I'm pretty sure you would have pretended to not be here. Plus, if it was locked, I would have known for sure you were."

She's got me there. My initial thought when I heard the knock was to be as quiet as a mouse and hide away from the world.

Pointing over her shoulder, she redirects the conversation. "I'm guessing you don't want to join in tonight."

"Not really, but if it's a requirement, then—"

"No, no," she interrupts, waving her hand at me. "If you don't want to make an appearance, then you don't have to. I just came to check on you. You can do whatever you want."

I don't know whether I'm more overwhelmed by the fact that I don't have to do exactly as I'm told and follow the expectations of me any longer, or that she came here because she cared.

I clear my throat. "When you say I can do whatever I like, does that include going outside to tinker with my bike?"

Her eyebrows pinch for a moment as she assesses me. "You have a bike?"

"Yeah."

"Since when?"

Her tone isn't accusatory, but I've definitely surprised

her. Although the memory of earlier today and the bullshit unraveling between Axel and Gray makes me want to stay as far away from the subject as possible.

"It's a long story," I finally reply, brushing a hand down my face, and I instantly hate myself for sounding like an asshole when it's not her fault. Standing from the bed, I tuck my hands into the sleeves of my hoodie as I smile softly at her. "I'm sorry. I'm not trying to be a bitch. Today has just been a day."

"And the remnants of your panic attack last night are still wearing you down."

My eyes widen as her words sink in. "Exactly," I mumble, my gut clenching as I take a half-shuffled step toward her. "How do you know that?"

I already know the answer, I can feel it with every fiber of my being, but I need to hear it from her to know it's true.

Her face is a mixture of a frown and a smile. It's not forced, barely meeting the corners of her eyes, but it's not filled with joy and happiness.

"It's the only reason I don't put up more of a fight when Emmett insists Duffer follows me everywhere."

Anger boils in my veins. "Do you need me to gut a bitch for you? Man or woman, we will make it happen."

Her chuckle is light and airy, thankfully void of any pain or heartache. "No, not today at least."

I want to know what 'at least' means. I want to know

what or who hurt her and take it all away, but I know the reality of being in her position. The fear that trembles through your body at the worry that someone will hound you with questions for answers you don't want them to have.

Taking a deep breath, I relax my shoulders and try to squash down the fury inside of me. I can save it for when it's truly needed, and that's not right now, not with her. "If you ever want to talk about it, I'm here. If you never want to talk about it, but you need me to show up at three in the morning with a shovel and no questions asked, count me in."

Before I can prepare myself, she launches herself at me, arms around my neck as she squeezes me tight. I tentatively hug her back.

When she releases me and takes a step back, I shake my head in disbelief. "Don't you think it's crazy as fuck that I only just got here, yet I trust you and want to protect you without question?"

"The craziest," she replies with a grin and steps back into the hallway. "Now, go and relax with your bike while I go and find the man of the hour." She wiggles her eyebrows as my own knit in confusion.

"The returning brother?" I clarify, and she blushes slightly as she nods.

"Do I need to tell Emmett about this?" I ask, completely

joking, and she laughs along with me as she shakes her finger at me.

"No, you definitely don't."

I find my Harley in the garage, sitting perfectly but a little dirty, which only makes me smile because it gives me something to do.

Searching for rags and cleaning solutions in the garage, I get to work bringing my baby back to life. It feels strange knowing Axel rode it here. Since it became my possession, no one but me has straddled that seat, but I'm surprisingly not as mad about it as I thought I would be.

I get lost in the rhythm and movements of sweeping my hand back and forth, forgoing the usual podcast I would have playing in the background when I was able to do this previously at the Reapers', instead opting for the sound of the late evening to keep me company.

I can hear birds, crickets, and the movement of a squirrel or two, along with the sound of cars in the distance. It's grounding. It's exactly what I needed. And it's at the top of my list to say thank you to Emily in some way shape or form.

Dipping my hand into the water bucket, I find the sponge I need and delicately trace it over the wheels, making sure to get the cleaning solution off, leaving them to sparkle.

"I heard I would find you out here."

My jaw clenches at the sound of the bitch's voice, and I can't keep the disdain from my tone as I reply, even when I don't turn to look at her. "What do you want, Molly?"

I'm bored of her bullshit, I'm bored of her thinking this is some competition when all I'm trying to do is keep my fucking head down and survive. I'm failing at it, but I'm fucking trying.

"I want you to leave."

Sighing, I reluctantly turn my gaze to find her standing with her arms crossed over her chest, her hip jutted to one side and a snarl on her face. Of course. I remain crouched beside my bike.

"And why would I do something just to please you?" I cock a brow at her, releasing my hold on the sponge as I drop it into the bucket.

"Because I'm the leader of the Ruthless Bitches and I'm going to make sure you're not inducted."

I wait for her to say more, for the threat to come, but when she continues to stare at me, I know that's all she has to say. There's nothing wrong with being a biker whore. If anything, I envy the women and the confidence in their every sway. Am I confident naked? Yes, but that's not the same as the swagger and sexiness they carry. It's exactly why I've failed at fitting in with them, but I'm not heartbroken by her statement.

"Do you want me to run along and weep into my pillow now?"

"Don't try me, bitch," she bites in response, taking a step toward me in her stilettos, and I sigh again.

"Molly, why don't you do us both a favor and fuck off back inside. Someone's waiting for their dick to get wet," I grumble, turning my attention back to my bike, hoping she leaves without another word, but I should know better than that by now.

"Hmm, you're right. But the question is, do I go back to Gray's waiting lap, or climb into Emmett's? I've heard the rumors about how hung he is. Maybe Ryker wants to feel how soft my folds are, how sweet my pussy is." Her purring words are like nails on a chalkboard as I try to gulp past the bile threatening to rise up my throat. I don't like the sound of any of that.

Not. One. Bit.

But it's not lost on me that she's only heard the rumors and not already seen Emmett for herself.

Bitch.

But I have to brush it off, I can't let her see what that does to me, what she's *hoping* it will do to me.

Fuck.

"Have you even heard yourself? Go, do whatever you

please and just leave me fucking be."

Without looking, I hear her take another step my way, irritating the fucking life out of me as her words turn darker. "There's nothing here for you. Nobody wants you. Nobody likes you. Nobody gives a shit whether you live or die. So why don't *you* be the one to do us both a favor and fuck off."

My heart races in my chest. If she had said those words to me two days ago, they would have washed off my back without leaving a mark. Now though, when I'm in my own mental depths of hell, all she's doing is saying the words that have been playing on repeat in my head since last night. Repeating my insecurities to me and they hit the mark she's searching for.

I clench my eyes closed, trying to swallow back the swirling ball of anxiety creeping up my throat, my senses overwhelmed, but I still sense her approaching among the chaos inside of me. I don't move, forcing myself to focus on her footsteps as she approaches.

One step… Two steps… Swipe.

I kick my leg out, hitting her legs, but the bitch manages to grip my hair before she tumbles to the floor, dragging me along with her. She lands on her back, and I fall to the side of her as she continues to tug at my strands.

Bitch.

I'm not cat fighting on the floor of a biker garage with

this woman. Rearing my fist back, I punch her in the gut first, before repeating the same swing at her face. Her hold on my hair loosens as she cries out in pain, and I stagger back so I can rise to a crouched position above her.

"What the fuck is going on?"

Shit.

Gray stands in the open entrance to the garage with his hands on his hips.

"Help me, Gray, she attacked me out of nowhere," Molly cries out, cupping her nose as blood trickles down the side of her face. I don't feel bad about it, not when she fucking started it. She just wasn't expecting me to throw punches.

"I highly doubt that," he retorts, taking a step toward us, but I don't move. Instead, I glare down at the bitch causing mayhem in my life once again.

Gripping her wrist, I yank her to me, making sure I have her attention when her eyes settle on mine. "The next time you lay a finger on me, I'll gut you and watch you bleed out for everyone to see. Until your eyes roll to the back of your head, before I let your body slump to the floor without care. Next time you touch me, I'll make an example out of you."

Standing, I make a bitch move and kick the bucket of water in her direction, and she screeches as the cold droplets coat her skin.

Gray covers his mouth with his hand, trying and failing to hide his amusement as I saunter past him. But one thing is for certain, that wasn't a joke, I meant that threat with every fiber of my fucking being.

Only time will tell if she heeds the warning.

RUTHLESS BROTHERS MC

THIRTY

Ryker

I shuffle down the hall toward the bathroom. I'm tired, groggy, and a little hungover from last night's celebrations. Shift is home, which means we will have our tech expert on hand to help us dive into these motherfuckers who keep attacking us.

I probably shouldn't have drank so much, but shit, I needed a second to not be drowning in the stress of figuring this mess out.

Something doesn't add up; I just can't pinpoint what. They gave us a time frame, and we're sure as shit not going to do what they want, but why would they continue to push us anyway? These aren't the kind of men I want to get the club into bed with, despite whether our previous prez was or not. It's not what we stand for.

Closing the bathroom door behind me, I flick on the shower before slipping my boxers down my thighs. I need to wake up, get a grip on myself, and get ready to make some moves today on behalf of the club and my brothers. The Devil's Brutes are clearly used to getting their way, but that's not happening here with us. The issue is they're one step ahead of us every time, and we need to change that.

I step under the spray, groaning as the water hits my body at the perfect temperature. Tucking my chin to my chest, I let the spray beat down on me for a few minutes, making my hair stick to my face.

When I can blink my eyes open, a little more awake now, I catch sight of my morning wood still standing to attention. My fist wraps around my length instinctively, a long tug making my toes curl against the tiled floor beneath me.

A memory flashes in my mind from last night. As I stumbled back to my room, I hovered in front of Scarlett's door, fist poised and ready to knock, then Emmett all but tackled me to the floor and told me to fuck off. He seems more clued up on the shit she was dealing with the other night than I do, and even with my alcohol infused brain, I still understood what he was saying. She needed space.

Shaking my head, I pull at my cock, remembering the feel of her sweet pussy around me as I fucked her in the garage. She's so responsive, so fucking hot as she comes apart in your hands, and the thought of her alone is enough to make me harder.

Maybe finding some kind of release will help me focus better today.

I laugh at myself, knowing all too well that I don't need any excuse to jerk off in the shower like a teenager. Splaying my left hand on the wall, I up the tempo on my cock with the other as I fuck my hand, thinking of *her*.

A breeze drifts over me, a shiver running down my spine, and I turn to find someone opening the bathroom door. It's on the tip of my tongue to tell them to get the fuck out, my cock still engulfed by my hand, when the woman herself walks in.

Her gaze is on the floor at first, but I see the moment her eyebrows pinch, noticing the sound of the shower and she lifts her gaze up to me. Her feet almost lift off the floor when she jumps in surprise, eyes wide as she stutters an apology.

Not that she's looking directly at me though. Nope. She's apologizing to my dick. Her eyes follow every sweep of my fist as she runs her tongue over her bottom lip.

"I'm so sorry," she repeats, waving her hand as she spins around and turns to leave. Her hand wraps around the door handle, pulling it closed behind her, as my hand continues to move. Faster now, after her heated gaze.

"Wait."

I almost panic that she didn't hear me over the spray

of the water, but the door freezes halfway closed. I tug once, twice, three more times before she tilts her head and glances around the door again. Three tugs that all have her name on.

She runs her tongue over her bottom lip once more as she trails her eyes from my toes all the way to my face, with an extended pause on the hand jerking me off. It's hot as fuck.

Dropping my hand from the wall, I turn to face her, crooking my finger for her to come closer. My grip tightens as she does just that. She doesn't shut the door behind her, but I don't give a shit, I'm too busy taking her in now that she's stepped back into the room.

Her hair is piled up into a messy bun on top of her head, she's wearing a long t-shirt falling mid-thigh, and there's a slight puffiness to her eyes which tells me she just woke up. There isn't a speck of make-up on her face, a brush hasn't gone through her hair, or any effort into what she's wearing, yet she's still the most stunning thing I've ever seen.

She comes to a stop beside me.

"See something you like, Scarlett?" Her teeth sink harder into her bottom lip as she nods in response, peering up at me through her lashes for the briefest moment before looking back at my cock. "Tell me what you want." It's not a question, it's an order, and any concern as to whether she'll participate or not is obliterated as she drops to her knees in one swift motion.

"Fuck my mouth."

She's like a siren calling out to me, spinning me under her spell. The order came from me, but her response makes me feel like I'm under her command.

I move closer to the opening of the shower, but she instantly shakes her head, nudging me backward as she shuffles on her knees until she's almost under the spray with me. Water droplets cling to her t-shirt, but she doesn't seem to notice as she trails her fingers over my thighs and leans closer.

Her lips part, inviting my cock so perfectly, and we groan as the tip of my dick feels the flat of her tongue. She twirls her tongue around my tip and drags it over my length. I'm on the verge of seeing stars and she hasn't even fully wrapped her lips around me yet.

I'm knocked off-balance as she nudges me, my breath coming in short, sharp bursts, my back hits the wall, placing her under the spray. The water drenches her, claiming her, just as she claims me for the first time with her mouth swallowing me whole.

My head falls back, hands clenched at my sides as she takes more and more of me, until I'm hitting the back of her throat every time. I can barely breathe, yet she's the one with water hitting her face at the same time as she takes me into her mouth, but it only seems to make her suction tighter around me.

Water droplets cling to her lashes as she digs her nails into my thighs. The pinch of pain mixed with the surrealness that is her mouth has me hurtling over the edge with no way to stop it.

She swallows every drop of me, humming around my length like it's me that's brought her to ecstasy. She doesn't stop until there's nothing left in me to give, but even as she releases my cock from her mouth, she peppers a few extra kisses along the veins.

Holy. Fucking. Shit.

Scarlett rises to her feet, the shower cascading around her like she's the fucking goddess of water or something as she brings her palms to my chest. My hands immediately find her waist, pinning her to me.

I trail a hand to her inner thigh, wanting to feel her warm cunt on my fingers, but she shakes her head and takes a step back, and I somehow let her go. "Come find me when you get home from whatever shit you have going on today." The rasp in her voice has my cock twitching again. "Then you can claim my pussy again."

She peels the t-shirt from her skin, letting it slap to the floor with a grin as she leaves the bathroom completely naked. Completely. Fucking. Naked.

Hot damn.

This war better be over sooner because I've got sweet pussy waiting for me.

I can't decipher what my mood is as I step into the Church. Longing. Annoyed. Desperate? Fuck, she's in my head in the best way possible. I don't want to stay behind and get lost in her, I want to go to fucking war and come back to find her sprawled in my bed, ready to take my dick.

"What's that grin on your face?" Gray taps my shoulder as he drops down into his seat, an almost knowing look on his face.

"I don't have a grin on my face," I grumble in response, forcing myself to relax the muscles in my face, and he waggles his eyebrows as he giggles like a schoolgirl.

"So it has nothing to do with Scarlett stepping out of the bathroom naked and soaked to the bone about fifteen minutes ago?" He cocks a brow at me, challenging me to lie as I fight the urge to grin from ear to ear.

Yes. It has *everything* to do with that. I refuse to admit it out loud though, so I toss him the finger instead. Somehow that only makes him grin wider.

Fucker.

Ignoring him, I glance around the table and focus on the Ruthless Brothers. Everyone's a little rough around the edges after last night, but we're all here to focus on bringing the Devil's Brutes down.

Emmett appears in the doorway, shuffling around to his seat without a word. The bruising on his face has ebbed a little, but there's still a slight limp to his walk from the blade he took to the thigh. Apparently the man has a target on his leg, summoning all of the weapons in his direction to cause him pain.

I *should* keep him out of today's fun, but I know he won't accept it. Not when the blood of the Ruthless Brothers runs through his veins. He'll be there whether I allow it or not. The main issue we have at the moment is we have nowhere to actually hit.

We don't know where the Devil's Brutes operate and we don't know where their compound is. So without something to go on, we're stagnant.

Axel grunts, mumbling under his breath with Euro as they step in, taking their seats like the rest of us, when Shift appears in the doorway.

I know that look in his eyes.

He's found something.

He pulls the chair out beside Axel, but doesn't drop down into it when he places his laptop on the table. "Prez, I think I have something."

He's far too chipper compared to how I feel this morning, but I don't hold it against him as I sit straight in my chair, ready for whatever information he has.

"Thank fuck for that. What have you got?" Relief washes over me as I wait with bated breath.

"A fucking weird-ass tingle in my stomach from finally being able to call you Prez. It's badass, man," he says with a smirk, holding his fist out for me to reciprocate, and I roll my eyes at him as I do.

Asshole.

A few brothers cheer around the table at his comment, but I wave them off, eager to get to the good stuff. Shift sighs dramatically as he spins the laptop toward me.

"Fine, fine," he mumbles, pressing a few buttons on the keyboard. "I've been tracking a shipment coming in and I'm certain it's theirs."

"How?" Axel asks, beating me to it.

"It's a repeat delivery that comes in every other Thursday. I've checked the surveillance cameras at the shipment yard, it's a bit grainy, but I'm certain it's their cuts." The screen comes to life with multiple still images.It definitely looks like their leather and emblem on the back.

"Can you tell if Kincaid is one of them?" I ask, getting more and more excited with every passing second.

"No, not for certain. But realistically, we don't have the upper hand here, so beggars really can't be choosers. This is the most solid lead we've got right now. I still can't pick anything up on their compound location."

I nod, seeing the bigger picture too, as I lean back in my seat. "Please, for all that is holy, tell me that it's today and we don't have to wait another week." Thursdays have always been inconsequential to me, until now. They've never been so important.

"Two hours."

Fuck yeah.

I don't need to look around my men to know their thoughts. I can feel the anticipation rising in the room as they wait for me to say go.

I speak the sweetest three words to leave my lips, before smashing the gavel into the wood.

"Let's roll out."

Sneak in.

Prepare for their arrival.

Hold positions.

Attack.

That's the plan. It's that simple, or so I hope.

Step one is already complete. The security guard is already in our pocket. Has been for a long time since he went to school with my dad and they got along. I slipped him an extra wad of cash to keep his head down and he is more than happy to do so.

Everyone is prepared and in their positions now, all eagle-eyed and ready for the moment to strike. It's just step four we're all eagerly awaiting, all thirsty for.

The container is in my direct line of sight. I'm in the club's blacked out SUV, with Emmett to my left and Gray to my right. Axel, Duffer, and Shift are stationed to the left of the target, while Eric, Becker, and Euro are camped out to the right. The rest are on the outskirts of the yard, keeping as many men on the ground as possible, ready to attack.

I tap my foot impatiently, completely unsure about Axel's decision for me to be holed up in the vehicle, but I placed him as the sergeant at arms for a reason. Even if I don't like it, I know it's the right choice. It just makes me even more impatient.

Gray clears his throat, glancing out of the corner of his eye at me and Emmett, his jaw opening like he's going to talk before he slams it shut again, twisting his gaze out of the window. He's done the same damn thing three times now and it's driving me insane.

"Whatever's going through your head, Gray, spit it out so we can focus on the job at hand," I grumble, tapping my fingers on my thighs and he sighs.

He clears his throat again, before finally blurting out what's on his mind.

"I think I'm in love."

My head rears back, and Emmett splutters beside me as we try to process his words.

"With who?" I ask, completely caught off guard.

"Himself," Emmett retorts before Gray can answer, and I have to stifle a laugh.

"Fuck off, assholes. With Scarlett obviously."

On what fucking planet is that obvious? Am I dense *and* fucking blind?

"You don't know what love is," Emmett states with a scoff, but that doesn't seem to deter Gray one bit.

"I know that, dickhead. That's why I said 'I *think*'." He holds his hand up to start listing off what's in his mind. "She's all I can think about. I want to smell her, feel her soft skin under my hands all of the fucking time, and not even just in the *fucking* kind of way. Like I want to hear her laugh, make her smile, lose badly to her on *my* video game, and finally fucking see her on my bike draped in my cut." He releases a breath like he's been holding those words in so tightly that it's a relief to get them off his chest.

Silence washes over us for a second before it's Emmett who clears his throat.

"Well, *I* like her too."

Gray rolls his eyes dramatically. "I gathered that when you fucking tattooed her arm, asshole." I blink at the knowledge, trying to recall if I saw it this morning. I remember seeing a glimpse of black ink with a flurry of oranges and reds, but I didn't get a good look at it with her consuming my dick and my mind. "Just like Ryker over here likes her too since they had some fun in the bathroom this morning."

"He did?"

"He did. Saw the aftermath on our girl as she stepped out butt naked with a grin on her puffed up lips."

"Fuck. Ryker doesn't ever go back for seconds."

"I'm sitting right here, motherfuckers," I grumble, swiping a hand down my face, but I can't deny any of it.

"So what does this mean?" I glance at Emmett, completely disorientated that we're having this conversation right now, but that doesn't seem to bother Gray.

"It means I need you to be honest with me about your feelings toward her. I want her, however that looks, so if that means sharing her with you two knuckleheads, then I have to wrap my head around that. Otherwise, I'm close to taking her off the table." His nod is firm as he holds my gaze.

"Off the table?"

I shake my head at Emmett's confusion, understanding what he's saying completely. "He means making an old lady out of her."

"No fucking way, man. She's ours."

"Ours." I test the word on my tongue, completely fucking blown away that I'm considering this right now.

"Can anyone actually handle the three of us?" Gray says with a smirk.

"Four."

"Four?" Emmett's brows knit at my correction, so I nod toward Axel.

"That's never going to happen."

I shrug, knowing full well I would have said the same thing a few days ago, but a lot has happened in a short span of time. "I don't know, the bike thing shocked me."

"So do his fucking overdoses, like he's not a danger to himself right now, but we're still taken by surprise," Gray grunts, pain and loss in his eyes as he looks at our brother. We know he's struggling, we just don't know how to help him, but Scarlett does.

"You can't make her an old lady and still give him what he needs from time to time too. You've got to be honest with her. We all do," Emmett explains, pulling at his beard.

"If Axel was sitting here right now, he would be saying the same for her," I add, knowing he doesn't trust her like we do.

"True," Emmett agrees.

"She's off limits to the rest of the brothers. No way in fucking hell is she ever going to be a Ruthless Bitch," Gray announces like this is all set in stone.

"Does she get a choice?"

"Of course she does… as long as she agrees." He rolls

his eyes at me again, like he's got all of this shit figured out already and he's just trying to get us up to speed.

Movement out of the corner of my eye halts my thoughts and pulls my attention. Someone's rolling up.

One bike, one leather cut, but I can't quite see it from this angle.

A gun pulls from his hip, pointing and aiming, as he continues to drive by without slowing to a stop. Before anyone can move, three shots are fired. Three men drop to the ground.

Eric.

Becker.

Euro.

My chest fills with anger as I push Gray from the SUV and clamber out after him. Adrenaline courses through my veins as I start to run toward them, but it's like I'm moving backward, aimlessly getting further and further away from the carnage. I don't miss the moment Axel steps out with his gun and pulls the trigger, dropping the Brute to the ground as the bike spins out in the distance before crashing into a container.

Axel's wide eyes meet mine and it speeds my world back up as we meet beside our injured brothers. Wounded at the hands of another Brute.

Fury burns through me, and I'm charging toward the fallen Brute before I even realize it. There's no question that this fucker is dead, but that was the whole point. I see it all now. He was a pawn, a sacrifice for their plans, as I read the words scrawled onto his t-shirt.

You will fall one by one unless you get in line.

THIRTY ONE

Scarlett

It's surprising what sucking good dick can do for your mood.

I was already feeling less groggy this morning when I woke up, but everything that followed with Ryker has me feeling practically normal again. Well, as normal as I can be. Admittedly, I wasn't quite ready for someone to touch me just yet, the anxiety I was swamped in bringing all of my pain and trauma to the forefront of my mind. I didn't want to admit that out loud though. A moment to myself is all I needed, and now I'm excited for him to get back.

A climax is calling to me, not one from my own hands, but from one of theirs, or preferably, their dicks.

My cell phone vibrates on the mattress beside me, pausing the podcast for a brief moment before it continues to play. I glance down at the message that pings on my screen and instantly tense, looking around my room like there's someone here to see me.

Kronkz:

Hey, weird hot guy check in. You're welcome. Everything okay? I know you usually drop off the face of the earth from time to time, but never this long. If you need me to come save you from something, then say the word, and ideally, where you are because you're impossible to track.

Let me know.

Fuck.

I consider any type of response that can explain the mess of my life.

Hey, I'm good. Just lost my entire home to a fake explosion that killed everyone I ever knew, but it's all good because I'm getting fucked like nobody's business and living my best life.

Hey, I'm alive, still keeping all of my secrets, surrounded by people who don't know the true me. So, nothing new, how are you?

Hey, come rescue me from myself, would you? I should have run immediately, but now my life is intertwining with what was once the enemy. Help a girl out?

Hey, everything is amazing. Fancy playing a video game later?

I don't send a single one of them. Instead, I toss my cell phone to the side again, pretending like I haven't seen it. Flopping back on my bed, I almost roll off it when my bedroom door swings open and Emily rushes inside.

My heart lodges in my throat, my eyes widening as I glance at my cell to make sure the message is no longer on the screen, but she's not paying any attention to it. Before I can utter a single word to her, she's thrusting her cell phone in my face, a panicked look in her eyes.

She gulps hard as I bring it to my ear, but I don't speak until I hear someone else on the other end of the line.

"Scarlett, are you there?"

Frowning, I glance at Emily. "Emmett?"

"Obviously, who else is going to be calling my sister's cell phone?" he grumbles, like I'm being stupid, but all I can see is Emily's face, the strain to her jaw, the tightness around her eyes, with unshed tears threatening to fall.

"I'm looking at an upset Emily here, Emmett, I had no fucking clue who would be causing her that pain," I snap in response, hearing him curse under his breath before he sighs.

"Shit, please keep an eye on her until I get there."

"What's going on?"" I ask as Emily takes a seat beside

me on the bed.

"You helped with my leg, so, how are you with bullet wounds?"

"What the fuck?" I blurt. That's not at all what I expected him to ask.

"I can't explain right now, I need to know if I'm bringing Euro to you or not?" He doesn't mention what the alternative is, and my stomach clenches.

Pinching the bridge of my nose, I squeeze my eyes closed for a moment. "I'm not trained."

"I'm not asking if you are trained, Scarlett, I'm just asking if you're more than a *Grey's Anatomy* certified doctor?"

Uncertainty wars inside of me, but I find the truth slipping from my lips despite it. "I've done it twice before... for the Reapers."

"Did they live or die?"

I scoff, shaking my head like he can see me. "Do you care? You shot them all to hell anyways."

Of course they survived, even though I might have been a little unsure the first time, but the second time didn't take as long.

"Shit, okay. We'll be there in ten minutes. Clear the fucking Church table."

The call ends before I can say another word and I slowly offer the cell phone to Emily, who is staring off into space.

"He's dead." Her words confuse me as I rise from the bed. I'm about to correct her, explain that Euro could still make it, but she must understand my confusion as she glances up at me through teary eyes. "My father, he didn't make it."

Before I even know what I'm doing, I drag her to her feet and wrap my arms tightly around her. We sway from side to side for what feels like an eternity as she clings to me. After a few more moments, she sniffles and takes a step back.

"I'm sorry, you go sort everything out like Emmett asked. I'll be okay."

"Duffer," I holler, knowing he's never far behind, and he peeks his head around my doorframe with a grim look on his face. "Stay with her. I need to help with Euro, but don't let her out of your sight. Stay in here if you need to."

He nods, so I spin to give her one last hug before reaching for my bag. It takes a second of digging around for me to pull the inconspicuous cosmetics bag from the bottom, before I rush for the door.

I barely take two steps into the bar area before Maggie is in front of me, a frantic look on her face. "Gray just called, tell me what you need."

Shit, okay. *Think, Scarlett, think.*

"I need a fully stocked first-aid kit, scissors, a jug

of boiling water, and something strong," I add, pointing behind the bar. "Oh… and rags, lots of clean rags."

I rush to the Church doors, but the second my hand wraps around the handle, Molly shouts for my attention.

"You can't go in there, whore."

I don't even have the time to roll my eyes at her as I shout back. "Fuck off, Molly."

Placing the cosmetic bag on the table, I unzip it to reveal pouches inside containing medical supplies I've gathered over the years for times just like this. I don't know in what other world I would need them, but it's imperative for myself more than anything.

I'm expecting more bullshit from Molly, but the main doors swing open and men rush inside, stopping whatever rampage she was on.

Maggie appears beside me with the items I asked for, and I quickly drop the stainless steel tools into the boiling hot water to sterilize them the best I can.

Murmuring my thanks, she waves me off, moving out of the way as Ryker steps in first, followed swiftly by Emmett, Gray, Axel, and Euro. The second my eyes land on the guy who needs my attention, the rest of them fade into the background.

He's clutching his arm tightly, pain etched into his face as he pants through clenched teeth.

"Take his cut off," I murmur, and Gray helps him do

it, before I cut through the white tee he has on underneath.

My gaze instantly falls to the wound as Euro drops his hand. Moving around him, I check the back of his arm without causing him too much discomfort from the movement, and I'm relieved to see it's a clear through and through. No fragments left for me to dig out. At least there's a positive in all of this.

Grabbing one of the rags Maggie brought in for me, I dig around in the first-aid box to find the cleansing alcohol solution, and quickly drench it in the liquid. Looking up at Euro, his teeth clenched together and jaw grinding with every breath, I finally focus on the room enough to realize there's a lot of fucking noise going on in here. The doors are open so that's not helping.

Tilting my head to the left, my gaze clashes with Axel's. Not the easiest brother to deal with, but they need my help. "Can we shut the door so I can at least think while I'm doing this? Please," I add, and he nods.

"What's going on?" My heart stills at the voice cutting through the air, my body stiffening in shock as I struggle to fucking breathe.

"Shut the door behind you, Shift," Axel grunts, and my gaze drops to the wound once more.

"Yes, sirrr."

I know that twang. That purposeful slur to the 'r'. It only confirms my worst fears as I stand here surrounded by Ruthless Brothers.

Fuck.

I'm screwed, I'm totally fucking screwed.

Gulping hard, I clench my eyes shut, trying to relieve some of the tension radiating through my body, but it's impossible.

Keep your head down and get this shit done, Scarlett. Then grab your fucking bag from your room and get your ass out of here.

I should have run to begin with. I fucking knew it, but I was blinded by the intrigue of the Ruthless Brothers. I was always called foolish, but this is the first time I'm seeing it in myself.

Taking another deep breath, I blink open my eyes and bring the damp cloth to Euro's wound. He grunts at the pain, and someone offers him the bottle of liquor Maggie brought in.

The room goes quiet, everyone watching my every move, and I think I'm going to be sick.

I can't be entirely sure that there are no fragments left behind, but I use the forceps from my kit to dig around a little, much to Euro's discomfort, and come up with nothing, so I proceed to patch him up.

He doesn't grumble at the stitches as I pinch both of the holes and thread them back together, before wrapping the bicep with bandages.

"You're good," I mutter, quickly packing away my things.

"Thanks," Euro grunts, dropping down from the table.

"At least one of them has survived," Gray states. I know from Emily that they lost Eric, her father, but there were more? Noticing my gaze, Gray shakes his head. "Our ambush was ambushed. We lost Eric and Becker."

I was hoping the casualties at least came from a victory, but that doesn't seem to be the case.

Searching out the blond Viking, I find him tapping away on his cell phone, lost in whatever he's doing so he's not giving much away.

I look back to Gray with a tight smile on my face. "I need to clean off." I wave my blood-stained hands at him before grabbing my things. His brow furrows at my short, clipped words, but I really need to get the fuck out of here, ideally without the new guy noticing me.

"For sure. Do you need any help?" Gray offers, but I shake my head tersely, not offering a verbal response as I rush for the door, ripping it open despite wanting to keep a low profile.

I need to get out of here. I don't know how or where, but I know one thing for sure.

I need to leave.

Right. Fucking. Now.

THIRTY TWO

Scarlett

I do one final glance around the room, making sure I've left nothing behind before I toss my bag over my shoulder. It feels weird. I didn't do a single thing to make this room my own, but seeing it without a few of my belongings scattered across the place makes me… sad?

Shit, I can't be getting consumed with the most irrelevant fucking feelings right now. I need to stay focused and get the hell out of here.

Hiking my bag up my shoulder, I open the bedroom door and peek out, making sure the coast is clear before I step into the hallway and head for the door to the rear. I gulp heavily as I silently step outside, closing the door softly behind me.

I tuck my hand into the slight opening of my bag, feeling for the weapon I know is there. I don't want to use it, but I will if I have to. I need to get out of here whether I like it or not. I got too comfortable and too damn foolish, but I didn't expect my world to start to implode quite like this.

Pressing my back against the wall of the compound, I glance toward the garage and check for any club members lingering around. There are two at the gate, maybe a few more in the opposite direction coming down from the mess the Devil's Brutes brought to them.

Indecision wars inside of me over whether or not I can escape with my bike. My heart says yes, but my mind says hell fucking no.

If I want to take my Harley with me, I'm going to need some kind of miracle. Not only would there need to be a distraction to clear the two Ruthless Brothers by the gates, but I'd need someone else to help open them so I could slip through with my bike.

There's potential, it could work if I went and found Emily, but I never would. Not only would that take too long, I would never put the weight of that on her shoulders. Especially not when she eventually found out who I was and what I had done.

Despite all of that, I need to see my bike one last time, before I figure out how to slip past the members on guard. With my heart racing, I take silent footsteps as I make my way across to the garage, before leaning my back against the side of that building.

I need to leave without anyone noticing.

I spy a small bush to my right and quickly tuck my bag in there. This way, I'll be able to sneak in and out without anything to worry about, before making my grand escape.

I take a deep breath, rolling my shoulders back before I turn toward the garage door. The shutters on the main openings are locked down today, but the usual door is slightly ajar. Perfect.

Moving the final few steps, I catch a scream in my throat as someone wraps their arms around my waist and lifts me off the ground.

No. No. No. Fuck, no.

My heart squeezes in my chest as my fight or flight kicks in, and I lean my head forward, ready to headbutt whoever the fuck has a hold on me, when Emmett comes to stand in front of me with a wide smile on his face.

I freeze despite myself, until Ryker says in my ear, "What are you doing out here, trouble?"

It takes me a second to catch my breath, and it's only when he places me back on my own two feet that I finally manage it. "I, uh, I wanted to see my bike."

Not a lie. Not the entire truth, but… still.

"Then why are you creeping?" Emmett asks as Ryker moves to stand beside him. It's not giving me interrogation vibes, but the confusion in their eyes is clear.

They don't know. They definitely don't fucking know,

but that will change, especially if I stay.

Clearing my throat, I glance toward the door before looking back at each of them, opting to go with another truth. "I wasn't allowed to see my Harley unless I was given permission when I was at the Reapers'. It's something they held over me, used as a weapon to keep me in line."

"What the fuck?" Ryker's eyes darken as he scrubs a hand over his chin. "If we hadn't already slaughtered them, we would now."

It's my turn to be overwhelmed as Emmett nods along with him. I offer them both a tight smile as he moves to my side and drapes his arm around my shoulders. "Let's go see your Harley," he murmurs, before kissing my temple, and I almost melt into a puddle beside him.

I can't deal with this. I can't deal with the reality of them being so close, but only for a limited amount of time now. The clock is ticking.

Stepping out of his hold, I keep my head down as I move toward the door, but as my hand wraps around the handle, I hear voices inside and it makes me pause.

"You need to get help with the drugs, Ax. You're tearing at those who care about you. I know that's selfish as shit to say, but I need you to see the pain you're causing."

"Pain is all I know, Gray."

"We know that, we fucking do. But you either need to let us help you or find a professional who can, because you

can't go on like this."

"I thought we were coming out here to suck dick, Gray, not hash out my fucking trauma."

"Fuck, Ax. I'm not sucking any dick until I have a fucking conversation with Scarlett. She's important to me. I don't know the how or why, but it's real, and until she knows who I truly am, I don't want to lie to her."

Emmett and Ryker aren't surprised; they're just staring at me like they're waiting for me to explode. With what… anger?

My gut is clenched tight with the fact that Gray admitted I'm important to him, but I swallow it down as I push the door open and step into the garage. Emmett and Ryker are hot on my heels, likely worried about what's going to unfold as Gray and Axel both turn to us in surprise.

"You weren't joking the other day." My heart gallops in my chest, my body heating from the memory, as Gray's eyes go wide, and Axel grunts.

"I don't fucking lie."

My mouth dries, words betraying me for a hot minute, before I finally speak again. "That's hot as fuck."

Their eyebrows practically touch their hairline as they stare at me, but before either of them can speak, I feel a body press against my back. Arms wrap around my chest before fingers ghost over my pebbled nipples, making me shiver as Ryker speaks against my ear.

"She's not lying, boys." He kisses my neck in the next breath, my body tingling as he continues to speak. "You want to see it with your own eyes now, don't you, Scar."

I nod, unable to find the words to respond. My head is overwhelmed with the fact that I'm supposed to be running, while my body, heart, and soul crave this very moment.

"Have you ever seen it before?" Emmett asks, moving to stand to my right, but my vision remains on the two guys standing in the open space, staring at me with shock and surprise.

"I've only ever seen it online when I've wanted to lose myself in an orgasm, but never in real life."

"You like man on man action, huh?" Ryker says, and I nod eagerly again.

I feel like I can't breathe as he trails his hands under my t-shirt and grazes my soft skin with his calloused hands. The feeling of his cock pressing against my ass only heightens my senses.

"What do you say, boys?" Emmett asks, confirming that he too wants to be a part of this.

I think I'm going to pass the fuck out.

I shouldn't be here, I should be fucking gone by now, but I can't deny myself this last farewell. The climax before my downfall. The instigator to my own ruin.

Fuck, I hate myself sometimes, but I know deep within my soul that I am who I am because I trusted my survival instincts, and I can never deny that.

I focus on the indecision in Axel's eyes, and I take it as a sign to put a stop to this, despite my own cravings. It's on the tip of my tongue to cut the mood and turn the direction of the scene unfolding before me, when Axel unbuckles his leather belt and unzips his jeans.

Holy fuck, he's just as big as Emmett.

His hand wraps tightly around his length. His hard, stiff, desperate cock, and my thighs clench together.

Before I can utter a single word of praise, of thanks, of fucking something to show my appreciation, just for him standing there with his dick out, Ryker grabs the hem of my t-shirt and pulls it over my head.

My breasts are on full display since I opted to go without a bra in my rush to leave. They're heavy and needy as Ryker teases his hands over my skin, touching everywhere but where I actually want him.

Emmett disappears from beside me, and a moment later, the garage door slams shut. The sound only solidifies the experience I'm about to go through right now. A flash of blond appears in front of me with my next breath, but it's a blur as my Viking drops to his knees in front of me.

Holy fucking shit.

I wet my lips as I glance from Emmett to where Gray and Axel are standing. Once Gray has my attention, he slowly drops to his knees in front of Axel.

I'm going to hell, I'm certain of it, but what a way to fucking go.

Emmett reaches for the waistband of my leggings and panties, dragging them down my thighs, and forcing me to kick my sneakers off as he discards the material completely. I'm naked and surrounded by four hot men. That's enough to make me climax on its own.

My jaw widens as I become transfixed on Gray's every move, watching with raw desire as he drags the pad of his tongue over the length of Axel's cock. As if that's not enough, Emmett inches closer and repeats the same motion with his tongue, but over my folds instead.

Ryker catches my head on his shoulder as I relax into him, his hands finally engulfing my chest as he peppers kisses over my neck.

Nothing matters but this moment. Not a single thing. It's all forgotten. All that exists is inside of these four walls.

My hips flex instinctively in time with Emmett's movement as I grind against him, hissing with pleasure as he grazes my clit again and again. I'm desperate for him to thrust his fingers into my core, but I'm too lost in their touch and the view before me to remember how to fucking speak.

Please.

I can think it, but I can't move my mouth to say it. Looking down at him, I'm surprised to find him looking up through his lashes at me as he twirls his tongue around my clit. I don't know if he can see the desperation in my eyes or just sense it, but he grins as he leans back.

"I'm not using my fingers to spread you wide, Scarlett. My cock is going to do all of it."

I gulp with need, my body heating as I manage a nod at the same time Ryker sweeps me off my feet. Emmett instantly catches my thighs, spreading my legs wide as he puts my pussy on display for him, and I groan.

"Show me that pussy," Gray grunts, his breath heavy as Emmett moves to the side, and when my eyes land on his, he's swallowing Axel's cock like a professional.

Emmett somehow manages to hold my thighs still, showing them how desperate I am to be fucked. I don't shrink under Axel's watchful gaze either, almost preening over the fact that he's taking in my pussy too.

"Hold her like this, Ryker," Emmett murmurs, and their hands switch and Emmett takes a step back before I hear the telltale sign of a condom wrapper.

I enjoy the view of Axel fucking Gray's mouth, watching his lips part wider with every pass before Emmett blocks my vision. His jeans are open and slid down to his thighs, leaving his cut and everything else in place.

Hot. As. Fuck.

There's something about being in so much of a rush that you can't even think about undressing fully that just makes me wet.

There's a filthy smirk on his lips, one I'm desperate to feel against my own as he retakes his position between my open thighs and lines his long, thick cock up with my entrance. His hands grab my legs as Ryker moves his hands to my waist, the pair of them working in silence to get me into position.

I manage to take a deep breath before he starts to inch inside of me, my mouth widening with every inch of friction as he takes his time filling me up. My back arches, my eyelids closing as a low, deep groan rolls off my tongue.

I've never felt so full. So close to tearing apart into a million pieces with pleasure. His touch, combined with Ryker's, and the knowledge of Axel and Gray in the room also has me wetter than he likely expects.

"Fuck, Scarlett. You're so tight. Fucking made for me," he grunts when he can't get any deeper inside of me.

I can feel Ryker's rigid cock behind me, sending me even closer to ecstasy, as Emmett begins to slide out of me slowly and slam back inside me in a battle of paces. Every time he takes a moment to pull out, I forget how fast he just slammed inside of me, making my body shudder again and again.

"Fuck, Scar," Ryker murmurs in my ear, leaving goosebumps to trail over my neck and chest. "What I wouldn't give to fill your ass too." His murmured words spike my blood with a new level of need.

"Do it."

"Shit, don't tease me like that, Scar. I wasn't saying right now, I just—"

"Do. It," I bite, pleading with him as Emmett continues to fuck me.

"Take her, Emmett, and spin a little so she can still watch her show."

Emmett pins me to his chest, fucking me just as ferociously as he was with Ryker's aid. He tilts my head to the side just in time to watch Axel come all over Gray's open mouth, his tongue lapping at the tip of his dick as he works him over to the edge.

I almost pout that it's over already, when I feel Ryker behind me once more. Lubed fingers graze my ass. The second he presses his fingertip inside of me, Axel drops to his knees before Gray, who loosens his jeans.

"Have you ever been fucked in the ass before, Scar?" Ryker asks, and I nod.

"It's my favorite."

"Fuck," he grunts in response, no longer being quite as gentle with me as he fucks me with one finger, alternating the motion between Emmett's thrusts in my pussy. I relax my muscles, falling into his hold as he adds another finger, before starting to scissor his fingers and spread me wide.

I'm a panting hot mess, on the brink of falling apart, but

it's like my body refuses to let it happen until I'm claimed for the first time by these two men at once.

Gray groans, forcing my attention to him as Axel takes him to the back of his throat, while Emmett retreats from my core and holds me still, ready for Ryker.

The press of his cock at my ass makes me shiver, before he's pushing inside. He takes his time as I try to relax my body. With my next deep breath, he's pushing past the tight ring and filling me.

My body sings, humming over every inch of my being as his hips meet my ass cheeks, and he holds me steady.

"Fuck, Scar." He gives us a second to adjust, but Emmett is too desperate to wait any longer.

Inch by inch, he takes my pussy as Ryker retracts, before they repeat the motion in opposite directions. All I can feel is them, all I can see is the ecstasy on Gray's face as he comes in Axel's mouth, his hand wrapped around Axel's long brown waves as he shatters.

Seeing his climax at the same time Ryker and Emmett brush against one another against the thin wall inside of me has me screaming with my own pleasure.

"Oh my god. Fuck, yes!"

I feel like shattered diamonds, blasting into a million pieces as they both continue to fuck me through every wave of ecstasy, my climax not waining as they both become staggered with their motions.

As my body begins to calm, it's Emmett I feel pulsing inside me first, releasing his load, and it sends another wave of my climax running through me before tipping Ryker over the edge too.

"Fuckkk," Ryker groans in my ear before he sinks his teeth into my neck, and I tense around them again.

Exhaustion clings to me, my body going limp between them as I manage to wrap my arms loosely around Emmett's shoulders. Perspiration drenches me, my muscles burning from the most intense workout of my life.

Is this what heaven feels like? I've never felt more content in my life.

Lost in euphoria, I'm semi-aware that I'm handed off to someone else, the murmuring happening around me not actually reaching my ears as I feel something draped over my shoulders.

A light breeze blows over my body, making me shiver, when I hear Gray's voice in my ear. "It's okay, sweet cheeks, I've got you."

I should protest, declare that he put me down, but it's inevitable. There's nothing I can do to stop him as I'm lulled to sleep with each step he takes. Moving closer and closer to my impending doom without an ounce of fight in me.

THIRTY THREE

Scarlett

My brain is fuzzy as I wake from the most blissful slumber of my life. My body aches in the most perfect way as I stretch out my arms and legs, and the reason why comes quickly crashing down around me.

Blinking my eyes open, my heart races faster in my chest as I try to place where I actually am. Disorientated, it takes me a moment to realize I'm in Gray's room. Alone.

I roll to my back as I catch my breath, feeling the soft sheets gloss over my bare skin. The clock on his nightstand shows that it's a little after six in the evening. I'm not sure how long I slept for, but it was clearly needed.

My gut clenches, far too aware that I should be long gone by now, and not lying here after having been distracted by Ryker, Axel, Gray, and Emmett, but I couldn't help myself. I was swept away in the moment, but now I have to focus on rectifying the shift in my plan and figure out how to get the fuck out of here for real this time.

Wrenching the sheets off me, I stand and instantly begin searching for some of Gray's clothes to wear. I manage to find a pair of black boxers and a navy t-shirt. I have to roll the waistband on the boxers a few times, but they hold in place, and the t-shirt falls to my thighs, so I'm covered enough to at least look a little presentable in public.

Everything else of mine is either in the garage or the bag I hid in the bushes near it. Shoes included. I just need to get to my bag and then I can figure everything else out.

Pulling my hair tie out, I run my fingers through the mess before re-securing it in a bun on top of my head. Double-checking around the room to make sure my things haven't magically appeared around me, I head for the door.

I place a hand on my chest as I will my breathing to calm down, feeling frantic with every breath I take, before swinging the door open.

The creak of the door gains the attention of the person standing across the hall in my doorway, a surprised look on their face as they glance back at me, before they grin.

"Girl, when Gray said that you were in bed sleeping, I didn't think he actually meant in *his* bed," Emily says with a smirk, wagging her eyebrows as she closes my bedroom door.

Panic starts to get the better of me as I worry she'll notice none of my belongings are in there, but she bounces over to me none the wiser.

"It also explains the smug-ass look on his face," she adds, and I realize I haven't said a word to her.

"I'm sure that's not quite the reason why," I mutter, forcing an eye roll, and she chuckles in response.

"Wait until you see it for yourself." Before I can protest, she links her arm through mine and pulls me along to the living room. "We can relax in here for a bit where it's quiet, then we'll likely be called outside."

"Why?"

"Maggie has the grill going again and all the old ladies and their families are here. She's throwing some kind of memorial celebration for my dad and Becker."

Fuck, in my own haze of panic, I forgot about that. "I'm so sorry for your loss, Emily," I murmur, squeezing her arm in comfort, but she shakes her head.

"Don't be. I was surprised at first, but I know in my heart that I lost the father I loved the day my mother was taken from us. He never recovered from that. He was harming himself, always lost in a bottle, and a shell of the big proud man I once looked up to. At least now they'll be together."

My eyes widen at her words and the impact they have on my heart. I can't imagine a love that strong, a love that sweeps you off your feet and causes you so much pain all at once. To not be the man your children needed you to be.

I'm just thankful she seems to be at peace with it.

It's on the tip of my tongue to offer a shoulder to cry on if she ever needs one, but I quickly slam my mouth shut, knowing full well that it would be a lie if I'm no longer here.

We step into the living room without another word and I find Gray sitting in his usual spot on the sofa. Emily was right; there's a huge fucking grin on his face and a twinkle in his eyes like I've never seen before. Fuck.

"There's my sweet cheeks, get your ass over here."

I move to dig my heels into the floor, but Emily is already dragging me toward him, and the second I'm within arm's reach, he pulls me down into his lap.

His heat engulfs me, my body preening that it's home, while my head starts to panic again.

This is the complete opposite of getting the fuck out of here, and I know it.

"Hey, have you seen Ryker anywhere?"

My body stiffens in Gray's hold, his face nuzzled in my neck. Of course I hear him right now when my guard is fucking down and my world is already crumbling.

"Yeah, he's out in the garage tinkering with his bike. But we can have a game first if you want to?"

No, Gray. No, he doesn't fucking want to.

"Sure." I feel the sofa dip to Gray's left as he loosens his hold on me, the new arrival and Emily chatting about nothing as I sit up straight in Gray's lap. "You must be Scarlett."

My pulse rings in my ears as I look at the Ruthless Brother before me, Shift to everyone here, and swallow down the mess of emotions inside of me.

"I must?" I cock a brow, showing way more confidence than I actually have right now and he smirks.

"Yeah, my brother doesn't shut up about you, like at all."

My brows pinch as I glance between the two of them and a sinking feeling washes over me. Wetting my lips, I gulp hard. "Brother as in Ruthless Brother or *brother* brother?"

It feels like an eternity before anyone responds, but I'm not foolish, I know the answer. It's in their eyes and the curve of their fucking chin.

Gray squeezes me against him as he chuckles. "Scar, we weren't both blessed to be this handsome and have different genes running through our veins. Shift just happens to be eighteen months older than me."

Of course he's his fucking real brother, that's what karma looks like. But the realization suddenly triggers more to swarm my brain. Maybe he wouldn't call me out, not when he's played a part in it all. But why? Why would he? Maybe it's actually me who has the upper hand here? But do I want to find out?

A tremble runs through my veins as my breathing becomes more ragged, but none of them seem to notice. "Are you playing this game with me or not, Shift? Otherwise my girl here will destroy me on it. At least I stand a chance against you."

"That almost sounds tempting to watch. I only know of one gamer girl who can bring a man to his knees and look awesome doing it."

I swallow hard, the lump in my throat not moving as I offer a tight smile. "Maybe another time, I need to go and get a drink," I murmur, slowly lifting from Gray's lap. Both of them seem preoccupied by the screen, but I don't speed up my steps as I try to remain as calm as I possibly fucking can. "Do you want anything, Emily?" I ask, glancing at her as she relaxes back into the sofa with a book in her hand. She shakes her head at me, not even lifting her eyes from the pages.

If I'm going, this is my moment. There might not be another.

I'm two steps from the door when Shift speaks, confusion thick in his tone. "Whose account is this?"

"Scarlett's. Why?"

At the sound of my name on Gray's tongue, I freeze, my mind willing me to fucking run while my heart pleads for me to stay.

"Scarlett?" Shift murmurs my name in confusion, but

it's not a question toward Gray, it's one for me, and despite my inner conflict, I glance back over my shoulder and meet his gaze. "Your gaming account is xGamerScar9x?"

I run my tongue over my lip nervously, struggling to answer, when Gray beats me to it with a chuckle. "Yeah, she's got like one friend, so we're increasing her popularity."

His joke doesn't hit the surface for Shift or me as we continue to stare at each other.

He. Knows.

He fucking knows.

His mouth opens, but before a single word can fall from his mouth, the sound of gunshots firing in the distance distracts us all.

"What the hell was that?" Emily gasps, fear in her eyes as she looks up from the book.

Gray and Shift jump from the sofa, glancing at each other in confusion as someone hollers from the bar area loud enough for us to hear.

"The Brutes, it's the fucking Brutes!"

Emily gasps again, her hand rising to her chest as her eyes grow wide. "There are women and children out there."

Fuck.

This shouldn't be my fucking battle, this isn't a war I want to place myself in again. This could be the exact distraction I need, but the fear in Emily's eyes and the knowledge that there are defenseless women and children out there has me pushing that all to the side as I glance straight at Shift.

"Hand me a weapon."

"Sweet cheeks—"

"I said, hand me a weapon."

Gray frowns at me, but I look directly at Shift. He cracks his jaw from side to side, uncertainty seeping from him, and I scoff.

"Do you want those women and children to fucking die?"

He shakes his head instantly, reaching for the gun at his waist, and I blindly wave a hand at Gray too. "You as well, give me your gun. Get whatever you need from wherever you keep your arsenal, but these two are mine. Mags too."

"Scar—"

"Just do it," I hiss, knowing we don't have much time, and to my surprise, Gray hands me his gun with an extra round of bullets without another word. I give the gun a quick once-over, making sure the safety is now off, before I hold out my hand toward Shift.

Gunshots sound in the distance once more, and that seems to edge him along a little more, but he's still not putting the damn thing in my hand.

"Kronkz, give me the fucking gun. Now."

THIRTY FOUR

Axel

My back is plastered to the floor, my hands scrubbing at the slight mark on my otherwise polished bike. I can't stop detailing the bike in my head, considering alterations and upgrades I could do. It's refreshing.

I haven't felt like this in forever. I know the darkness and shadows are still lurking over me, but at this moment, they cease to exist.

Ryker is toying with his motorcycle beside me, each of us basking in the silence as my eyes cast to the new bike now being stored in the garage. Hers. It's here because I brought it here, so I shouldn't feel uncertain about it. It was my doing, but it's a change, and I'm the worst at adapting.

"So…" Ryker starts. I tilt my head to look at him. He's standing with his hands on his hips, his feet shoulder-width apart.

"So…"

"Are we going to talk about earlier?"

Fuck. I should have known this was coming. I've been waiting for it, but the more time that passed, the less likely it seemed. More fool me for being wrong. He's going to want to understand every thought, every inch of my actions, and every piece of my mind afterward. It's not a grilling, he's a concerned friend and I understand that, but we're not a bunch of pussies who discuss this shit, or at least I'm not.

"What is it I'm supposed to say?" I stop what I'm doing, tucking the rag into my pocket as I stand, pulling out a cigarette and lighting it instantly.

He gives me a glare, the one he gives me every time I light up near the bikes, but I ignore him, just like I do every other time. With a sigh, he folds his arms over his chest and gets back to the point. "I don't know, man. But it felt like a huge moment."

I shake my head at him as I take another pull of my smoke. "Well, it wasn't."

"Are you sure about that? You have never, in all of the time we have been friends, allowed a woman in the same room as you while your dick was out if her hands weren't tied and her ability to touch you was zero."

"I knew you and Emmett had her occupied."

"We did, but you've also never willingly stayed in a room if you've seen one of us fucking someone either." He raises a brow, like he's got me there.

"I don't know what you want me to say, Ryker. Gray sucks good dick and I was horny."

"You also reciprocated that exact action, which you have never done in front of someone else. *Ever*." Glaring at him, I pull at my cigarette before exhaling heavily. Fucker does have me there. But I don't know how he expects me to explain it to him when I can't even explain it to myself. "It feels like there's fucking hope for us, Ax. Like there's more to the blood and bullshit we have to deal with every day."

"We like the blood and bullshit," I interject, stubbing my cigarette out into the sand bucket I have placed by the door.

"I'm not saying we don't, but today, despite all of it, we got a fucking minute to unload. Literally." I almost chuckle at his attempted joke, but I manage to hold it back and shake my head instead.

Laughter catches my attention, drawing my gaze out over the yard, which is filled with people. A sense of sadness washes over the compound, the death of two brothers combined with another injured has left us hurting once again. Emmett is with the coroner, making all of the arrangements. It helps that we have them on the books, so we don't have to go through the whole mess with the authorities, but it's still a longer process than preferred.

Maggie has the grill out, manning it like a total boss as always, while the old ladies, the families, and the Ruthless Bitches are all gathering at the picnic tables or sitting around on the grass in groups.

Nothing brings a family together quite like loss.

The kids don't really understand, that's their magic I think. They're running around with water guns and causing mayhem, but it also brings a smile to everyone's faces under the late evening sun.

"You have to admit it, Ax. Despite all the bullshit with the Brutes and the losses we took today, when we were in this garage earlier, it made us feel invincible."

He likes her. They all do, yet there's something we don't know, and I'm the only one who seems to see it.

Grunting, I don't offer him any further response as I lie back down on the floor and pull my rag back out. The second I lift my hands in the air again, my whole body stills as gunshots ring out around us.

Panic kicks in as I quickly jump back to my feet, smacking my head on the damn bike as I go and I stumble for a second. Rubbing at my head, I stare with wide eyes as I glance from Ryker to the chaos outside. Women and children are screaming as the Brutes trample the compound, and my blood boils like an inferno.

"What the fuck?" Ryker grunts, a snarl on his lips as he reaches for the gun at his hip.

"It's retaliation for the fact that we *didn't* get the hit on them like we wanted. That we even attempted it to begin with," I grumble, reaching for my own handgun and making sure the safety is off. "Do we have any other weapons out here?" I ask, knowing the answer as frustration bubbles in my veins.

"No."

"Then let's make it work with what we do have," I grunt, ready to tear these motherfuckers to shreds and not feel any remorse about it.

Gunshots sound out again, the commotion getting louder, and it moves us into action. With my gun raised, I start to rush toward the enemy. We're at a disadvantage from this angle, coming up behind the Brutes, when what we want is someone placed between the innocent and the Devils.

As if sensing my thoughts, the double doors to the clubhouse swing open with a whoosh, but where I expect to see our men barreling out in droves, I see the last person I expect.

Scarlett.

She's in nothing but a long t-shirt, with her hair twisted up into a bun on top of her head, but that's not the part that has me surprised. It's the gun in each hand raised and ready to take aim.

"What the fuck is she doing?" I grunt, not turning to

look at Ryker as I feel his presence beside me.

Two steps. Two steps is all she takes before she starts firing. The guns pop with precision, hitting the closest two Brutes to the children, and they drop to the floor.

"Round the back!" she hollers to the women and families, turning to her right to glance at them while firing two more rounds from each gun and dropping four more men in the process.

Holy shit.

I spot one of the guys to the left as he raises his gun at her, and before I can consider if it's worth it or not, I point my own at him, pulling the trigger and watching him drop to the floor instantly.

Her eyes find mine through the chaos, her pupils so dark from here I would swear they were black. With a small nod, she continues.

"Maggie. Move." The order falls from her lips, making our mother hen frown for a moment, glancing down at her grill before she relents and rushes inside.

Moments later, Shift and Gray rush from the clubhouse with more weapons, and this time, the only weapons sounding off belong to the Ruthless Brothers as more men load up and come out.

There must have been two dozen of the Brutes when they first arrived, and now only four remain, their guns dropping to their feet as they surrender. It was either a ridiculously easy attack in their opinion or a suicide mission, because I can't see Kincaid anywhere.

Rushing across the ground, I slow my pace when I fall in line with where Scarlett, Shift, and Gray stand, and Ryker joins us from the other side as the Brutes drop to their knees at Scarlett's order.

Her chest heaves with every breath she takes, beads of sweat clinging to her temple as she continues to keep a firm grip on the guns in her hands.

"Are all the women and children accounted for?" she asks, glancing over to the doors to the compound where Duffer stands, nodding in response.

"Yes, ma'am."

"Don't fucking call me ma'am," she mutters, then takes a step back. "You can do what you want with these assholes, they're not my concern." With that, she marches back toward the building, barefoot.

"Ax?" I pull my gaze from the crazy fucking woman, who just kicked ass in a gun battle wearing a fucking tee and no shoes, to turn and stare at Shift at the mention of my name. "What are we doing with them?"

"We're sending a message," I grunt, before pulling my trigger three times and watching the men topple over. Blood pours from their heads, their skulls shattered from the brutal attack, but I don't give a fuck.

The fourth and final guy sobs, preparing for his bullet

too, but instead, I drop to my knees so we're eye to eye. "It's your lucky day, Grant," I state, reading his name on his cut. "You get to be the one to go home and tell Kincaid that he's fucked with the wrong crew."

He nods, his eyes red with snot trailing from his nose. He's as big as me and sobbing like a baby. He staggers to his feet, swiping at his face as he runs for the gate. He gets about fifty yards away from me when I pull the trigger using the final bullet in my chamber.

"Nah, I changed my mind. No survivors is the message I want to send."

After hollering out orders to get rid of the dead Brutes, I point my finger at Ryker, Shift, and Gray, before signaling for them to follow me inside. Making my way toward the door, I falter when I hear the sound of an engine approaching, but I relax the moment I see it's Emmett.

We wait by the doors, watching the horror and shock on his face. "What the fuck? I was gone for two hours."

"And all of this happened in less than fifteen fucking minutes," I grunt, waving him closer.

Pulling the double doors open, I'm not surprised to find the women, children, and bitches filling the bar area. What I am surprised by is the brunette standing with her arms folded over her chest as she leans her back against the Church doors.

It's like she knew I was coming for her.

I give her a nod, and she steps inside, and I follow her without a word. Emmett, Ryker, Shift, and Gray slip inside too, closing the door behind them. No one takes a seat. Everyone stands and stares at each other. I'm highly aware that Emmett has no fucking clue what's going on, but he'll soon catch up.

"What the fuck was that?" There's a bite to my tone, but she doesn't wilt at it.

"An expensive clean up. If you need me to contribute to the cost, just let me know."

Is she for fucking real?

"No, what the fuck were you doing?" Ryker interjects, clearly as bewildered as I am.

She fidgets like she's searching for the guns that were there a moment ago. Guns we had no clue she knew how to handle.

Shift breaks the silence with the sound of his boots thumping along the floor as he cuts the distance between him and Scarlett. His brows are knitted as he reaches out and grips her chin, tilting her head back. "It's actually you in the flesh." Scarlett glares at him, a defiant gleam to her eyes, as he laughs. "That was definitely like watching *Tomb Raider* in live-action."

"What is going on?" Emmett asks, scrubbing at his chin as he looks back at Ryker, Gray, and I for answers, but we're just as in the dark as he is.

"Yes, someone explain to me what the fuck is going on." Ryker grunts, folding his arms over his chest.

Shift turns to look at us while maintaining his hold on Scarlett. "When you said there was a new club whore called Scarlett that you took from the Reapers, I never expected it to be the Scarlett I knew."

"She's just a club whore we picked up from the Reapers," I grunt, refusing to listen to his bullshit about her being anything special to him before she got here, but he pushes on.

"Club whore? You're fucking with me, right? I wouldn't be surprised if she was still a virgin."

"Definitely not a virgin," Gray interrupts, a smirk on his lips despite the mess unraveling between us.

"I've never been a club whore, ever. That's just what you assumed," Scarlett clarifies, which makes even more sense, but she doesn't turn her gaze to glance at any of us. What else is there to know?

"What does that mean?" Emmett repeats as my head starts to spin with the unknown.

"Explain, Scarlett. He's doing a shit job and I have no patience," I bark, giving her a pointed stare, but Shift waves me off.

"Everyone knows I bring money in for the club by setting up transactions on the dark web."

"We know, but what does that have to do with her?" My irritation is getting more noticeable in every word I speak as he talks forever instead of getting to the point.

"Again, what does that have to do with her?"

He pauses, looking back at the woman in front of him with a hint of wonder in his eyes, shaking his head in disbelief. "Gamer Scar Nine is my number one assassin contact."

My body goes rigid with shock.

"What?" Gray takes a step closer to them, clearly not frozen in place with the new information like I am.

Shift nods like it all makes sense. "After her last job a few weeks ago, she went off the grid and I was getting worried." He looks back at her with his eyes wide. "I didn't realize you were even from Jasperville, never mind a Reaper."

Scarlett shrugs, offering nothing to the conversation.

"Get to the fucking point," I hiss, bracing my hands on the chair in front of me, and Scarlett sighs, rolling her eyes dramatically as she hits at Shift's arm and it drops from her chin.

She faces us, lips thinned, as if she's accepting her fate. "My last assignment was to kill the Ruthless Brother's Prez. A transaction set up by my contact, Kronkz, aka

Shift."

My blood runs cold, my jaw slack as I stare at her through a new lens.

Ryker prowls toward Shift, then points a finger at him. "Wait, you put the job out for someone to take out *our* Prez and profit from it? Who the fuck ordered that, and why the hell did you allow it?"

My heart pounds ferociously. Surprised, the words slip from my mouth.

"I did."

TO BE CONTINUED...

AFTERWORDS

Yesssss, welcome to the craziness that is the Ruthless Brothers MC!

Am I making you wait until book two to have all the answers? Well, some of them at least haha, book three will hopefully cover the rest. We both know I'm mean like that.

I'm obsessed with Scarlett so much. Emmett's caring nature, Gray's playfulness, Ryker's leadership, and Axel's – nope he's got nothing going on for himself haha They're all going to rock out world. And Shift, what a motherfucker, huh?

This has been one of the harder books I've written, some topics playing heavy on me as I try and make it work as beautifully as possible. Which has made the stress worth every second.

I hope you've enjoyed these guys as much as I have!

Keep reading to find the revealed release date for book two!

Much love.

THANK YOU

I know I do a big shout out to Michael and the babies every time, but writing this while in the process of moving house and juggling all of the things, including a new puppy, wasn't easy. But you guys made it possible for me. Thank you from the bottom of my heart for supporting me know matter what, and making me smile when it feels all doom and gloom.

I love you all infinity war.

Thank you to my Queen Bee's; Tanya, Nicole, and Jen. Nobody alpha reads like you badass women. You get me excited about my own damn books and make me smile with your negotiations haha You mean the world to me, thank you!

A million thank yous to my beta's; Michelle, Monica, Brianna, Kaz, Keira, Lorna, and Kerrie! You rock!

Kirsty. Imagine my life without your organization and queen badass-ness? LOL None of this would be here that's for sure. Thank you for sailing this crazy boat of disaster with me!

Laura and Katie. Wow. Just wow. After searching all of the exclusive sexy images, we finally found our guys, and you turned it into a masterpiece. Thank you!

Sloane and Sarah, queeeeens! Thank you for taking

care of all of the pretties and making me love my work even more!

Zainab, thank you for not giving up when the world threatened to cave in around us. You work magic, and you're awesome. Thank you.

ABOUT KC KEAN

KC Kean is the sassy half of a match made in heaven. Mummy to two beautiful children, Pokemon Master and Apex Legend world saving gamer.

Starting her adventure in the RH romance world after falling in love with it as a reader, who knows where this crazy train is heading. As long as there is plenty of steam she'll be there.

ALSO BY KC KEAN

Ruthless Brothers MC
(Reverse Harem MC Romance)
Ruthless Rage
Ruthless Rebel

Featherstone Academy
(Reverse Harem Contemporary Romance)
My Bloodline
Your Bloodline
Our Bloodline
Red
Freedom
Redemption

All-Star Series
(Reverse Harem Contemporary Romance)
Toxic Creek
Tainted Creek
Twisted Creek

(Standalone MF)
Burn to Ash

Emerson U Series
(Reverse Harem Contemporary Romance)

Watch Me Fall

Watch Me Rise

Watch Me Reign

Saints Academy
(Reverse Harem Paranormal Romance)

Reckless Souls

Damaged Souls

Vicious Souls

Fearless Souls

Heartless Souls

Made in United States
North Haven, CT
06 December 2024

61739353R00259